MARRIAGE
CAN BE
MISCHIEF

Books by Amanda Flower

The Amish Candy Shop Mystery series

Assaulted Caramel

Lethal Licorice

Premeditated Peppermint

Criminally Cocoa (ebook novella)

Toxic Toffee

Botched Butterscotch (ebook novella)

Marshmallow Malice

Candy Cane Crime (ebook novella)

Lemon Drop Dead

The Amish Matchmaker Mystery series

Matchmaking Can Be Murder

Courting Can Be Killer

Marriage Can Be Mischief

MARRIAGE
CAN BE
MISCHIEF

Amanda Flower

KENSINGTON
PUBLISHING CORP.

www.kensingtonbooks.com

KENSINGTON BOOKS are published by

Kensington Publishing Corp.
119 West 40th Street
New York, NY 10018

Copyright © 2021 by Amanda Flower

First Kensington Books Mass Market Paperback Printing: December 2021

ISBN-13: 978-1-4967-2405-2

ISBN-13: 978-1-4967-2406-9 (ebook)

10 9 8 7 6 5 4 3 2 1

Printed in the United States of America

For Kim, Ken, Gunnar, and Norah

ACKNOWLEDGMENTS

Thank you always to my readers who welcome a trip back to the Amish and *Englisch* world in Harvest, Ohio. The Amish Matchmaker mysteries and Amish Candy Shop mysteries would not be possible without your love of the books.

Thanks always to my super-agent, Nicole Resciniti, who makes all the books possible. You have been guiding my career for a decade now, and I'm just as grateful for all you do as I was on day one. Thanks too to my amazing editor Alicia Condon and the great team at Kensington. You are the best of the best in publishing.

Thanks to my husband, David Seymour, for his support and love while I struggle with each and every deadline and for his surprise food deliveries on tough writing days.

Thanks too to Kimra Bell for her help on this manuscript.

Thanks to my dear friends Delia and Suzy, who supported me during the writing of this book while I planned (and re-planned due to the pandemic) my wedding.

Finally, thank you God in heaven for friendship. This series is really about the lifelong friendship between Millie Fisher and Lois Henry. I have friends just like them, and I pray when we are Millie's and Lois's age, we have just the same amount of spunk.

A house is made of walls and beams;
a home is made of love and dreams.

—Amish Proverb

CHAPTER ONE

Lois Henry pulled at her multicolored geometric print blouse. "It's so hot this evening, I feel like I'm baking bread in my shirt. When is this concert over? Is it running long? Or is that just me because I'm perspiring like Jethro the pig in the noonday sun?" She fanned her red face with the concert program.

Lois and I sat side by side in lawn chairs on the Harvest village square just before twilight. Around us, other villagers both *Englisch* and Amish shifted in their own seats as the middle school band concert dragged on. I felt the hair on the back of my neck curl from the humidity that at last report was at sixty percent, making the warm night air feel that much hotter. It was one of those few times that I saw the benefit of Lois's air-conditioned house and car.

The businesses that encircled the square—the candy

shop, cheese shop, and pretzel shop—had long been closed for the night. The only business still open was the Sunbeam Café, which was trying to take advantage of the Harvest concert series for a few extra sales. The large white church next to the café glowed in the sunset, looking more like a painting of a church than the real thing.

I patted away the dew on my forehead. "Pigs don't actually sweat," I said. "That's why they wallow in mud and water on hot days to cool down."

"I didn't say it for an animal husbandry lesson," Lois said. "Did you see what this humidity is doing to my hair?"

I turned in my lawn chair to have a better look at her. The chair, which Lois had purchased at the local flea market, was far from sturdy. In fact, I had a feeling it might break apart any second. I stopped twisting.

Lois's typically upright red-and-purple spiky hair drooped to the left side of her head. I didn't say it, but it reminded me of a grassy field that had been bent over by the wind. "Your hair looks different from usual." I felt this was the nicest way to put it.

"It's going to take me an hour to set my hair again after tonight. People really don't know how hard it is to look like this." She picked at her hair with her long purple fingernails, but it did little to put her hair upright again.

I certainly didn't know how hard it was. Lois's appearance and mine could not be more different from each other. Although we were the same age, nearing the end of our sixties, and had grown up on the same county road, our upbringing had been very different. I grew up Amish, and Lois grew up *Englisch*. Even so, we had been the best of friends as girls and remained the best of friends to this very day.

However, I knew to many people we appeared to be an odd pair. I wore plain dress, sensible black tennis shoes, and a prayer cap. My long white hair was tied back in an Amish bun. Lois wore brightly colored clothes, chunky costume jewelry, heavy makeup, and had that striking haircut.

She leaned across the arm of her chair, and the seat made a dangerous creaking sound. "Did I sweat my eyebrows off?"

I shook my head. "*Nee*, they're still there." I did not add that they were looking a tad more wobbly than usual. It was certainly due to the trickle of sweat running down the side of her forehead. I had to agree with Lois: It was a hot night, and the concert should have been over an hour ago. We weren't the only ones who thought it had gone on too long—several couples and families had gotten up and left.

Lois shifted her folding lawn chair, and I found myself wincing with every creak and rattle the chair made. I didn't want her to be hurt if it broke. Even though we were sitting on the grass square in the middle of the village of Harvest, anytime you fall at our age, it can leave a mark.

"Careful, Lois, that chair is not as sturdy as you think it is," I warned.

She bounced up and down in the chair. "Don't be silly. It's as sturdy as they come. They don't make chairs like this anymore." With her final bounce, there was a loud crack, and Lois and the chair went down.

I jumped out of my seat. "Lois, are you all right?"

The children playing in the band froze and stopped

playing. The leader held his hands suspended in the air. Lois waved from the grass. "Keep playing. I'm fine."

Several people from nearby blankets and chairs ran over to us. Two *Englisch* men helped Lois to her feet.

"Are you hurt?" I asked.

"Nothing more than a bruised ego, and that stopped bothering me twenty years ago." She smiled. "If I became upset every time I fell over, I would be in a perpetual state of nerves." She smiled at everyone who'd rushed over to help. "Thank you, you're all too kind. Now, hurry back to your seats, so the concert can continue."

After they were out of earshot, Lois said, "Because we need to move this concert along. It's going on forever." She rubbed the side of her leg. "I spoke too soon about not being hurt."

"What's wrong? Should we find a doctor or nurse?"

"No, no, it's nothing as serious as all that. I just banged up my knee."

"Let me at least get you some ice for it, and here—" I moved my chair next to her. "Sit in this until I get back."

My chair was as unstable as hers had been, but it had to be better than her standing if her knee was bothering her. "Stay there. I will find the ice."

She rubbed her knee. "We can only hope by the time you return, this concert will be over," she whispered. Well, mostly whispered, but luckily the band had resumed playing, making it hard to hear much of anything over the cymbals and drums. "I don't know how much more of this I can take."

"All right," I said. "Please, stay there, and I will find some ice."

On the far side of the square there was a small concessions booth. I thought I would start there. If I didn't have any luck, then I would run across the street to the Sunbeam Café and grab a cup of ice from Lois's granddaughter, Darcy Woodin. I didn't want to scare Darcy until I knew how badly Lois was hurt.

"Excuse me," I said to the man waiting in line. "Can I just ask for some ice? My friend fell out of her chair and bumped her knee."

The *Englischer* stepped aside. "I saw her go down. It looked like a nasty tumble."

The girl inside the food trailer handed me a cup of ice and a fistful of paper towels.

I smiled at her. "*Danki*, this is so kind of you."

"I'd hurry back to your friend, if I were you. Margot Rawlings is headed this way, and she's staring right at you."

I looked over my shoulder and found that she was right. I thanked her again.

"Millie Fisher, can I have a word with you?" Margot called.

I sighed and stopped in the middle of the grass. Margot walked up to me and put her hands on her hips. Margot was an *Englisch* woman who was just a few years younger than me. I had known her most of my life. Although she was *Englisch* like Lois, their appearances were very different. Margot wore her hair short like Lois, but it was a pile of soft curls, which she had a habit of patting and pulling when she was frustrated. She also had a much simpler wardrobe of jeans and plain T-shirts. She was a no-nonsense woman who was doing everything within her power to make sure that Harvest, Ohio, became the number one tourist destination in Amish Country.

The concert tonight was one of her events. Throughout the summer she had been hosting a concert on the village square every Friday evening from seven to eight. It was almost nine now. The concert had certainly outlasted its allotted time. I had heard from Lois that Margot thought these concerts would bring people back into the village in the evenings. Typically, everything in Harvest closed at five or six, even in the summer. The concerts were popular, and tonight's had had a nice crowd before the performance ran a little too long.

Margot tapped her sneaker-clad foot in the grass. "What is this I hear about Lois Henry falling out of her chair?"

I held up the cup of ice. "She's not seriously hurt. We're taking care of it."

"What happened?" she asked.

"Lois found the chairs we're using at the flea market for what she calls 'a steal.' I think they were past their prime when she got them. I'm very careful when I sit on them and try not to breathe."

Margot shook her head and her curls hopped in place. I would never say it to her, but her signature curls always reminded me a little bit of tiny baby bunnies skipping up and down on the top of her head. I didn't think it was a comparison she'd appreciate.

"Lois and her flea-market finds. Her house is just one big warehouse. You can barely walk through the living room, it's so jam-packed with her yard-sale and flea-market finds. She needs to purge some of those pieces."

I made no comment because Lois was my friend, but at the same time, I agreed with Margot. Lois had an addiction to shopping and shopping for furniture in particular. She loved to collect interesting pieces, but she really didn't have anywhere to put them in her two-bedroom rental house on the edge of downtown. She lived alone and her collection wasn't hurting anyone; it made her happy, so who was I to offer criticism? It wasn't like she was a hoarder. Lois was a collector.

And she was one of the most giving people I knew. If someone needed a piece of furniture, she wouldn't think twice about giving it to a friend, no matter what it cost her to buy it.

Margot looked over her shoulder at Lois. "It's not the village's fault she bought a rickety chair. I hope she doesn't think she can file a complaint."

"I don't believe she's planning to do that."

"Hmm."

"And if you are so concerned about Lois, why not go speak to her? She's sitting right over there. This ice is for her, and it's melting quickly in the heat."

Margot seemed to think about my suggestion for a moment. "Well, I'm glad she's all right. I'll check on Lois later. You know when there is an event on the square I'm very busy. I always have to run from one thing to the next."

I pressed my lips together to keep myself from saying something I would regret. I still thought she should ask *Lois* how Lois was doing.

"But I am glad I caught you alone. I very much wanted a word with you in private."

I shook the ice in the cup and listened for the rattle. At Margot's raised brow, I steadied my hand. I wasn't shaking the ice to wave her off. I only wanted to know that it had not completely melted away. I had no idea why Margot would wish to speak to me alone. As an Amish person, I could not be on any of her village committees, and I did not have a business or service that would lend itself to events on the square. I was a quilter by trade and a matchmaker by avocation. I subsisted on my small income from selling quilts to local shops and from special orders, and I helped the young Amish men and women in the county to find their matches at no cost. I have had this gift since I was a small child. I knew in my heart when two people were right for each other. I also knew when two people were wrong for each other.

I didn't charge for the matchmaking because it was a gift from *Gott*. It was not meant to be a business venture but an adventure in true love.

"What can I help you with, Margot?" I asked in the friendliest manner I could manage. Because if Margot was asking you something, most likely she wanted you to do something for her. She always did.

"When was the last time you saw Uriah Schrock?" Margot asked in her businesslike way.

"Uriah?" I asked. That was not what I'd expected her to ask at all.

I knew Uriah, of course. We had gone to the same Amish schoolhouse as children, and when we were young, he had been sweet on me. But that made no difference to my feelings. I'd only had eyes for Kip Fisher. Kip and I were married young and had twenty wonderful years together, but then he passed away from cancer when he was in his forties.

Today, Uriah was the groundskeeper of the village square, and that made Margot his boss. If anyone should know where he was, it was she. It made me very curious as to why she was asking me where her employee was. Shouldn't she be the one who knew his whereabouts?

"Uriah was supposed to be here today to set up for the concert as usual." Margot tugged on her curls. "But he never showed up. I called the shed phone at the farm where he's been renting a room, and there was no answer."

My stomach dropped. That wasn't like Uriah at all. He was typically a very responsible man. He would not ignore his work.

"I just wondered if he said anything to you about going back to Indiana. I know the two of you are special friends." She narrowed her eyes at me when she said that last part.

I pressed my lips together and willed myself not to blush. I was far too old for blushing. I wasn't sure what "special friends" meant, but I did not like the sound of it. Special or not, he was my friend, and it worried me Uriah hadn't shown up for work. It was not like him at all.

"Where is he renting a room?" I asked, realizing for the first time that I didn't know where Uriah had been living since he'd returned to Ohio. Had I never asked him?

"He's renting from the Stollers. They are a young couple who live on an alpaca farm."

"Alpaca?" I asked. "I didn't know people in our community were farming alpacas."

"It became very popular in Ohio while you were away."

Ten years after my husband died, I moved to Michigan for a decade to care for my ailing older sister, Harriet. Only after she passed away did I return to Ohio.

I nodded, feeling a little surprised that Uriah had never mentioned that he lived on an alpaca farm. I would think that would be an interesting bit of information to share.

"So have you seen Uriah?" Margot started tapping her foot again. Apparently, it was taking me far too long to give her a straight answer.

"*Nee,* not for a few days. I expected to find him at the concert tonight."

I did not admit to her that I had been looking for him when I first arrived. Usually when Lois and I came to the square for an evening concert, Uriah made a point of stopping by our chairs and saying hello. Months ago, Uriah had asked me to accompany him on a buggy ride. I had been so taken aback by the request that I declined. Somedays, I wished I had the nerve to tell him I had changed my mind.

Margot tugged on her curls, and like some miracle, every time she let them go, they bounced perfectly back into place. "It was very poor form not to tell me that he wouldn't be here tonight. I had to scramble and tell everyone where to put the chairs and where the band should set up. In the past, I have always relied on Uriah to do that sort of thing. You don't think he found himself in some kind of trouble, do you?"

I folded my hands on my lap and held them tightly. "Trouble? What do you mean when you say *trouble*?"

"Could he have gotten lost or hurt? He's just not the type to blow off work. I expect that sort of behavior from the high schoolers we hire during the summer to help out with the grounds, but not from someone like Uriah."

"*Nee*, it does not sound like him." My worry grew. "There must be some sort of explanation. Maybe his buggy broke down."

"Maybe," Margot said. "I'd be lying if I didn't say I'm more concerned than ever now that I know you haven't heard from him either. I thought if anyone in the village would know of his whereabouts, it would be you. He mentioned that he wanted to move back to Indiana this summer, but I can't believe he would do so without telling me first."

My chest tightened. "I did not know that was his plan. When did he tell you?"

"A week or two ago," she said as if the exact date did not matter. "It was always his plan to go back. All his children and grandchildren are there. What would keep him here?"

"Nothing, I suppose . . ." My voice trailed off.

"He said he wanted to tell me"—Margot stopped tapping her foot—"so that I had plenty of time to find a replacement caretaker for the village square. That doesn't sound like someone who would leave without a word."

She was right, it didn't. "Then it can't be that. He'd tell you he was leaving. I'm sure it's something else." I hoped he would have told me too, but I didn't say that.

She stood up. "Well, if you hear from him, let me know. And he'd better have a good reason for not being here tonight. I won't be happy if he doesn't have a good excuse."

I swallowed hard and watched her walk away. At the time, we didn't know how *gut* his excuse really was.

CHAPTER TWO

My hands were shaking after Margot left. I had a sinking feeling that something bad had happened to Uriah. I told myself I was overreacting. There was no reason to assume the worst. My dark thoughts had to be the result of the recent murder investigations I had been involved in since moving back to Harvest. What kind of Amish woman was I that murder was the first thought to come to my mind when someone was reported missing? And I did not know Uriah was, in fact, missing. He simply had not shown up for work. People did that all the time, but not Uriah Schrock.

I glanced at the cup of ice in my hand. Between the hot air and my warm hand, most of the ice had melted. I hurried across the green to Lois.

"You were gone so long, I thought for sure you had flown to the North Pole to harvest the ice."

"Margot stopped me. I'm so sorry." I handed her the cup of ice.

"It's no problem. My knee feels all right now that I've been off it for a bit." She peered inside the cup. "Looks more like ice water to me. I'll drink that. I'm so hot. The concert is finally over, praise be, and we can leave." She stood and gulped down the water. Wiping at her mouth with the paper towels I had also brought, she said, "Much better. Now, what did Margot want with you?"

"She asked me about Uriah," I said and then I went on to tell her what Margot had said about Uriah's uncharacteristic behavior.

"You know, I was surprised he didn't come over and greet us before the concert the way he's always done. I didn't say anything because I didn't want to upset you. I know Uriah is a touchy subject with you."

"Uriah is not a touchy subject." I let out a breath. "I'm sure there is a simple answer as to why he is not at the concert today. I'm sure we will know it very soon. And I'm ready to go home too."

"You can't head home without me. I need to give you a lift."

Then I remembered she was right. My buggy was in the shop for repairs. Lois had picked me up to bring me to the concert.

"It's a nice night for a drive with the air conditioner on full blast," Lois said.

The student musicians hugged their parents and packed up their instruments. "Let's just drop off these chairs at the café, and I will take you home. Maybe I can fix the broken one."

"Maybe." I had my doubts but dutifully folded my unbroken chair.

Lois and I were walking across the grass when a young Amish woman called my name. She hurried toward us. "I thought it was you, Millie," she said.

"Marie Beiler? How are you?" I recognized her as a young employee from my niece's greenhouse.

"I'm so well!" She beamed from ear to ear. "I just wanted to tell you that Jeremy proposed to me yesterday."

I smiled. "And you accepted, I take it."

"Of course! I had to tell you because without you, we would never have been matched together since we are from different districts. You really are blessed by *Gott* to match couples."

I set the chair on the sidewalk and leaned it against my leg. "I am very glad to hear it. And is your family happy?"

She clasped her hands in front of her. "Both families are so very happy."

"Gut."

She looked over my shoulder. "Oh! There is Jeremy waving at me now. *Danki*, Millie." She ran away to the waiting courting buggy.

"Another satisfied customer," Lois quipped. "You really should charge for the service you do."

"I can't charge money for my gift from *Gott*."

She eyed me. "But your quilts cost money."

I wrinkled my nose because I didn't have a *gut* reply to her statement. Even so, it would feel wrong to ask young couples to pay me to find their matches. Love should have no cost.

In silence we crossed Church Street right in front of the big white church with the purple front door. We were headed to the Sunbeam Café, which was still open because Darcy was trying to take advantage of people who might want a bite to eat after milling around the square following the concert. Hers was the only *Englisch* business on the square and the only one still open. I supposed that Swissmen Sweets was semi-*Englisch,* as it was run by Bailey King, an *Englischer,* and her Amish *grossmaami,* Clara. The candy shop was on Main Street on the opposite side of the square.

The café was doing a brisk business, and Lois tucked our lawn chairs just inside the door. "I'll move them tomorrow, but they will be fine there until Darcy closes up." She waved at Darcy. "I'm just going to run Millie home, and then I will be back to help you close up for the night."

Darcy waved back without a word as she rang people out at the cash register.

Lois's sedan was parked in front of the village playground. It was a prime spot, and one that she managed to get almost every day. Children ran around the jungle gym and swing set. Several of them were still wearing concert clothes that were now peppered with dirt and grass stains. I supposed their parents wanted them to run off some steam after sitting through such a long performance.

Lois and I climbed into her car. Even though it was late, I had some work to do when I got home. I had been working on a quilt for an exacting *Englisch* customer. Considering how much she was paying me for the custom quilt, I knew that it had to be perfect. One stitch off and she would ask for her money back.

I sat in the car and let my muscles relax. I'd held myself so still on the lawn chair, thinking it might snap, that it was nice to relax into the car seat. I was also sore from working with my niece at her greenhouse two days a week. Now that it was late summer, the annuals were all but gone and the greenhouse was in the process of preparing for the fall onslaught of orders for mums and pumpkins. Even though my niece would not let me do the heavy lifting, I was sore from reaching above my head over and over again to move and water the greenhouse's hanging baskets.

After a bit of quilting, a *gut* night's sleep would set me to rights. The next day was Saturday, and Edith said she would only need me in the morning at the greenhouse. She would have extra help from some of the young Amish in the district during the afternoon.

The sun disappeared behind the horizon as Lois drove out of the center of the village.

Not far from my little farm, Lois turned onto the county road, which had been under construction all summer. Workers were widening it to accommodate the increased traffic through Holmes County. A flagger stood up ahead of us and held a stop sign high.

"They are never going to finish this road," Lois grumbled. "This is so Ohio. There are two seasons: winter and construction." Just before the flagger, there was a rural, loose gravel crossroad that was more frequented by Amish buggies than cars. "Let's go this way. I need to get back to the café quick to help Darcy. She's been overwhelmed lately, and I'm afraid all those hungry concertgoers will make her lose her head."

"What's wrong with Darcy?" I asked.

She pressed her lips together. "I don't know exactly. She just keeps crying. At first I thought it was over her last boyfriend, but that's been done with for almost a year now. There has to be something else going on. She won't tell me, and I'm trying to be understanding and not press her for information, but it's hard for me. You know I like to get right down to business."

I knew that would be difficult for Lois. She wasn't the type to just wait until someone told her what was going on. There had been many times in my life when I didn't want to discuss something that was upsetting me, and she forced it out of me.

The car kicked up gravel and dirt.

"They shouldn't worry about widening that road when there are other roads in the county that aren't even paved. I wouldn't dare travel this way if it was rainy out. The threat of becoming stuck is just too great."

I chuckled at a memory. "Kip and I got stuck on this road once in a rainstorm. He was fit to be tied that day. By the time he got the buggy wheel unstuck, he was covered from head to toe in mud." I laughed at the memory of my usually mild-mannered husband kicking the buggy wheel when it wouldn't turn. When he caught me laughing, he started to laugh too and pulled me out of the buggy and kissed me in the rain. He got mud all over my dress, but I didn't mind. It was one of the happiest moments of my life. So fleeting and so sweet. We had been young then, just married for a few years. We had no idea what life held for us—that we'd try to have children and fail or that Kip would die when he was still young and strong. I shook the memories from my mind.

I looked out of the window of the car so that Lois would not see the tears that had suddenly gathered in the corners of my eyes. That was over now, and there was no point in shedding any more tears for time lost. Instead, I needed to take comfort in past joys, not bemoan the void left behind.

"What on earth is going on up there?" Lois asked.

Her voice was just the distraction I needed. On the side of the road there were at least four vehicles: two sheriff's department SUVs, an ambulance, and a construction truck. Behind the *Englisch* vehicles, a single Amish buggy stood along the side of the road. The horse stamped its hoof on the dry gravel road.

"Is it some kind of accident?" I asked. "I hope a car did not hit a buggy." It was a tragedy that happened in Amish communities much more often than we cared to think about.

The emergency vehicles and buggy were parked just shy of the weathered covered bridge to the right of the gravel-and-dirt road. The bridge was impassable and had been for years. Large logs blocked the bridge entrance, as it had been decided decades ago the structure was no longer sturdy enough to carry a buggy's weight. Some members of the Amish community claimed it wasn't even fit to carry a squirrel across its length. With newer roads available, like the one under construction, even the Amish communities saw no reason to fix it.

Lois slowed her car. A young deputy stood at the edge of the ravine, staring down below. He wasn't the only one. There were several men and women in uniform peering into the ravine and shining search lights below as they looked. The deputy glanced over at us and paled.

"Hey, it's Deputy Little." Lois pulled the car over to the side of the road and waved at the young officer. "Little! Little, over here! Can't you hear me?"

Deputy Little's shoulders sagged. I guessed he wasn't as happy to see us as Lois was to see him.

CHAPTER THREE

Deputy Little was a short man with concerned eyes. He had recently become engaged to Charlotte Weaver, a formerly Amish young woman from the village and the cousin of Bailey King of Swissmen Sweets. Charlotte had recently left the Amish way and was still in the process of adjusting to what it means to be *Englisch* and what it means to be in love.

Despite all the changes in her life, I wasn't surprised by their engagement. The moment I saw how the pair looked at each other, I knew Luke Little and Charlotte Weaver were destined to be together. What I didn't know was whether their cultural differences would get in the way of their happy ending. First, Charlotte had to decide whether she could leave the Amish. It was my opinion that she hadn't left the Amish because of Deputy Little. It was a decision she was going to make whether or not she fell in love with an *Englischer.*

The young deputy looked around as if to make sure no one was paying him any mind. They weren't. Everyone seemed focused on what was happening at the bottom of the ravine. He walked over to our car. "Lois, Millie, what are you doing here? You shouldn't be here."

Lois wrinkled her nose. "I can be anywhere that I please to be. Last time I checked, this was still a free country, and I, for one, will exercise my rights."

The young deputy sighed. "I know you will. But what are you doing out here at night? No one comes down this road anymore," he said.

"They do if they want to avoid that mess of construction on the state route. We were headed to Millie's home, and I decided to take a shortcut rather than wait for them to clear the road," Lois said.

He appeared to be unconvinced. "You didn't come because someone told you to?"

I leaned across the seat for a better look at the deputy. Holding on to my seat belt so that it wouldn't cut into the side of my neck, I said, "Lois was just taking me home after the Friday evening concert on the square. Why would anyone tell us to come here?"

"No reason." His mouth twitched.

Lois narrowed her eyes. "Deputy Little, do you know that we are both old enough to be your grandmother? Would you go and lie to your grandmother like that?"

He flushed.

"What's going on here, Deputy Little?" I asked. "Was there an accident? I hope a car didn't go over the side of the ravine. Was a buggy hit?"

Deputy Little rocked back on his heels, and his eyes

flitted from side to side as if he was in search of escape. I don't know why he felt trapped. To be honest, if it came down to it, the young, fit police officer would always be able to outrun Lois and me, not that Lois wouldn't try to throw her giant purse and its questionable contents at him if she was pressed.

Lois clicked her tongue. "I have been saying for years that they should put a guardrail along this stretch of road, but no one ever listens to me. At night in the rain or anytime in the winter, this can be a dangerous way to come. A nimble cat could slide right off into the ravine."

"It hasn't rained for days," I said.

"I'm just making a point," she said. "They should have done something about this road, and the bridge, for that matter, decades ago. The ravine has inched its way closer to the road as the banks are eroded by rain and harsh weather."

He shook his head. "It's nothing like that. There wasn't an accident. There isn't a car or a buggy in the ravine . . ."

Lois folded her arms. "Then what is it?" She sat back in her seat, making it clear that she had no intention of moving her car until she had a satisfactory answer.

Deputy Little wiped sweat from his forehead with the back of his hand. Even after sunset, the humidity was high on this muggy August night. "I can't talk to you about it right now, if ever. The sheriff is here."

"The sheriff!" Lois stuck her head out the window for a better look, forcing Deputy Little to jump back or be hit in the stomach. "Why, he is there! It must be something big for the sheriff to come out on a Friday night, much less show his face so deep into Amish territory." She ducked her head back inside the car. "Come on—dish, Deputy."

Deputy Little's Adam's apple bobbed up and down. He shot furtive glances over his shoulder. "I can't."

"Leave him be, Lois," I said. "Deputy Little is right. The sheriff would not like it if he caught him talking to us. You know how Sheriff Marshall feels about the Amish."

"I'm not Amish," Lois said. "Sheriff Marshall shouldn't have a problem with me."

"You're my friend. You associate with the Amish."

Lois rolled her eyes. "Name me one person in Holmes County who doesn't have Amish associations. The sheriff can't even make claim to that."

As she said this, I spotted the sheriff speaking to a paramedic at the back of an ambulance. The ambulance bay was open, and I could look inside. Part of me expected to see a person on a gurney, either injured or, worse, in a body bag. But the bay was empty except for a lot of medical equipment that I couldn't name.

Sheriff Marshall was a large, forbidding man. In his uniform, his ample stomach hung over his belt. Lois was right. It was odd to see him outside of the office. He usually let his deputies do the footwork. If the case went well, he took the glory. If it went poorly, he could blame everything on a deputy or two. He'd been recently re-elected a year ago, so he had three more years in office, but from what I heard, he was always campaigning to keep the top spot in the department. I guessed he was here because he could use whatever was going on in the covered bridge or ravine for his next campaign. Not that he needed the help. The last three times he ran, he was uncontested. No one wanted to go up against the larger-than-life sheriff.

Lois leaned her bare arm on the bottom edge of the

window. "Are you really not going to tell us what happened? Do I have to ask the sheriff?"

"You wouldn't," Deputy Little whispered.

Lois narrowed her eyes. "Wanna bet? I'm always game for a healthy wager."

"Lois," I started to say, feeling bad for the young deputy. Working for such a difficult man like the sheriff had to be challenging. Lois wasn't making it any easier.

Before I could finish my thought, Lois said, "Deputy Aiden would have told us what the problem was. Goodness, I miss that man, and he was easy on the eyes too."

Deputy Little blushed. "He wouldn't have told you outright, and besides, Aiden Brody no longer works for the sheriff's department. He works for the state in the Bureau of Criminal Investigation now."

Lois sighed. "It was a real loss to the county when he left the sheriff's department for BCI, but who could blame him? The sheriff made it a point to make poor Aiden as miserable as possible." She looked at Deputy Little. "I suppose he's doing that to you now."

Deputy Little didn't comment.

"Little!" the sheriff bellowed.

"I have to go. Please leave," he whispered.

"If we leave now, will you tell us what is happening later?" Lois wanted to know.

"I'm sure you will hear all about it. Knowing the people of Harvest, I guess it won't be long before the whole village hears the news." He turned and walked to where the sheriff stood.

"Well, that's all very strange," Lois said as she started the car. She rolled the car by the spot where the sheriff and Deputy Little stood. Sheriff Marshall was glaring at Deputy Little.

I slid down in my seat, so the sheriff wouldn't spot me.

Lois poked me. "Did you drop something? What on earth are you doing?"

I lifted the lever that lowered the seatback and lay as flat as I could. "I'm hiding. I don't want the sheriff to penalize Deputy Little for talking to an Amish person. We need the deputy to stay in the department if we want the Amish in this county to be treated fairly at all. Deputy Aiden's departure was a big loss for our community too, not just for the *Englisch.*"

Lois shook her head. "You look like an international spy . . . well, the schoolmarm version. Maybe I should change your code name from Amish Marple to Double O Bonnet. I actually like the ring of that."

"Don't," I said from my semi-prostrate position. "I was just getting used to Amish Marple."

"You're no fun at all." She chuckled. "Maybe I will just give myself an international spy name. It goes with my hair, don't you think?"

As Lois drove away from the covered bridge, I peeked out the passenger-side window. A lone Amish man with a long white beard stepped behind the ambulance, illuminated by the vehicle's flashing lights. It could have been my imagination, but I was almost certain it was Uriah Schrock.

CHAPTER FOUR

Lois pulled into my driveway a few minutes later, and my two Boer goats, Phillip and Peter, raced down the driveway. They were out after dark and having the time of their lives. Typically, I penned them in the barn just before dusk.

"If it's all the same to you, Millie, I'm going to skip the goat hugs tonight. I need to get back to the café to help Darcy."

I nodded and got out of the car, lost in thought.

Usually, I would have mentioned to Lois that I thought I'd seen Uriah, but something stopped me. I wondered if I had just imagined seeing him there. Was it another man with a white beard? In the dim light, I might have been mistaken, but deep down, I knew I wasn't. Phillip leaped into the air next to the car as I shut the door behind me.

"Don't you dare nick the paint with your hooves!" Lois cried through the open window.

The goats danced away from her car but kept up their playful antics. Phillip and Peter wanted to play, and that was a sure way to run Lois off. She loved my goats, but being chased by them wasn't her idea of a good time.

When I got the goats into the barn and settled myself in the house, I worked on my quilting as planned. As I sewed, I was preoccupied with my conversation with Margot and the scene with the police on the side of the road. I wished that I had told Lois I'd seen Uriah before she'd left.

There was no way to tell her until the next day. The middle of the night was not the time to walk the half-mile to the shed phone I shared with the Raber family, my closest neighbors. The phone was on their farm, and they were kind enough to let me use it whenever I had a need, but I didn't believe that extended to after dark. Plus, I would risk turning an ankle or, worse, waking up the goats.

When the quilting was a flop, I went to bed, but I tossed and turned on the mattress. I was so restless, my cat, Peaches, aptly named because he was the color of a ripe peach, hissed from his post at my feet. He didn't like being bounced like a ball on a trampoline.

"I'm sorry," I said to him in Pennsylvania Dutch.

He mewed softly as if filing one last complaint before closing his eyes. I had always believed cats were night creatures, but Peaches proved that not to be true. Maybe it was because he was on the same time clock now as Phillip and Peter, my goats. The three of them ran the farm and got into as much mischief as possible.

Thinking of the goats made me wonder what they

were up to. I hoped they were sleeping peacefully in the barn and not eating something they shouldn't. It was amazing to me what they would eat. Once Phillip took a bite out of the wire fence around my vegetable garden, and I rushed him to the vet. Thankfully, he was fine, but he gave me quite a scare. The two of them were ornery rascals, but I loved them dearly.

I lay in bed and must have fallen asleep from sheer exhaustion at some point because the light coming in through the window the next morning woke me up. The sun was not completely up yet, but it inched toward the horizon. That told me it was time to get up. I had an idea forming in the back of my mind, and it was best to start to work on it right away.

Peaches did not share my feelings about the dawn. He rolled over and burrowed under the down quilt. He had no interest in rising early. I walked into the kitchen and boiled hot water on my propane-powered stove. A morning like this called for a strong cup of coffee made in my French press.

The French press had been a gift from Lois, and I had to admit that I'd grown quite fond of it. It made the perfect cup of coffee. By the time the water boiled and the coffee steeped in the press, the light was breaking through the trees. I let out a breath. Sunrise was my very favorite part of the day. Each morning offered new opportunity and ways to give thanks to *Gott* for this life.

I took my steaming plain white mug and went outside to watch the sunrise over the barn. I let out a breath. An old Amish saying came into my mind as I watched the sun come up. "Contentment is not getting what we want but being satisfied with what we have." That had been true in my life. There were many things I had wanted that

I did not receive, and yet, I was content with my life . . . on most days. No human I knew was content on all the days, nor did I believe the Lord expected that any more than He expected human perfection this side of heaven.

As quiet as I was trying to be, the goats must have heard me, because plaintive bleating came from the barn. From the way they were carrying on, you would have thought I locked them inside the barn all day and all night, never letting them see the outside world at all.

I left my mug on the edge of the planter by the back door. I had learned long ago, it did not work to have hot coffee around the goats unless you wanted it to be spilled.

The dew on the grass dampened the toes of my black tennis shoes, but I enjoyed the fresh scent of wet earth.

I slid open the barn door. "Good morning, you two," I greeted the goats.

Both goats lay in their large pen on the fresh bed of straw that I'd thrown down for them the day before. I change their straw at least twice a week. Ruth Yoder claimed they were the most spoiled goats in Holmes County. That might be true, but they also brought me much joy. Changing the straw more often than another Amish farmer might was the least I could do for them, even if they seemed to have a knack for finding trouble.

Phillip, my black-and-white goat, was typically the instigator, but Peter, who was brown and white, wasn't without fault. I'd bought them when I first moved back to Holmes County, to help me clear the brush around my house. Nothing is better for clearing brush than a couple of hungry goats, but after the project was completed, I decided to keep them. I learned the goats were fine companions. They amused me. They were also *gut* guard goats.

They made sure I didn't receive any unexpected guests on the farm.

I put my hands on my hips and peered at them over my glasses. "Well, aren't you both a pair of lazybones. You're not even going to bother to get up and say *Guder mariye*?"

Phillip struggled to his feet as if it was a tall order to stand. He was a dramatic goat to be sure. He shuffled over to me and bumped his hard forehead into my hand. It was gentle bump, more of a *hello* than *I want to knock you over*. He peeked behind me. I knew he was looking for the cat. Those goats loved Peaches something fierce, and Peaches chose to love them back when he felt like it, which was not quite as often as the goats hoped.

"*Nee,* Peaches is not with me. He's still sleeping inside. Neither of us got much sleep last night."

If Ruth Yoder, the bishop's wife, knew that I spoke to my goats as if they were people, she would tell her husband and insist I have some type of interrogation about my beliefs as an Amish woman. Ruth Yoder liked to stage any number of interventions. I knew the goats didn't understand what I was saying, but they listened in their own way, and when you live alone as I do, that's just about all you can ask for.

"Boys, I was wondering if you are up for a morning walk."

Peter hopped to his feet when he heard the word "walk." Maybe the goats understood more than I thought.

Phillip jumped in place as if he knew exactly what I'd said too.

The goats, Peaches, and I each proceeded to eat our breakfasts. The goats had feed, Peaches had cat food, and

I had a piece of lemon blueberry pound cake left over from a quilting circle meeting a few days before. All right, that was not true—I had two pieces. At my age, I thought I had a right to indulge now and again. Worry always made me hungry, and there was nothing I loved more than blueberries. I could eat blueberries or anything with blueberries in it for breakfast, lunch, and dinner. I not only could do it but thought it sounded like a delightful plan.

With full bellies, the goats and I hit the road. Peaches stayed behind and watched from the porch while I walked my bicycle to the front of the house. The bike had been a gift from my niece. She'd found it at a local salvage yard and took it to a local Amish bike shop to have it refurbished. She'd had it painted bright red of all colors. It wasn't very Amish to have a bright red bicycle, but Edith insisted that I was a bright red person.

I was tickled by the gift but a little wary too. At first, I must admit, I was a little afraid to ride it. It had been such a long time since I had ridden a bike any distance, but the old saying is true: You never forget. I tucked my skirts around my ankles so that they wouldn't get tangled up in the spokes. This would be a *gut* time to wear trousers like the menfolk, and Lois was quick to point out how impractical skirts are in situations like these. But after sixty-some years wearing skirts, I don't think I could bring myself to wear anything else.

"Let's go!" I called to the goats.

They ran after me. Usually when we went on these walks, I turned right on the road, toward Edith's greenhouse, but this time I went in the opposite direction. Phillip and Peter were confused by my change of direction for a moment, but then trotted along behind me as if we went this way all the time.

"Goats, want to go on an adventure?" They galloped along. I smiled. Walking the goats was something I had started earlier in the summer, and I had come to realize that we all liked it. Phillip and Peter were an active pair, and they needed things to do or they found trouble. The bike rides were *gut* exercise for all of us.

My first ride with the goats had been unplanned. I rode the bicycle around the farm, getting used to the feel of it again. I also wanted to practice the old skill without an audience. It turned out I did have an audience of sorts. It was my cat and the goats. Almost immediately, when I began riding up and down the driveway, Phillip and Peter fell in line behind me. Then, to test them, I turned onto the street. They followed me there too. I rode all the way to the greenhouse that day, and the goats were always a few steps behind me. The next morning, I saw them standing by the bicycle with eager faces. It seemed that a new family outing had been born. Not that Ruth Yoder would approve of my thinking of the goats as family. Then again, Ruth did not approve of many of my ideas.

Amazingly, this morning the goats stayed with me even though I'd changed their normal route. Lois would say it was because I was the one who fed them, so they associated me with food. Being ravenous eaters, they would follow me wherever I went. Just in case she was right, I always carried some vegetables from the garden in my bicycle basket in case I might have to lure the goats back home. As of yet, I hadn't had to use them.

I slowed my bicycle when the weathered covered

bridge came into view. I had thought that I would be able to ride up to the bridge, peek over the side of the ravine, and maybe see whatever Deputy Little and everyone else had been investigating the night before. That wasn't to be, because I wasn't the only person near the bridge. The deputy's car was there. There was also a silver van with a watermelon-sized dent in the right side and a cracked rear window.

Deputy Little stood on the side of the road with his back to me. Across from him, a young *Englisch* man bounced back and forth on the balls of his feet, waving his hands around while he spoke.

The young man brushed his artificial-looking black hair away from his forehead, but it flopped right back in his face to cover his eyes. Despite the hot and humid summer morning, he wore black jeans and a black T-shirt. Not the most practical outfit for standing in the hot August sun.

I parked my bicycle beside the deputy's car and climbed off. "You two stay here," I whispered to the goats. "I don't want Deputy Little to see you. I don't think he would look kindly on my bringing goats here."

Phillip whimpered.

"Shh. Now, stay here with the bike. I'm just going to see what's happening, and then we are going straight home. Do you understand?"

Phillip and Peter shared a look. I didn't have high hopes that they would stay put as I'd asked.

I peeked around the side of the deputy's car. Then, seeing that neither man noticed me, I hurried over to the other side of the van, so I could hear them better.

"I told you, man," said the *Englischer* in black. "We're making a documentary about the unsolved murder of

Samuel Zook. I think it really has potential. True crime is hot right now!"

I sucked in a gasp and clasped a hand over my mouth for fear they might hear me breathing. I had not heard the name Samuel Zook in a very long time. He was an Amish man who had been found dead in his buggy forty years ago on a cold January morning in this very spot. From what I remembered, he had been stabbed in the neck with a knitting needle. He was also Uriah Schrock's brother-in-law. Was that why Uriah had been here last night? Was he participating in this documentary?

"With all the interest in Amish culture lately," the young man went on, "we thought it would be timely. We were even thinking of entering it in a film festival. We have the skills to do it. We all graduated at the top of our classes in film school. I mean, Sundance can't be that hard to get into, can it?"

"Tell me again about the skull," Deputy Little said.

Skull? Had I heard him right? Did he say *skull*?

I heard the click-click of hooves on the gravel road behind me. I spun around and waved at the goats to hide behind Deputy Little's SUV. They stood there and grinned at me as if we were all playing a fun game. This would not end well, I thought. The goats would certainly give my presence away.

"How did you find the skull? Tell me again," Deputy Little said.

The young man sighed. "Oh, all right. We were trying to get an aerial shot of the ravine, and the drone malfunctioned. The aerial would have been perfect for the opening credits. This is a really creepy, rundown place, and it's great for atmosphere. Xander was on the controls, ran the drone into the—"

"Xander is one of your colleagues?"

"Yeah, but probably not for long. That drone cost me a couple grand, and he busted it." He scowled. "I'm going to have to cut him loose."

"The skull?" Deputy Little prodded.

"Right, so I told Xander he had to go down into the ravine to retrieve my drone. I still hoped I could save it. When he got down there, he screamed his head off. He sounded like an extra in a horror film. I climbed down and found him staring at this skull half buried in the mud. It was creepy, man, like right-out-of-a-movie creepy. We both knew right off it was a human skull, so that's when we called you guys. Xander and I weren't going to babysit a skull, so we grabbed the drone and climbed out of the ravine. When we reached the top again, there was this old Amish dude standing on the side of the road like a statue. He scared us all half to death. I swear to God, I thought it was the ghost of Samuel Zook come back to the scene of the crime."

"That wasn't a ghost," Deputy Little said.

"Yeah, I know, but I'd just found a human skull and that shakes you up a little. I mean, it was dusk, and this Amish dude just stands there without saying a word like an apparition. It had us spooked. Xander wanted to bolt, but I had a good head on my shoulders and started to film. I think it's going to make a spooky take."

"I'm going to need to see that film, Tyler," Deputy Little said.

Tyler frowned.

"What did the man look like?" Deputy Little asked.

The goats came closer to me, and I held my finger to my mouth to tell them to keep quiet. Usually when I was eavesdropping, it was with Lois. That could be stressful, but not as stressful as snooping with goats.

"He had a white beard. I mean, it's hard to say. He was Amish. It wasn't like his clothes were unique, you know. They all wear the same thing."

Deputy Little folded his arms.

"You saw him yourself last night. He was that same Amish dude who was hanging around last night. It freaked me out how he was just staring down the ravine with this ghostly, blank look on his face. If you ask me, something is wrong with him. It's like he needs to be put in a mental hospital or something." He shook his head. "How can a person stare that long? It's not natural."

"Did he say anything to you before the authorities arrived?"

"He told us to call the police because there had been a murder. It was creepy. Do you think he was the killer?"

My stomach dropped.

Deputy Little made a noncommittal sound.

Peter stepped out from behind the van, and I leaned over to grab him.

"Is that a goat?" the young man asked.

The goats seemed to think that was an opening greeting of sorts because both of them tottered around the van.

The young man opened and closed his mouth. "There is an old Amish woman and two goats standing by my van. Like, I'm not making this up."

Deputy Little rubbed the back of his neck as if he had a sudden pain in it. I wondered if I was the one who'd caused it.

CHAPTER FIVE

"Millie Fisher, what on earth are you doing here?" Deputy Little asked.

Then he turned around and found Phillip and Peter on either side of me. He gave a great sigh. Without any better idea of what I should do, I waved. "*Guder mariye*, Deputy."

The young man opened and closed his mouth. "I feel like I'm in another universe. Is it normal for old Amish people to just appear on the side of the road like this? I mean, this is the second time, so I'm starting to think it's a thing around here."

I put my hands on my hips. "Who are you calling old, young man?"

The goats lowered their heads as if they planned to butt him right into the ravine.

He swallowed hard. Maybe I was as scary as Uriah had been to him.

"Millie, what are you doing here?" Deputy Little asked again.

"I'm taking my goats for a walk. Or a bike ride, really. They walk, and I ride my bicycle. We were just out for a little exercise on this fine summer morning before it grows too hot for it."

"I've definitely entered the Twilight Zone. Is this something the Amish do? Walk goats?" Tyler asked. "Are we done here? Because I have to finish shooting film so I can go back home to Cincinnati and get this production in the can."

Deputy Little looked back at him. "You can't leave the county until this case becomes clearer. We don't know the identity of the person you found at the bottom of the ravine, but we need to determine whether foul play was involved."

"Foul play? Like murder? Another murder? I know that's what the old Amish dude said, but do you think he's right?" Tyler's voice became increasingly excited. "If it ties in to Samuel Zook's death, it will be epic for my film. I mean, maybe we will be going to Sundance and Cannes."

Deputy Little frowned at him and then turned back to me. "If you are just walking your goats as you say, Millie, you should continue on your way."

"I'm going to go too," Tyler announced. "I have more film to shoot."

"I have a few more questions for you," Deputy Little said to the young man.

Tyler held up his hands. "Hey, man, you can't keep me

here. I don't know anything about this situation. That skull was down there for a long time. I'm no bone doctor or anything, but it could have been longer than I've been alive. Xander and I have nothing to do with it."

"Even so, you have to stay in the area until the sheriff's department says you can leave."

Tyler opened and closed his mouth. "I'm going to end up making a documentary about you. My company and I are determined to document social injustice through film."

Deputy Little scowled at him. "It's not injustice. It's protocol."

Tyler shook his head as if Deputy Little was naïve. "When we decided to come to Amish country to shoot this film, we never for a second suspected how weird it would be. And who is she anyway?" He pointed at me. "Maybe she's the Amish dude's wife and knows all about the murder."

"Tyler, she's a neighbor, not his wife," Deputy Little said.

Tyler didn't look convinced. "If you ask me, the skull is related to Samuel Zook's murder. I mean, part of the story is that his wife went missing the night he was killed, right? Could it be her? I'm not a detective, but I've watched a ton of true crime to get ready for this film, and I'd put my money on that."

A chill ran down my spine, and Peter must have sensed my nerves because he scooted closer to my side.

Deputy Little glanced at me. There was a pained expression on his face. Was it because he was aware I had known the missing woman, Galilee Zook, Uriah Schrock's older sister? Everyone had called her Gali. Everyone but her husband, Samuel.

"We don't know who it is yet," the deputy said in a clipped tone.

"Could it be Galilee?" I asked. Now I was beginning to understand why Uriah would be at the scene, but how could he have known that the filmmakers would find the skull? And was Gali the reason he'd come back to Ohio after so many years away? Why had he never said that to me?

"Whoa," Tyler said. "Did you know her? You knew Galilee Zook?"

"I knew both her and Samuel. They were members of my district."

My memory traveled back to the day I'd heard the news. Kip and I had been at home making breakfast on a cold January morning when a neighbor stopped over to say that Samuel's buggy had been found on the side of the road near the covered bridge. Samuel was dead, and Gali was missing. The entire Amish community had been shocked. Nothing like that had ever happened in our village before. No one knew what to think. There was so much fear in the community that someone was out to kill Amish members.

I tried to remember what I knew about the night of the murder. Weather conditions had been poor, and Samuel had picked up Gali from her job as a waitress at the Amish Corner Bench, an Amish restaurant on the outskirts of Harvest. It was unusual for Samuel to pick her up. Most nights she rode her bicycle home. But neither one of them made it home that night. Samuel and Gali had no children and no one else living with them on their small farm. No one knew they were missing or in trouble until the buggy was found the next day by an Amish farmer.

The sheriff's department had investigated, but it was a halfhearted attempt. The Amish community was even more nervous about communicating with law enforcement back then than they are now. From what I remembered, the sheriff's department didn't press the community to tell them what they knew about Samuel and Gali.

Then, a few weeks after the murder and Gali's disappearance, there was an article in the *Englisch* newspaper saying that the police believed Gali was the killer. The Amish community was shocked, but no one protested the article. No one wanted to become involved with the police.

At the time, my husband, Kip, said someone should look for Gali and that she could not have killed her husband. When he said that, I asked him to go to the bishop and the sheriff. He claimed it wasn't our place, and we shouldn't get involved. That was the end of the conversation. I was a young Amish wife who was doing her best to follow her husband's lead. It was what I'd been taught to do. Sometimes, in the dead of night, I wondered how Kip and I would get along these days, had he lived. After twenty years on my own, I was surer of myself. I don't think I'd take his decisions as law any longer.

I swallowed hard as I thought back to that time. We stood on the spot where Samuel had died; a skull had been found at the bottom of the ravine; and Uriah was at the scene last night. I could see how Tyler had made the leap that it was all connected. I found myself making the leap as well.

"Oh, wow, this is great," the young *Englischer* said. "Could I interview you for the documentary? I think it would add a lot to have first-person accounts of that time. Maybe you can put me in contact with other Amish people who were around back then? How old were you at the time?"

"Tyler," Deputy Little said. "You're here so that I can interview *you* about what your drone found, not so you can interview Millie."

"Drone?" I asked. Tyler had said that word before, but I hadn't known what he was talking about.

"I'll show you," Tyler said and ran over to the van.

"We have your drone in evidence," Deputy Little said.

"Dude, do you really think that's the only drone I have? You never know when these things will malfunction or run into a tree. It happens a lot if I have Xander piloting the drone. The guy never learned to fly it well. I should have taken the controls."

He opened the sliding door of his van and rooted around inside. Deputy Little stiffened and put a hand on his duty belt near his gun.

The inside of the van was a tangle of cords, plastic food wrappers and containers, crumpled sheets of paper, and precarious towers of cardboard boxes. I didn't know how Tyler hoped to find anything at all in the mess, but in less than a minute, he came out with a black contraption that looked like a mini airplane with a propeller on top.

He held it out to me for a better look. "A drone. Isn't she a beauty? This one is my favorite. She's great for long distances. Thankfully, this was not the one that fell into the ravine. That one cost me twenty-five hundred, but this one was four times that." He pointed to the bottom of it. "This is where we attach the camera." He turned to Deputy Little. "I will be getting my other drone and camera back, won't I?"

The deputy nodded. "You should be, in a day or two."

"Good. I need to protect my gear. Being an independent filmmaker takes money, most of which I don't have. I don't have a big studio backing me."

"Did I hear right that you said you found a skull in the ravine?" I asked.

Deputy Little opened his mouth as if he wanted to say something, but Tyler was faster. "Oh, yeah. Yesterday, we were doing aerial shots of the ravine for our film. My friend Xander crashed the drone into a tree, and it took a nosedive down. We climbed down there and it landed right near a human skull. It looked like an animal had dug it up."

I shivered.

"That's enough, Tyler," Deputy Little said. "You're free to go now. I will find you if I need to ask any more questions, and I'll let you know when you can come to the station to claim your drone."

"All right," Tyler said and set his drone back into the messy van. "But it can't take too long. We have to get this project done if we want to submit it to the film festival. I need to edit at home in Cincy. I don't have the right equipment here."

Deputy Little frowned but made no promises. Peter and Phillip stepped around me, closer to the ravine's edge, as Tyler climbed into his van and drove away.

After he was gone Deputy Little looked at me. "Millie, what are you really doing here? And don't tell me that you were walking your goats."

"I *was* walking my goats. I have walked my goats every day this summer." I paused. "But I was snooping too."

"At least you're honest," he muttered.

"Now, tell me about this skull. What does it have to do

with Uriah?" I peered down my nose at him, which was a bit hard since he was taller than I was.

The young deputy frowned. "Who said anything about Uriah?"

"I heard Tyler talking to you about the murder that happened here. Uriah's brother-in-law was killed on this very spot and his sister went missing. Also, Uriah didn't show up to work the Friday night concert last evening, and Margot was fit to be tied."

"I'm sure she was," Deputy Little said. "I think it would be more newsworthy if Margot was calm."

"You won't have that when it comes to her special events on the square." I paused. "Also, I know that Uriah is somehow involved in this. I saw him on the side of the road when Lois and I were leaving last night."

Deputy Little sighed.

I studied the deputy's face. "Is he in trouble?"

Deputy Little wouldn't look at me; instead, he rubbed the back of his neck. "Millie, I can't talk to you about this case."

"Why not? It clearly has connections to my Amish district, and I was living here at the time of the murder. I knew Samuel and Gali Zook. Not well. They were a bit older than I was, but I knew who they were, and I certainly know Uriah."

He sighed. "This is the first big case we've had since Aiden Brody left the department."

"Is it a murder investigation?"

"Not yet," he admitted. "Right now, we're considering it a suspicious death. When the coroner tells me how old the bones are, whether they are male or female, and how the person might have died, then we can make a better determination."

"You found more than the skull?" I shivered.

He made a face, and then said finally, "We found most of a skeleton. It was buried. How long ago, we don't know."

I shivered. "If it was buried like that, doesn't that mean murder?"

"Depends how long the body was there. Mud and leaves could have covered it over time."

"But you said most of it was there. Wouldn't—" I paused and closed my eyes. Then I opened them and forced myself to go on. "Wouldn't an animal have scattered the bones if the body was left out in the open? Or wouldn't someone have stumbled on it before? I know that not many people come down this road anymore, but a hunter or a hiker should have seen something."

Deputy Little studied me. "You know way more about murder than the average Amish matchmaker."

"Is that a compliment?"

Instead of answering, he removed his ball cap and smacked it on his knee. "If this is a homicide investigation, I can't mess it up."

"And with my help—well, Lois's and my help—you won't. You know that Lois will want to be involved too."

"I wouldn't expect anything else."

Phillip ran to the edge of the ravine and peered down. The goat's movements made me forget the skull and Uriah for the moment.

"Phillip." I put my hands on my hips. "You come away from there. You could fall."

He looked at me, then back into the ravine. He was a surefooted climber, but he wasn't a mountain goat. If he got down to the bottom, I didn't know if he'd be able to get back up to the top.

I pointed at my feet. "I want you over here right now."

Phillip looked at Peter, and Peter backed up. Usually, Phillip could convince Peter to go along with all his hare-brained schemes, but that didn't seem to be the case when it came to galloping into ravines. Peter feared heights. Once, Phillip had climbed on the top of my buggy, and Peter watched from below. It didn't matter how much Phillip bleated at his brother; Peter never climbed to the top.

"Do you want me to grab him for you?" Deputy Little asked.

"*Nee*, if you try to, he will think it's a game and run down into the ravine twice as fast. You both might be hurt."

I reached into my bicycle basket and came out with a carrot that was as thick as my wrist. The vegetable garden had done very well this year. Peter jumped after the carrot.

"*Nee*, Peter. I will give you one in a moment for being a *gut* goat just as soon as we convince your brother to stay out of trouble." I shooed him away. "Phillip! Phillip! Come get your carrot."

The black-and-white goat stared down into the ravine as if mesmerized by the possibility of adventure.

I called again, and he finally turned his head in my direction. I held out the carrot to him. "Shame on you, Phillip. You can't get in the way of police work."

He didn't seem the least bit remorseful, but he did look very interested in the carrot. He moseyed over to me to chomp on his treat.

Peter stamped his hoof like the prodigal son's older brother, and I reached into the basket to remove a carrot for him as well. I held it out to him, and he delicately took it from my hand.

Deputy Little shook his head. "I thought Jethro the pig was the only animal in Harvest with a personality."

I folded the linen cloth over the remaining vegetables in my basket. I didn't want the goats to think that this was going to become a regular thing. "*Nee,* all animals have personalities if you are willing to get to know them."

Phillip and Peter stood sweetly on the side of the road as if they had never done a thing wrong in all their lives. I knew better.

"I'll take your word for that, Millie," he said. "Now, I will have to ask you and your hooved friends to leave. I have to get back to the station. I would much rather not leave the three of you standing so close to the edge of the ravine."

"I have to go too," I said as if it had been my idea all along. "I'm helping my niece at Edy's Greenhouse today. Saturdays in the summer are always busy."

He nodded. "And that's where you're going to be all day?"

I put my hands on my hips. "I don't know why you need to know where I will be all day, Deputy." I pointed at the ravine. "You don't think that I have something to do with all this, do you?"

He shook his head. "I don't have a reason to, but it would be helpful to me if you gave me a bit of time to start investigating this case before you poke your nose into it."

"How much time do you need?" I cocked my head.

"How much are you willing to give me?" he countered.

"The morning," I said. "And then I'm talking to Lois."

"I suppose I will have to be happy with that."

I nodded. "You will."

"Be careful, Millie. Both you and Lois should be careful. We could be dealing with an accident here, but there is a chance too that it's murder. A very good chance."

I said good-bye to the deputy and climbed back on my bicycle. Pedaling down the country road, I whistled for the goats. Phillip took one last long look at the ravine, and then the two of them trotted behind me all the way back to the house.

CHAPTER SIX

A fter being home for a short while, I rode my bicycle to Edy's Greenhouse. My niece Edith's greenhouse was the largest in Harvest. It was a popular shopping destination for both Amish and *Englisch* looking for the perfect plants and flowers for their gardens. Thinking that the goats had had enough adventure for one day, I left them home with Peaches. Besides, Edith wasn't always glad to see them at the greenhouse as they tended to eat the flowers.

Even though I had been up for many hours, it was just before nine in the morning when my bike tires crunched over the gravel driveway of Edy's place. Edith and her three children were in the front of the greenhouse. Edith was telling the older boys where to put the flower displays for the day while their younger sister sat in the grass and played with the family cat. The little girl wore a pale pink dress and her skirt was spread across the grass like a blanket. The white cat that was Peaches' mother lay on her back on the girl's skirt and patted at her fingers with her paws. It was just like a postcard of an Amish girl sold in the gift shops in the village.

"Micah, put the pot of sunflowers there. Be careful not to break their stems." Edith waved at me.

I came to a stop next to her on the driveway.

"Micah has been around plants so much of his life, you would think he'd be mindful of the stems." She glanced around. "What? No goats? I thought for certain they would be with you today."

"I was up early and already took them for a walk," I said, removing my large black bonnet. I should have left it at home. It was too hot for a bonnet on such a warm summer's day.

She laughed. "*Aenti* Millie, you're the only person I know who would walk her goats while riding a bicycle. It's one of the oddest things that I have ever seen."

I smiled. "I think you need to spend more time with Lois then. She does three or four odd things a day."

She chuckled. "I'm glad you left Phillip and Peter at home. We have beautiful weather, so it promises to be a busy Saturday. I can't be worried about what trouble your goats might get into and serve my customers at the same time."

I was about to comment on that when a buggy turned into the driveway.

Edith shaded her eyes. "I wonder who that could be. We don't open until ten." She dropped her hand. "Although I know there are many in the district who come whenever they like. They think since I live a few yards from the greenhouse, I'm always available to them to sell plants."

Edith might not know who was coming, but I did. I recognized the horse and buggy right away as Uriah's. They weren't his specifically. He had been renting the horse and buggy since he returned to Ohio.

Ya, the Amish can rent buggies and horses just like the *Englisch* can rent cars. It's not our first choice, though. We prefer to own rather than borrow. For an Amish man in particular, owning his own horse and buggy is a source of pride and self-respect. However, in Uriah's case it made sense for him to rent. He wasn't planning to be in Harvest long, or so he'd said over a year ago now.

"Is that Uriah Schrock?" Edith asked. "He doesn't have a garden, as far as I know. What is he doing here?"

A knot formed in my stomach. He was here to talk to me. I knew that. I would not be the least bit surprised if Uriah had seen Lois and me drive by the ravine last evening. He would guess I had questions. He would be right. I had so many questions.

"He must be here to speak to you, *Aenti* Millie. The children and I will finish getting ready for today's customers. Take your time." Edith waved to Uriah's buggy and then stepped into the large greenhouse, followed by the children. I was sorry to see her go. I had so many questions for Uriah that they all threatened to come out at the same time.

Uriah climbed down from his buggy and tethered his horse to the hitching post at the edge of the driveway. He then adjusted his black felt hat and strode over to me. "Millie, it's *gut* to see you." He removed his hat. "When I didn't find you at home, I hoped this was where you'd be and not at the café."

I arched my brow. "Why wouldn't you want to see me at the Sunbeam Café?"

He frowned. "Not everything should be said out in the open."

I studied him and felt worry rise in my throat. "Are you well?"

He pressed his lips together. "Physically yes, but I'm sick at heart. So sick at heart, Millie. I thought I would find the cure for it, but it has only become worse."

He was speaking in riddles. "Margot thought you were ill when you didn't come to the concert last night."

He nodded. "I have called her this morning. I knew it was early, but I wanted to tell her how sorry I was before she heard the rumors. She gave me quite a lecture. My ears are still ringing."

"I'm sure she did. Lois and I drove by the old covered bridge last night. I saw you there."

He nodded. "*Ya*, I thought it was you. The two of you have been in cahoots since you were schoolgirls."

I cocked my head. "You make our friendship sound like it's a bad thing."

"*Nee.*" He held his hat in his hands. "I don't think anything in the least. I wish I had a friend to rely on the way you can rely on Lois."

I wanted to say that he could rely on me in that way, but I stopped myself. "I was walking my goats this morning."

He chuckled and rocked back on his heels. "Millie, you are the only woman I know who would say, 'I was walking my goats.'"

"*Ya,* well, they need exercise. More exercise than I can give them on my little farm, and I don't like them running over to the Rabers' farm to pester their sheep. Raellen's husband said that my goats teach the sheep bad habits."

"I don't believe it in the least. Those sheep had poor habits before Phillip and Peter came along." His eyes twinkled with amusement, but I saw some pain and sadness there too. It was the same haunted expression I had seen on his face a handful of times since he'd returned to Ohio. Something was hurting Uriah Schrock at his very core.

"The goats will be happy to know they have your support."

"The goats are not the only ones, Millie."

The way he looked at me caused my gaze to drop. When I looked up again, he had turned and faced the road.

"Deputy Little was by the covered bridge this morning. I saw him on my walk," I said, deciding not to mention that Tyler had been there too. I wasn't sure what Uriah knew about Tyler and the other young *Englisch* man who'd found the skull. I wanted to hear his side of the story first.

When Uriah didn't say anything, I went on. "He said that some young *Englischers* found a skull at the bottom of the ravine."

He faced me again. "This is true. It's my sister."

He said it with so much certainty, the words took my breath away.

"The police have not determined that yet."

"Maybe they haven't," Uriah said with a sad smile. "But I know it's her body. As soon as I saw the skull, I knew it was hers. I have been looking for her for such a long time. As soon as I saw what the young men discovered, I knew my journey had come to an end."

"Your journey?"

"I promised myself before I died I would find out what happened to her. I have been looking for her for over forty years. I never believed the story that she ran away to become *Englisch*."

I swallowed. "Why didn't you believe it?"

"Because it was just a story. A story her husband's family made up and spread around the district in order to discredit her and protect themselves, so they wouldn't have to answer hard questions about Samuel. He was not a *gut* man. Samuel was unkind to Gali. I knew it. My parents knew it and even the leaders of the district knew it. They did nothing. It is not the Amish way to meddle in a church member's marriage—even if the husband is in the wrong."

I thought about this for a moment, thinking back to what I knew of Galilee and Samuel. It wasn't much. They were at least ten years older than Uriah and I. They seemed like a normal Amish couple. Gali was quiet even when she was just around Amish ladies. I thought she was shy. When Samuel died and she disappeared, I attended the prayer vigils that the church held for them, but I didn't do much more than that. I never asked the many questions I had. Kip told me not to, and I did what my husband had asked me to do. Nothing.

And I hadn't felt like I could comfort Uriah either because of our history. When I married Kip, Uriah and my friendship fell away. We'd say hello and wave to each other in passing, but we no longer had in-depth conversations about our lives. We never talked about why we'd stopped our friendship, but I think we both knew it was the best way to respect my marriage to my new husband. Because of this, I never spoke to Uriah back then about his sister's disappearance. I never asked him what he thought might have happened to her. I never asked him how he was.

"I didn't know he was unkind to her," I said softly. Guilt washed over me that I hadn't asked more questions at the time.

He shook his head. "There was no reason for you to know. Our family kept it a carefully guarded secret. The only reason the bishop was aware of the problem was because Gali went to the district leaders for help." He balled his fists at his sides. "They sent her back to her husband."

"They didn't do anything at all?" I asked, feeling ill.

"They spoke with Samuel about being kinder to his wife, but that didn't help. If anything, Samuel was even crueler after having his wrist slapped by the bishop."

I winced. "The bishop at that time was Bishop Yoder's father."

Uriah nodded. "It was."

I didn't know why, but that bit of information felt important. The elder Bishop Yoder, who was long dead by now, had been a severe man. His son, the current bishop and Ruth Yoder's husband, was more relaxed and seemed to be receptive to church members' need to have more technology for their businesses. He was more compassionate too. Many of the older members had mentioned how different the present bishop was from his father. The district had changed quite a bit under the current bishop.

"I went to the bishop myself and asked for help," Uriah said. "I was scared for Gali. I thought Samuel would kill her one day, but they turned me away and said that they'd spoken to Samuel. My brother-in-law promised them he would change his behavior, but I knew it was a lie."

"But Samuel was the one who was killed," I said.

"I know this, and my sister disappeared at the same time. The two things had to be related. But neither the police nor the church leaders took any action. Many believed Gali killed him and ran away. I even believed it for a time—that's why I waited so long to look for her. I suppose it was easier than thinking she was dead. I liked the idea that she had escaped him. If she had killed him, I wouldn't have blamed her."

I had heard others say the same thing those many years ago. "Was he always unkind to her? Why did they marry? Did she love him?"

"I don't know if she ever did. She might have thought she did. She was pressured into the marriage by our parents."

"Why? Galilee was one of the prettiest young women in the district. She could have married any number of young men."

"The family farm was not doing well. Samuel promised to help my parents keep the farm if he could marry my older sister. His family's buggy business was doing very well. He made enough from the buggy shop to keep my parents' farm going until they could get back on their feet."

I knew the buggy shop well. Zooks' Amish Buggies was where my own buggy was currently being repaired. It seemed to me that I would be paying a visit to them very soon. Not just for my buggy but for information.

"And Gali agreed to be part of this bargain?" It made me ill just thinking about it, even though I knew marriages like this happened in the community. Perhaps not as often as they once had, but they still happened.

"Of course. What choice did she have? Our father said that Samuel loved her and she had to marry him. I don't think for a moment that she thought there was any other option open to her." He tugged on his long white beard. "After she disappeared and Samuel died, the farm failed. There was no work for me here, and I couldn't live in the county anymore. My parents went and lived with one of my aunts. I had to leave. This district had too many sad memories. My sister was gone, and you . . ." He trailed off.

"Me?" I asked, surprised. I hadn't had a thing to do with Gali's disappearance. I didn't see how I was tied in to all of this.

He shook his head. "I heard there was work in Shipshewana, Indiana, so I left. I met my wife there and built a new life, but I never forgot my sister. I always thought that she would come and find me if she'd disappeared by her own choice. She never did. As the years passed, I was less and less confident she was still alive. After my wife died, I promised myself I would come back here and find out what had happened to Gali. After forty years, my worst fears are confirmed that she is dead."

"You don't know that for sure. The police haven't determined whether the bones found in the ravine are hers."

"I know they are," he said. He pushed up his sleeve. There was a bandage in the crook of his elbow. "I went to the coroner's office this morning to give blood. Deputy Little said it would be the easiest way to determine if the remains are of my sister."

I shivered. It must have taken great courage on Uriah's part to do that. Also, I was not sure the district elders would have approved. I guessed that Uriah had not asked them before he went. Also, technically he was no longer a member of our district. His district was in Indiana.

"And what if it is Gali? What does that mean for you?" I asked. "Will you have your answer and be at peace? Will you return to Indiana?"

"I thought as soon as I knew the truth, the anxiety I have felt over the loss would go away." He looked into my eyes. "So many times I prayed to *Gott* to help me, to soothe my agony over Gali's disappearance. My guilt for not doing more to help her. I can't say that the severity of the pain has been constant. It has come and gone many times, but not knowing what happened to her festered in the back of my mind. I thought when I knew, I would be cured of what I can only view as chronic grief. But it's not over. The pain is still there." He looked up at the heavens as if petitioning *Gott* Himself. "It's only gotten worse."

"I don't think anyone truly recovers from losing a person they love," I said softly. "Your longing for that person never goes away. But we have hope in the Lord that we will see them again. In the darkest times, that can be our only source of comfort." I folded my arms to steady myself as Kip came to my mind. He was never far from my thoughts.

"That may be true, but I thought there would be a settling in my soul when I knew." His hands bent the brim of his hat in half.

"And that did not happen?" My grip tightened on my bonnet.

"*Nee*. I know she is dead, but I don't know how she died. I don't know how she came to be at the bottom of that ravine. And I must know this."

"I'm not sure you will ever find those answers. She passed away so long ago."

"That may be true, but I have to try." He grabbed my hand, and his hat fell into the grass.

Carefully, I pulled my hand away, picked up his hat, and held it out to him.

His cheeks reddened as he took the hat from my hand. "I am sorry, Millie. But, you see, this is why I had to talk to you. You have to help me find out what happened to my sister."

"What can I do?"

"You can help solve this mystery. If anyone can, it is you."

I had essentially said the same thing to Deputy Little barely an hour earlier, but this felt different. It was one thing to want to find out what had happened of my own accord. It was quite another to be given the charge by another person so close to the tragedy. "I'm not sure I am the right person for this. Deputy Little is on the case. He's a *gut* man and will do his very best."

"But he's not Amish, and he was not alive when my sister disappeared. You can go places where he cannot go. You can speak to people he cannot approach. You have a history with the community he doesn't."

It was all true.

"Besides, is it not true that Lois calls you Amish Marple?" Some of the humor was back in his eyes. "Do not tell me that you haven't already been thinking of sticking your nose into this mystery. If you have not, why did you go to the covered bridge this morning?"

I did not have a *gut* answer to that question, so I said nothing.

CHAPTER SEVEN

Uriah put his hands in his pockets. "I know you will want to speak to Lois about all of this. She will be your helper on the case as usual."

"Lois does like to be involved in most things, and she has been a *gut* friend to me," I said.

He nodded. "She always has been. I envy your friendship. I don't have someone like that in my life. At least I haven't since my wife died. I wish now you had met her. I think the two of you would have been great friends."

I smiled. "If you want my help with all this, you will have to tell me why you were at the covered bridge last night with the police."

Uriah's eyes went wide and then he said, "I had been walking around the covered bridge for the last several days. I knew it was the road that my sister traveled on her way home from work. It was a cold night in January when she disappeared. She was a waitress at the Amish Corner Bench restaurant on Route 39. She usually rode her bicycle to work, but Samuel picked her up that night because it was snowy and cold."

I nodded.

"So you just happened to be there when the young *Englisch* men found the skull?"

"Ya," he said, but he wouldn't meet my eyes.

I didn't want to say it just yet, but I was certain there was something that Uriah was keeping from me about why he'd been near the covered bridge.

I wanted to question him, but he distracted me by saying, "I'm not sure how much you knew about what was happening to my family back then. I'm not sure how much I need to tell you."

I stared at him. "What do you mean? Samuel and Gali were members of our district. Of course, I knew."

"I didn't hear from you after." He wouldn't look at me.

"I—I'm sorry. I sent the family a card and dropped off a cake. I went to Samuel's funeral."

"I know, but I thought since we had been such *gut freinds* as children, you would have visited me."

My stomach tightened. I had thought about visiting Uriah at that time, I had, but Kip said the family needed their privacy. In my heart of hearts, I knew that Kip didn't like the idea of my friendship with Uriah. When I was young, it was not common for young Amish women to have friendships with men outside the family.

Kip thought it was best that I kept Uriah at arm's length, and I had out of respect for my husband. However, I didn't know what *gut* it would do to tell Uriah my reasons now.

I swallowed. "I am sorry I wasn't there for you when you needed support. I should have been."

His shoulders relaxed. It was as if he had been gearing up for an argument of some sort, but when I responded with an apology, all the air went out of him. *"Danki."*

Uriah had been back in Harvest for over a year. I wanted to ask him why he'd never said anything to me about feeling hurt over how I reacted to Gali's disappearance. I wanted to ask him why he had not mentioned Gali at all since he'd returned to the village if she was the reason he was back. I shook these questions from my head because I knew they would not be helpful. Right now, we had to concentrate on what had happened the night before near the covered bridge and how much trouble Uriah might be in over it.

"The restaurant where Gali worked is still open. Have you spoken to anyone there?" I asked.

He nodded. "It's owned by the same family, although the grandson of the man who was the owner when Gali was there is now in charge. His grandfather passed away decades ago. The grandson, Nathaniel, worked at the restaurant then as a busboy. He knew Gali, and I have spoken to him many times about her. I'm afraid that I have made myself a bit of a nuisance at this point. Now, every time he sees me, he dashes away and has one of his workers tell me he's too busy to talk to me."

"Is he Amish?" I asked.

"Nee, he's not. The food is Amish and everyone working in the kitchen and waiting on the tables is Amish, but the owning family is not. They might have been at one time. Their last name is Zurich. I think I remember hearing that the original owner's father was Amish. At some

point a member of the family fell away from the faith. As you know, when that happens, it's very hard to return to it. I think folks get the taste for *Englisch* life, and they just can't come back even if the bishop would allow it."

I nodded. "Is there anyone else in the restaurant who was there at the same time as Galilee?"

He shifted his feet. "*Ya*, the cook, but she won't talk to me."

I wrinkled my brow. "Why not?"

"We have a history." He shoved his large hands into his trouser pockets and shuffled back and forth. "She was sweet on me when I was a young man, but I didn't feel the same. She never forgave me for that."

"What is the cook's name?"

"Alice Springer."

"Do you think Alice would talk to me?"

He shrugged. "Maybe. In my case, she's still sore that I didn't ask her on a buggy ride all those years ago." He rubbed the stubble on the side of his face. I realized he must not have shaved that morning. Though they wear long beards that indicate whether or not they are married, Amish men are dedicated to shaving their cheeks and upper lips every day. Uriah had said that he gave blood that morning so the *Englischers* could run their scientific tests to see if the body in the ravine was his sister. Had he forgotten to shave as a result? I knew it was silly for such a small detail to bother me, but it did.

"I'd be obliged if you tried to talk to her, though." He cleared his throat. "I best be getting on to the square. Margot will have choice words for me because of my absence yesterday. *Danki*, Millie, I feel better having you on my side." He gave me a lopsided smile. "I suppose I should have asked you for help months ago. You and Lois would have found out what became of Gali much sooner than I did. I was only afraid."

I wrinkled my brow. "What were you afraid of?"

"I came here to find out the truth, but in my heart, I knew she was dead. I knew she didn't kill her husband. Gali wasn't built that way. Even if she left to join the *Englisch* like everyone wanted me to believe, she would have found me at some point if she was still alive. We were close. I made myself easy to find even after moving to Indiana. She would have come looking for me. But she never did. That's how I knew she was dead." He shook his head. "It will never make up for losing her, but maybe finding out what happened to her, I will be able to find some peace concerning this matter."

He looked at the ground. The grass was long. I knew it was Micah's job to mow that week. Edith's two sons took turns. Knowing Edith's younger son, I guessed he was putting it off until his *maam* gave him a gentle reminder.

"Is there anything else, Uriah?" I asked, wondering what other surprising news he had to share with me.

"When I went to the station today, Deputy Little had many questions. He wanted to learn everything he could about my relationship with my sister and brother-in-law. He asked who their friends were, which of those friends were still around the village, which had moved away." He met my gaze. "He wanted to know where I was the night Samuel died and Gali disappeared."

I bit my lip and let out a breath. "This is just part of Deputy Little's job. Remember, he was trained by Aiden Brody, and Aiden was always thorough as a deputy."

"*Nee*, Millie, it is more than that. Deputy Little thinks I might have killed them both."

"*Nee!* That can't be! If you did, why would you come

back all these years later to find out what happened to her?"

"Guilt?" he suggested.

I shook my head. I refused to even consider it. "Why would you kill her? What could your motive possibly be?"

"I might not have a motive to kill Gali," he said. "But I knew that Samuel was unkind to her. She cried on my shoulder so many times about it. I was the one who encouraged her to go to the church elders and tell them. I thought they would help. They spoke to Samuel but did little else. Gali was still afraid of him. Deputy Little said I could have killed Samuel, causing Gali to run away in fear, when she fell to her death in the ravine."

I shivered. It was a plausible theory, just as Gali's killing her husband and running away was a plausible theory. However, there wasn't proof for either one.

"Deputy Little is only playing devil's advocate."

He nodded. "That may be true, but it does not change the fact that people in the village will start to talk. Before long, I will be seen as a killer in all their eyes."

I wished that I could tell him he was wrong, but I knew he wasn't.

CHAPTER EIGHT

"*Aenti* Millie, are you leaving?" Micah asked as I climbed onto my bicycle, which I'd parked under a shady tree near the greenhouse.

It was mid-afternoon and the rush of customers had begun to slow down. Edith had said I could leave if I wanted to.

I wanted to. It had been four hours since Uriah had asked me to help him find out what had happened to his sister. After he'd left, customers had flooded the greenhouse and my niece put me on the register. There was no time to even think of what I had learned from Uriah.

My great-nephew looked up at me with imploring eyes.

"I'm leaving," I said. "I need to get to the village to see Lois."

"Can I come too?" He clasped his hands together as if in prayer.

I raised my eyebrows. "And how would you travel with me? My buggy is in the shop."

"I have my own bicycle," he said proudly. "I can just ride behind you. *Maam* doesn't want me riding into the village by myself, but she said I could go with you if it's not too much trouble for you." He looked up at me with imploring blue eyes. "I'm not too much trouble, am I, *Aenti* Millie?"

I ruffled his hair. "You are a whole bunch of trouble, but I love you for it. Let's go double-check with your *maam* first. I'm not taking you with me unless I hear that it's all right with my own ears."

"I would never lie to you, *Aenti,* about being allowed to do anything."

I squinted at him. Micah was the mischievous one in the family. Maybe he would not lie to me outright, but I knew he had a way of playing his mother and me against each other to get what he wanted. "We will double-check."

He sighed as if the weight of the world lay on his thin shoulders.

We found Edith in the greenhouse. Her little girl sat at her feet playing with her faceless Amish doll. "Micah told me that you said he could go to the village with me."

Edith looked up from the handwritten receipts she added up at the sales counter. A dusting of dirt covered the counter's surface, but that wasn't unusual for a greenhouse.

"I did." She smiled. "Micah would like to go to the general store, but we are far too busy for me to take him today. He wants to buy something for himself with his birthday money and with the money he made working at the greenhouse this summer."

Jacob was across the greenhouse, dutifully watering a pot of geraniums. "I would not waste my money in such a way. I'm saving my money to go to the county fair with my friends."

Micah glowered at his brother. "I'm going to the fair too."

"You can go." Jacob went to the next pot with the hose. "But how will you enjoy the rides if you don't have any money to buy tickets?" He shook his head as if he could not understand how irresponsible his younger brother was being.

In the Hochstetler family, Jacob was the conscientious older brother and Micah, the dreamer. In my opinion, we needed both kinds of people in this world, and they needed to learn from one another.

As the boys scowled at each other, I doubted they would agree with me on that last point.

"Are you sure you don't want to save your money for the fair?" Edith asked. "I won't be able to give you any extra money when the time comes."

"I've saved some money for the fair." Micah straightened his shoulders. "It's enough to ride the Ferris wheel and eat a corn dog. I don't need more than that. The best part of the fair is people-watching, and that's free." He gave his brother a look. "I would rather buy something that lasts than waste all of my money on just one day."

Jacob rolled his eyes and moved on to another geranium pot.

Edith shook her head. "Micah, you sound just like your

grandfather when you say that. If that's what you want and if *Aenti* Millie is willing to ride alongside you, then, *ya*, you can go."

Micah pumped his fist in the air in triumph and ran off to get his bicycle.

Edith shook her head. "You will keep watch over him, *Aenti*?"

"Like a hawk." I winked at her and went back outside to my own bicycle.

Micah's bicycle was an old-fashioned ten-speed, and he walked it over to the spot where I was waiting under the shady tree. "It's an *Englisch* bike," he said proudly. "*Maam* found it at the thrift store. I have the fastest bike around. Jacob thinks his bicycle is better because it has a basket and a longer seat, but he's wrong. Faster is always better."

I smiled. "You may have a fast bike, but remember your *aenti* is riding ahead of you and doesn't want to be bowled over."

"I would never run you over on purpose, *Aenti*."

"I should hope not. Try not to do it by accident either." I wagged my finger at him.

He sighed. "All right." He looked as if I had taken all the fun out of our trip to the village.

It was a nice late summer day, and Micah and I had a pleasant ride. We only passed a few *Englisch* cars, and all the drivers were courteous, slowing down and giving us a lot of space. I wished I could say it was always like that riding a bicycle or driving a buggy on the country roads of Holmes County. It wasn't.

When we reached the general store, which was a short walk from the square and the Sunbeam Café, I got off my bicycle as Micah pulled his bike to the rack. He finished parking the bike and stared at me. "You're not coming inside, are you, *Aenti*?"

I stood next to my bike. "You don't want me to go inside?"

"Well." He licked his lips. "There really is no reason for you to, is there? I know what I want, and I will be out quickly."

"Maybe I need something at the store too," I suggested.

"If you do, just let me get it for you. You have an account with the store, don't you?"

I nodded.

"I'll just tell them to put whatever it is on your account."

I engaged the kickstand on my bike. "You really don't want me to go inside, do you?"

"I don't really see a reason for you to . . ."

"I told your *maam* that I would keep an eye on you."

"And you can from here." He wiped his sweaty palms on his pants. He was definitely up to something, and it didn't appear he had any plans of telling me what it was.

I pressed my lips together. "All right. I'll just wait outside the store until you are done shopping. You had better hurry, though. I'm giving you ten minutes or I'm going in there after you."

"You don't have to wait."

I folded my arms. "*Ya*, I do. You are in the village under my care. This is my final offer or I'm going inside too."

"All right." He sighed again.

What on earth could he be buying in there that he wanted to be so secretive about? I could not help wondering.

He disappeared into the building, and I sat on a bench outside the shop.

The scent of lavender hung in the air from a large planter on the table next to me. It mingled with the smell of fresh dirt and manure from nearby farms. It wouldn't be long before the farmers, Amish and *Englisch* alike, would be harvesting their fields and plowing them for winter cover crops. Many farms would plant winter rye or wheat, or red and white clover. The clover would be plowed under in the spring to give nutrients to the soil for another profitable growing season.

Kip had been a farmer. I remembered how busy he was this time of year. He would work from sunup to sundown. Sometimes he came home long after the sun had set. As a young wife, I fretted during the evening hours. I would run around the house and make sure that everything was spotless before my husband came home. I made sure he had a warm meal waiting for him on the stovetop or in the oven. Many times, I would have everything ready hours before he arrived back from the fields. I would just wait for him and wait some more.

I had always thought I would have children who would fill those anxious hours at the end of the day, but a child was not a blessing that *Gott* bestowed on us, despite the hours I prayed for one. Kip prayed fervently too.

As the years passed without a *kind* to tend to, I came to love those quiet evening hours while I waited for Kip to return from his work in the fields. As time went on, I worried less and less about being perfect. It was a gift that came with age and stability in love. It was my time to spend quilting and chatting with the Lord. By that time, I had long since accepted that it would just be Kip and I until the end of our days. I never for a moment thought Kip's end would come so soon.

I smoothed my skirt over my knees even though there wasn't a wrinkle or crease in the fabric. I had been thinking about Kip often lately. I wondered if it was because of my friendship with Uriah. Or was it Uriah's focus on the past as he tried to discover what had happened to his sister? For me, it was impossible to think of days gone by without thinking of my late husband.

"Mildred Fisher, what are you doing sitting on that bench like you have all the time in the world? Don't you have a quilt to piece?" a sharp voice asked me.

I looked up. There was only one woman in the district who would give me a difficult time about sitting and resting a spell or call me by my full name, which I hated. I couldn't see anyone wanting to be named Mildred. "Hello, Ruth."

The bishop's wife folded her arms over her chest. Ruth was a strong, tall woman with steel-gray hair, glasses, and the most disapproving stare I had ever seen on another person. Her stare was so powerful, I had seen it cause people to admit things they hadn't even done.

"Millie," she said, using my preferred name this time. "What are you doing sitting on a bench twiddling your thumbs? Shouldn't you be working on your quilt commission? If you want the ladies in the circle to help with the quilting, you must get on with the piecing. You can't expect us to do all the work for you." She sniffed and patted the white prayer cap on the back of her head as if to be sure it was perfectly in place. Of course it was; a prayer cap would know better than to move on Ruth Yoder.

I smiled at her. Unlike the people who confessed their

transgressions to Ruth when faced with her fearsome glare, I said nothing. She didn't scare me, which I was certain annoyed her. She didn't scare Lois either, which I knew infuriated her. It was difficult to be afraid of a person I'd known since she was in pigtails on the schoolyard. She had been bossy then and she was still bossy today. She was the bishop's wife and the self-declared leader of our Double Stitch Quilting Circle, but her bark was worse than her bite, so I didn't even flinch when she criticized me.

"I appreciate your concern, Ruth. I have been working diligently on the quilt. I am very grateful that Double Stitch is willing to help me with the hand-quilting part. I know it would take me far too long to do it on my own. The *Englisch* buyer is eager to receive her quilt. I should have it all pieced by this evening, so we can stretch it on a quilt frame and go straight to work."

She made a huffing sound, mostly because she hadn't caught me twiddling my thumbs. She always wanted to catch someone doing something that she thought was wrong, so she could correct them.

"That is *gut* to hear. If we are working on a quilt frame, we will have to do it in your home. There is not enough space in the Sunbeam Café for that type of work," she said happily.

I shook my head. What she said was true, but I knew she was pleased to have a meeting outside of the café. Ruth didn't care for the Sunbeam. She liked Darcy well enough—as well as she like any *Englischer*—but Lois's antics and mannerisms set Ruth's teeth on edge. It had been that way since we were all girls. In Ruth's defense, Lois liked to get a rise out of Ruth, so she might be a little more outlandish than she normally would be when

Ruth was around. She made a point of saying things that would irritate the bishop's wife.

Lois was my closest friend, and despite her penchant for pointing out flaws in people, Ruth was my friend too. I knew underneath that tough, judgmental exterior, she really cared for the people in our district and truly thought she had their best interests at heart.

"We have a lot to talk about at the quilting meeting," Ruth said. "I suppose you've heard about the body that was found at the bottom of the ravine by the covered bridge and the connection to Uriah Schrock."

I knew it had been too much to hope that Ruth only wanted to speak to me about the quilt.

CHAPTER NINE

Ruth rubbed her forehead as if she were getting a headache. "It seems as if every time I turn around there is another tragedy in the district. My poor husband. This is not *gut* for his heart."

My eyes went wide. "Is Bishop Yoder unwell?"

"No, but he is not a young man. I have taken great care of him," she unknowingly boasted. "I worry about him constantly."

It was true that the bishop was not a young man. He was years older than Ruth. His first wife had died young and afterward he'd married Ruth. He was the bishop's son, and many thought *Gott* would choose him to lead the district in the future. The more cynical women in the church said that Ruth had set her sights on him even before his first wife was in the grave. I couldn't believe that.

I knew Ruth to be ambitious but conniving seemed a tad too far.

She clicked her tongue. "I have told my husband many times that Samuel Zook's death would come up again. He claimed it would not because it happened when his *daed* was bishop." She shook her head. "I knew better. Uriah should not have come back to stir up trouble."

I stood up from the bench. "Uriah has every right to come back to Harvest. This is where he grew up."

"That may be so, but why does he want to open old wounds after all this time? What we need in this district is peace, not trouble. He brought us trouble."

"The wounds never healed for him," I said. Which, when said aloud, seemed like a fairly obvious reason for his return.

"If that is true, he should have not run away from the village. Why didn't he deal with what his sister did back then? Why did he wait forty years?" She put her hands on her hips.

I bit the inside of my cheek. I didn't have a *gut* answer for that, nor had Uriah, actually.

"Samuel Zook has been dead for forty years," she went on. "And Galilee has been missing just as long. Shouldn't this be a case of the dead burying the dead?"

"If you think that," I said, choosing my words carefully, "why would you want to discuss anything about this at the quilting circle meeting? I would think you'd just want it to die away."

She held her hands aloft. "Because I have no choice. Uriah has brought it to the forefront and put the district under the scrutiny of the sheriff's department again. I was home when he came to speak to my husband about it. Do you know he accused my husband's father of ignoring Galilee's pleas for help? It is not the bishop's job to come between a man and his wife."

"It wasn't Gali's fault either. It was Samuel's, and I believe the church could have taken a harder stand on his abuse." I put my hands on my hips and matched her stance.

"You didn't say anything about it at the time."

I dropped my arms to my sides. What she said was true and intensified my feelings of guilt over not saying something.

"I always believed the police were right." Ruth sniffed.

"Right about what?" I asked, afraid that I already knew the answer.

"That Galilee Zook killed her husband and ran away to be *Englisch*. That theory makes the most sense. She would have to change her identity after committing murder."

I blinked at her. "How can you say that? What about the bones in the ravine? They could be Gali's."

"They could be from anything. Maybe a deer, even," she argued.

"They found a human skull." I folded my arms.

"That's what the *Englischers* say, and Uriah is making it worse."

"How?" I asked.

"He came to my husband this morning and insisted that the district covered up his sister's murder."

I rolled my eyes. It was a habit I had picked up from Lois.

By the look on Ruth's face, she didn't appreciate the mannerism. "Uriah can't be going around blaming the district for this, and he is putting Bishop Yoder's father in a bad light." She lowered her voice. "He mentioned abuse. He said that Samuel hit his wife. He can't say something like that. Doesn't he think about how that will look to the outside world? If it's true, it will hurt the district. Just the rumors of such things hurt the district. There are already enough misconceptions about our people among the *Englisch*. We don't need this too."

"I think Uriah has a right to find out what happened," I said quietly.

"What is the point of speaking about it now? It's in the past. Very far in the past, I might add. So much of the district has changed. Everyone knows that my husband would not tolerate such a thing. Why hurt the bishop's family name in this way when everyone involved in this tragedy is dead?"

"Uriah is not dead," I said in a quiet voice.

"But he left! He has not been here for forty years. He came back to stir up trouble. Now that he has, it could be to the detriment of our district."

"I think the discovery of the skeleton at the bottom of the ravine puts the theory that Gali ran away in serious doubt," I said.

Ruth gasped. "But that's what we were told by the district elders and by the police. You think they lied to us?"

"*Nee*, I didn't say that, but it was the easiest explanation of what might have happened to her, and sometimes the easiest explanation is just that, easy. Easy doesn't mean right. I'm afraid both the district elders and the sheriff's department may have wanted to end the chatter over Samuel's death as soon as possible. Finding a simple solution to Gali's disappearance was the best way to do that."

She pressed her lips together. "Bishop Yoder's father would not lie to the district."

"I don't think that he lied. But he also didn't press the

deputies to look for another answer. Samuel and Gali's relationship was a problem for the district. With them out of the way, it was no longer a concern."

She glared at me. "You make it sound like some kind of conspiracy theory, as if the bishop and other leaders in the church had a hand in it."

"That's not my intention." I knew that Ruth and I were never going to see eye to eye on this. She would defend her husband's father to the bitter end because she was also defending her family and her husband as bishop.

"You are discrediting the bishop by saying such things."

"It was the time. Every Amish bishop back then wanted everything to be neat and tidy and for everyone to fall in line. It was the 1980s and everything in *Englisch* life was changing so rapidly. There was a lot of fear that our culture would not survive. It was simpler if problems disappeared on their own."

"And what is wrong with neat and tidy?" she wanted to know.

"Nothing on the surface," I said. "I just don't believe it's sustainable. I don't think *Gott* tells us to ignore complicated and difficult questions. We have to be willing to ask them. If we cannot find answers that suit us, we have to be comfortable enough to sit in that discomfort. To openly talk about our discomforts."

Ruth stared at me as if I had a cauliflower sprouting out the top of my head. "What are you going to do about it, then? I assume you plan to stick your nose in all this."

"How could I be doing that when you think I should be home working on my quilt?" I asked.

She narrowed her eyes. "Don't you sass me, Millie Fisher."

"I'm not sassing you, and besides, that's something

you should say to someone younger than you. We're the same age."

She glowered at me.

"I'm going to help Uriah the best I can. He is my old friend. He's your old friend too," I said pointedly. "But right now, we just have to wait and see if the body is that of Gali Zook. If it's not, it still represents a tragedy. Someone died in that ravine, and we owe it to that person to find out what happened to him or her."

Ruth scowled. "We need to discuss this tonight with the quilting circle to see how we are going to deal with it. Perhaps you're right that Uriah and the district deserve to know what happened to Gali, but we have to do it in a way that respects the church leaders."

I raised my brow. "I thought you would want to leave this with the church leaders, the men, to handle."

She put her hands on her hips. "You know the men will be no use in this situation. It's the women who root out the gossip and the truth. We will discuss it when we work on your quilt tonight. There is no time for idleness."

Just then, Micah came out of the Harvest Market clutching a brown bag to his chest. When he saw the bishop's wife standing with me, his eyes went wide. Ruth instilled a healthy fear in the children of the district.

"Micah," Ruth said. "I hope you are being a *gut* son for your mother."

I wrapped a protective arm around my young great-nephew's shoulders. "He's doing a wonderful job. We're actually here today because he wanted to spend some of his hard-earned money at the general store."

"Oh, what did you buy?" the bishop's wife asked with an appraising gaze.

A panicky look crossed Micah's face.

"Ruth," I interrupted. "I will let everyone in the group know about the quilting meeting at my home tonight. I'm sure we will have everything sorted out soon."

She looked back at me, seemingly forgetting Micah and his purchase—which had been my intention all along.

"Don't let Lois distract you from finishing that quilt. I hope she's not coming tomorrow." With that she walked away.

"She scares me," Micah said in a small voice.

"She scares a lot of people, but she's a marshmallow inside. Trust me."

"Maybe a burnt marshmallow," Micah muttered.

I had to look away, so he wouldn't see me laugh. "Micah, that is not something you should say about the bishop's wife. She deserves your respect."

"Oh, okay." He kicked at gravel under his feet with the toe of his scuffed sneaker. "*Danki* for stopping her from asking me what I bought in the store."

"I could tell that you didn't want to share it with her. Would you share it with me?" I asked.

He held the brown bag to his chest and chewed on his lower lip. "Do you promise not to tell anyone?"

I cocked my head. "I can't make that promise if it puts you or someone else in danger."

"Oh, it's nothing like that," he assured me.

"I'll try my best. I won't know if I will keep it a secret until I see what it is."

He considered this and then reached into the paper bag. He pulled out six plastic-wrapped stacks of professional baseball cards. "I have an *Englisch* friend. He collects them. He gave me some of the old cards he didn't want. Ever since then, I've wanted more. I've studied the players."

"Do you know much about professional baseball?"

He looked right and left. "I listen to it on the radio when *Maam* is busy at the greenhouse. It's the radio that she uses to listen to the weather every night. It's important to be on top of the weather, so that we know how to take care of the plants," he said as if he was reciting it from memory. I guessed it was something that Edith had said to her children many times.

"I don't listen to any of the music," he said quickly. "Just the games. At the beginning of the spring, my friend gave me a list of the Cleveland games and the ones that would be on the radio. Listening to and learning about the games and the players is my favorite thing to do."

"It sounds to me like this has become an important hobby to you," I said.

He tucked the baseball cards back into the bag. "Is it okay to like baseball and be Amish, *Aenti*?"

I smiled. "There is nothing wrong with having interests. It's when those interests lead you away from *Gott* that you run into problems."

"Baseball won't lead me away, but . . ."

"But what?" I asked.

"I wish I could be on my friend's Little League team. He has a uniform, cleats, and a catching glove just like the real baseball players. Do you think I could go to one of his games?"

I shook my head. "That is something you will have to ask your *maam*."

He lowered his head. "She will say *nee*."

"She might surprise you."

He shook his head. "Amish mothers never surprise their children."

CHAPTER TEN

"How would you feel about a piece of blueberry pie?" I asked Micah.

"I'll take any kind of pie. I'm not picky when it comes to pie. You're the one who loves blueberry, *Aenti*." He smiled so widely, I spotted the gap of a missing molar in the back of his mouth.

He knew me too well. In general, I stayed away from sweets. I drank my coffee black and ate more vegetables than candies. But that all stopped when blueberry desserts were around.

"Then let's go over to the Sunbeam Café and eat a slice or two."

He tucked his paper bag into the satchel that he had tethered to his bike. "*Maam* never lets me have sweets in the middle of the day like this."

"Then this will be our secret." I winked.

He grinned. "I want a big slice of pie. If we are going to be sneaky, it needs to be worth it."

I cocked my head. "Have you been spending time with Lois lately?"

We arrived at the Sunbeam Café just a few minutes later. We both locked our bicycles in a bike rack in front of the playground next door and went inside. It was close to three in the afternoon, and the café was quiet. We were between the lunch and dinner rush. It was the perfect time to stop by for some blueberry pie and to pick Lois's brain.

"Millie," Lois said as soon as I stepped into the café. "I expected you a while ago. I thought you were done working at the greenhouse at noon."

"The greenhouse was busy, so I stayed a bit longer. Then Micah and I had to stop at Harvest Market for a few minutes."

Lois waved at Micah. "Well, hello there, young man. Can I interest you in a piece of pie?"

He nodded vigorously. "*Aenti* Millie said that's why we are here."

Lois nodded. "On quiet afternoons, your aunt drops by more often than not for a piece of my granddaughter's blueberry pie. We have to save her a slice every single day. I think she lives on the stuff."

"I don't eat blueberry pie every day," I scoffed.

Lois raised her eyebrows at me. "You would if you could."

I couldn't argue with her there.

"I like blueberry," Micah said. "But what else do you have?"

Lois grinned. "I like a young man who wants to know all of his options. It shows me that you aren't hasty. We have peach, apple, cherry, key lime, chocolate silk—"

"Chocolate silk!" he cried. "That's my very favorite."

"Then you are in luck. We just have one that's finished cooling and is ready to be cut. We buy the very best chocolate from Swissmen Sweets across the square. You're about to eat the best piece of chocolate pie you have ever had in your life."

Micah grinned from ear to ear. Lois sold the chocolate pie so hard, I considered changing my order for a full second until I remembered nothing was tastier than Darcy's blueberry pie. Absolutely nothing.

Lois disappeared into the kitchen. While she was gone, I told Micah to pick a table. He chose one in front of the window just one table away from local author Bryan Shell. Bryan was bent over his laptop, pecking away at the keyboard. As always, his long legs stuck way out from under the table and his back was hunched. Since the café had opened, he had been there almost every day working on what he called the "great American novel."

Lois suspected, and I tended to agree, he was there less for the writing and more to see Darcy Woodin, Lois's granddaughter and the owner of the café. He had a crush on her. A few months back, he'd worked up the courage to ask Darcy on a date. At the time, she was still reeling from losing a man she loved. She told Bryan she would think about it. She was still thinking about it—over nine months later. Maybe a different kind of man would take that as a hint and stop working at the café every single day, but not Bryan. I had been watching him and Darcy together for a long while, and I was not convinced they were a *gut* match, so I had made no effort to push them together.

Lois returned and set Micah's piece of pie in front of him. It was a huge wedge that was as big as three pieces combined. It would certainly spoil his dinner and I would hear about that from his mother. However, I didn't have the heart to take it away from Micah or to ask Lois to cut it down to a more manageable size. He just appeared to be so blissfully happy when he looked at it.

"Millie," Lois said, "I have your piece at the counter, so we can talk." She gave me a knowing look. It didn't take much imagination to figure out that Lois wanted to talk about the skeleton found near the covered bridge. I suspected that part of the reason for the triple-sized slice was to buy us as much time as possible.

"Enjoy your pie, Micah," I said. "I'll be right over here visiting with Lois, and then we will ride back home."

He nodded. He was unable to speak since his mouth was full of chocolate.

When I reached the counter, Lois slid a piece of blueberry pie and a coffee in front of me. The pie was warm, just how I liked it. The coffee was hot and black. That was just how I liked it too. That's how I knew something was amiss. Lois hated black coffee and felt it was her personal mission to convert me into a flavored coffee, latte, or at least cappuccino drinker. As of yet, she had not been successful. Despite the steady stream of Americanos, mocha concoctions, and frozen-layered café treats she made me drink. The fact that she had not tried at all this time was concerning.

I picked up the mug of coffee. "Uh-oh, what did I do?"

She poured herself a coffee, added cream, sugar, and so much caramel sauce to it that my teeth ached just looking at it. "When were you going to tell me that Uriah is involved in all this skull business?"

"Skull business?" I asked.

"It's the best way I can think of describing it. We don't

know if it's a murder yet or an accident." She shrugged. "Skull business it is."

"I'm thinking it's a murder." I pressed my lips together as I remembered Deputy Little telling me that the body had been buried. An accident victim wouldn't have buried him- or herself.

"Maybe there was a troll under the bridge that snatched the person off, causing them to fall to their death," Lois suggested.

I blinked at her. "A troll?"

"Didn't you ever hear the fairy tale of the 'Three Billy Goats Gruff'? It happens." She paused. "It happens in fairy tales."

"I didn't grow up reading fairy tales." I picked up my fork and took a bite of pie. The blueberry was sweet yet tart, and the perfect crust melted in my mouth. I had no idea how Darcy made crust so perfect. In my opinion, she made better pie than any of the Amish bakers in the district, not that I would ever say that aloud. I would have a lot of district members angry with me if I claimed an *Englischer* could outbake an Amish woman. Whether she admits it or not, every Amish woman takes pride in her cooking and baking.

Lois clicked her tongue. "There was so much of childhood that you missed." She sipped from her oversized mug.

"My childhood was just fine and you know it. You had a front-row seat."

She nodded. "That I did, and I'm sorry. Let's not bicker over all of this. We have another case to solve, Amish Marple. I assume that's what you want us to do. Where to next? I've no doubt you have a list of people you want us to talk to. Let's get down to business."

I glanced at Micah, who happily ate his pie while looking at some of the new baseball cards on his lap. I didn't see any harm in the baseball cards, but I didn't know whether his mother would feel the same way.

"We can't speak to anyone until I take Micah home."

"Hogwash. The boy would love it if he were in on one of our investigations."

"Oh, I know he would. Micah is the most curious of Edith's children, but Edith would not want us to put her son in harm's way. Nor would I." I popped a blueberry into my mouth.

Lois shook her head and drank her super-sweet coffee. "I don't see us taking him anywhere dangerous, but I suppose you're right. If we've learned anything about all of these killers we have encountered, it is that they can be anywhere and anyone."

I nodded. "But you're right. I have a couple of places that I would like to go today, if we can. It's already late afternoon, so we don't have much time before everything closes up for the night."

Lois sighed. "If only Amish Country kept casino hours. Then we would get so much more sleuthing done."

Before I could respond, she said, "Listen, I have to help Darcy with a few things in the kitchen to make sure she's all set for the dinner crowd. Thankfully, one of her part-time waitresses is coming in tonight, so I get the evening off." She pressed a hand to her lower back. "Carrying those heavy trays is no easy trick for someone of my age." She took a breath. "Take Micah home and I will pick you up at the greenhouse. Since you two are on bikes, I will only be a few minutes after you."

I finished my blueberry pie. My fork made a scraping sound on the plate. I was surprised to see it gone.

"I think that's a fine idea, Lois." I reached into my apron for my change purse and, when Lois wasn't looking, I tucked enough money under my plate for both pieces of pie and a little extra. She didn't like me paying her for food at the café. "Micah seems to be done with his pie too, so we will be on our way."

Lois smiled. "I'll be right behind you, Millie, like any good sidekick."

CHAPTER ELEVEN

Micah and I were almost back to the greenhouse when we came upon the crossroad where the construction was happening. Micah, who was in the lead on the way home, slowed. The flagger stood in the middle of the road holding a stop sign as a dump truck poured gravel into a large hole in the street.

Micah stood on his bike pedals. "This is going to take forever. Let's go this way!" Without waiting for me to respond, Micah turned down the dirt-and-gravel road that led to the edge of the ravine and the covered bridge.

"Micah! I don't think we should go that way," I called.

But it was no use. He either didn't hear me or chose to ignore me as he pedaled quickly down the road. I had no choice but to follow.

I caught up with Micah as he stopped his bike beside Tyler's van. Micah was talking to Tyler and another young *Englisch* man. Tyler still wore all black even though it was in the high eighties that afternoon. His friend was a little more practical in khaki shorts and a white T-shirt. Both of them were sweating in the heat, though. Above our heads flew the drone Tyler had shown me that morning.

Tyler pointed up to the sky, and Micah watched in amazement as the other *Englischer* made the drone dip into the ravine. Or at least I believed he was the one controlling it since he held a black device in his hand.

"How did you do that?" Micah asked.

"Micah," I called as I climbed off my bicycle and walked it over to the young men.

"*Aenti*, did you see that thing fly?" he asked. "It's like a metal bat in the sky."

"Hey, you're the Amish lady who was walking your goats this morning," Tyler said. "Are you back because you want to do an interview? I have everything we need right in my van. Xander can set it up in no time."

His friend looked at him as if Tyler might have a serious case of heatstroke. "Did you say walking goats? You mean like how you walk a dog?"

"Oh *ya*," Micah piped up. "*Aenti* Millie walks her goats every day. She even comes to our greenhouse with the goats." He lowered his voice. "My *maam* doesn't like it all that much since the goats eat the flowers if we don't watch them."

Xander shook his head. "That's rad, man. I wish I had been here to see it. Tyler, did you get any of that footage? It might just be the local color we need to make this film stand out to the Sundance judges."

"No, man." Tyler shook his head.

"Could we maybe do a reenactment?" Xander asked. "We'd make it look completely unscripted. That's how all reality TV works these days. They reenact everything for effect."

"Reality TV?" I asked.

"Oh, wow," Xander said. "You don't know. You're, like, *real* Amish."

I cocked one eyebrow. "There are fake Amish? I wasn't aware of such a thing."

"I love a witty Amish person," Xander said. "She's going to be great on camera. Where do you want me to set up?"

Tyler glanced around the road as if searching for a place. "In front of the covered bridge. It makes everything look more country."

I waved a hand at both of them to remind them that I was still there. "I'm not doing an interview. My nephew and I were just riding home from town when he decided to take a shortcut." I gave Micah a disapproving look.

Micah kicked at the gravel with the toe of his black tennis shoe.

"Oh," Tyler said and then his face cleared. "We'd still love to get the perspective of someone who lived back then."

I made a face. I know the 1980s were a long time ago for these young men and before they were born, but the decade wasn't ancient. At least not in my memory.

"You'd be our third interview for the documentary."

I raised my brow, surprised. I did not expect anyone in the community to give them an interview. "Who are the other two?" I asked.

Tyler grinned as if my question was somehow proof

that I was waffling about the interview. I wasn't, but if I could learn of other people who might know something about Galilee Zook, all the better.

"The sheriff, for one. He was the deputy on the case at the time of the murder," Xander said.

"Yeah, the sheriff was super keen on the idea when we told him that we might get into Sundance." Tyler grinned. "For some, all it takes is the promise of bright lights."

I didn't know what this Sundance business was, but I suspected, as an Amish woman, I wanted no part of it.

"Murder?" Micah asked.

I patted his shoulder. "It was a long time ago. Before your *maam* was even born."

His mouth fell open. "That must have been forever ago. *Maam* is pretty old."

I shook my head. "When do you speak to the sheriff?" I asked as casually as I could.

"Tomorrow. He says it's a good day to do it because it's a Sunday and the county all but shuts down." Tyler shook his head. "I would never get anything done if I didn't work on Sundays. We're going to talk to him on the village square. He says it will be a nice setting."

It certainly would be, and I was happy to know about the interview. I tried not to work or sleuth on Sundays. It was the Lord's Day, after all, but sometimes I had to make exceptions. This would be one of those times. "And who is the other person?" I expected him to mention another *Englischer* name. Maybe it would be a member of the *Englisch* family that owned the Amish Corner Bench restaurant.

"Uriah Schrock," Xander said. "He's that old dude who scared us half to death when we found the skull."

"Skull?" Micah asked. His eyes were huge.

I winced. I hoped he wouldn't tell his mother any of this. Or I would most certainly hear about it later. "It's nothing to worry about, Micah."

"A skull has something to do with Uriah?" Micah twisted his mouth as if he didn't quite believe me. "Uriah is here by the covered bridge all the time. I see him all the time."

The three of us stared at him, and his face flushed red.

"How do you know that, Micah?" I asked in Pennsylvania Dutch.

"Umm . . ." Micah kicked more gravel.

I gave him my best *aenti* stare. "Micah."

"You know I told you about my *Englisch* friend who has the baseball cards? He lives that way down the road with his grandparents." He looked this way and that. "We meet at the covered bridge to trade cards. It's halfway between our houses, so I'm never away for so long that Mama notices I'm gone."

I pressed my lips together. "You should not leave home without telling your *maam*."

He dropped his head. "I know, *Aenti* Millie, but I wasn't sure she'd let me trade cards."

"We can discuss this later." It wasn't a conversation I wanted to have in front of Tyler and Xander, even if we were speaking in our own language and they couldn't understand us.

"What's your friend's name?" I asked Micah in English this time.

"Caplan Stoller. But everyone calls him Cappy."

I frowned. Stoller was the name of the family that Uriah rented a room from. If they lived so close to the place where his sister had disappeared and his brother-in-law died, he had to have chosen to live there for that reason.

As if he were confirming my supposition, Micah added, "Cappy said that Uriah is living in an old outbuilding on their property. We always talk to him when we see him at the bridge. He said that he wouldn't tell anyone about my baseball cards." He bit his lip. "I hope you won't either, *Aenti*."

That wasn't a promise I was ready to make.

"That's cool," Xander said. "We would love to talk to the Stollers too . . . Maybe they know something. Are they old enough to have been around forty years ago?"

Micah shrugged. "They have gray hair."

The two young men looked at each other. "That sounds old enough," Xander said.

Tyler nodded. "The more we can learn from people who lived back at the time of the murder, the more compelling our film will be."

And the more I learned from people who lived back then, the more likely I would be to find the person responsible.

CHAPTER TWELVE

I managed to leave Tyler and Xander filming by the covered bridge without agreeing to be interviewed, but I knew it would not be the last time they asked. They were certainly persistent.

Micah took the lead riding home. Since he had been to the bridge so many times visiting Cappy, he knew the way well. I was a *gut* five bike lengths behind him when I turned into the driveway and spotted Lois's large sedan.

Micah hopped off his bike and leaned it against a tree. "Bye, *Aenti*," he called and sprinted into the house, clutching the paper bag from the market to his chest. I knew he wanted to avoid more questions about Cappy and the baseball cards.

Lois stood by her car and tapped her foot. "I never thought I would beat you here. What was the holdup?"

"Micah went down the road with the covered bridge."

"Ahh, and you took it upon yourself to do a little snooping while you were at it." She sighed and shook her head. "You couldn't wait for me."

"*Nee*, Tyler and his friend Xander were there." I hurriedly told her who the two men were and what I had learned from them and from Micah.

She waved her hand and the plastic jewelry on her wrist clattered together. "It sounds to me like Uriah has been snooping around the bridge for a long time. Did he think he would find his sister's body there?"

"I don't know," I said. "Maybe. Why else would he go there so often?"

"After forty years? It seems unlikely." She paused. "I know you're not going to like me saying this, but it seems unlikely he'd find anything unless he knew it was there."

I blinked at her. "You don't think Uriah killed Samuel and his own sister, do you?"

Lois wrinkled her nose. "I don't like to think that, but we have to keep it as a possibility in the back of our minds. We can't be certain that he doesn't at least know something he's not saying to you. Uriah has always been vague about why he came back to Holmes County. Why? If he was looking for his sister, why didn't he just come out and say it? You have to admit, it's odd behavior. I can't imagine Uriah killing anyone. Then again, I have thought that about other murderers we've caught too, and they did turn out to be guilty."

I knew she was right. I hoped that my affection for Uriah wasn't clouding my view of him.

Lois folded her arms. "It cannot be coincidence that he's renting from the Stollers either. Their alpaca farm is the closest property to the bridge."

"You're right," I said, much as I hated to admit it.

There was something about the situation that worried me, but I just could not put my finger on it. I didn't know if it was because Uriah hadn't told me where he lived. But again, I reminded myself that I hadn't asked him where he was living.

Another thought struck me. "We still don't know that the skeleton Tyler and Xander found is Gali."

"That doesn't make me feel any better."

"Why not?" I asked.

"Because if it's not Gali, someone else was killed and buried in that ravine. The saddest part about that possibility is that it would be someone no one is looking for."

She was right. That would be incredibly sad.

"Where are we off to now, Amish Marple?" Lois opened her car door.

I patted the back of my prayer cap. I wanted to go to the Stollers and find out what they knew, but not yet. I felt I should talk to Uriah first. I believed Lois was right that he might have known something or still knew something that he wasn't telling me. I wasn't sure how he expected me to help clear his sister's—and possibly his own—name when he was keeping information about the case from me.

"Let's go to the Amish Corner Bench. It was the last place anyone saw Gali and Samuel alive. Uriah told me that the grandson of Gali's own boss is the owner now. He was young when she disappeared, but he or someone else might remember something."

"My favorite Amish restaurant." Lois clapped her hands together. "I love it when investigating includes Amish fried chicken."

I raised my brow. "And why do you think this trip includes fried chicken?"

"Well, if we are questioning the staff, it would be rude not to buy a meal at the restaurant. And they have the best fried chicken around."

Lois had a knack for putting things in the simplest of terms.

"Leave your bicycle here. You can come back and get it later." Lois smacked the roof of her car. "Let's ride!"

The Amish Corner Bench restaurant stood on a hill overlooking a state route and the rolling countryside. There was a vineyard just a few yards from the edge of the parking lot, and behind grapevines, cattle grazed on the green hills. The restaurant itself was a broad, white-washed building with black trim and window boxes over-flowing with vining annuals that I recognized from my niece's greenhouse. On the wide front porch that ran the length of the building, there were a number of white rockers. About a third of those rockers were occupied by customers, and there was a line of people standing out-side the entrance, waiting to be seated.

"They are all here for the chicken," Lois said as we ap-proached the porch. She lifted her nose in the air. "Do you smell that? It's like they have a full chicken dinner in there waiting for us."

"We aren't here to eat."

She put a hand on her stomach. "But I'm starved. And as I said before, people will be more likely to talk to us if we put down a little money. The Amish are no different from the English in that regard."

"Well, it's no matter. I'm not sure we will get inside. There's a long line of people waiting for a table. And we are just at the beginning of the dinner rush. This is a bad time. We should come back tomorrow."

"Tomorrow is Sunday. They will be closed. This is our one chance."

I wrinkled my nose. "But we can't get in."

"Are you going to deprive me of my chicken?" Lois asked, aghast. "Leave this to me and I will get us a table in no time at all."

I frowned and watched her confidently walk down the porch, smiling and saying hello to people as she went. None of them seemed to be offended that she cut in line. Lois just had this way about her that caused people to give her room. It was certainly a gift that I hadn't been given as I fought for every inch of my own space.

While I waited for Lois, I listened to the *Englisch* conversations around me. Most of the customers spoke of the scenery or people from back home. One woman was sharing with a friend all the details about her daughter's good-for-nothing husband, but it was the third conversation I heard that caught my attention.

"From what I heard, the body they found under the covered bridge has been there for years. At least that's what my neighbor said," a man was telling his female companion.

"It's hard to believe someone could be down there that long without being found."

"Millie." Lois waved to me. "We are being seated. Come on." She stood a few feet away from me with a triumphant smile on her face. I had been so engrossed in eavesdropping that I hadn't heard her approach.

She reached me and tugged on my arm.

"How on earth did you get a table?" I asked in a low

voice, so that no one else could hear me. I didn't want the diners around me getting upset because we'd jumped the line.

"Money talks, my friend, even to the Amish." She winked and gave my arm a tug.

I turned back to the couple talking about the covered bridge, but they were gone. I bit my lip. Gossip was already starting to circulate about Gali, and before long it would be about Uriah too.

As we made our way to the door, Lois greeted everyone she passed and thanked them for moving aside for her.

At the entrance, an Amish hostess called from the front of the line. "Henry? Party of two!"

I stared at Lois. "What did you mean when you said money talks?"

She just smiled back at me.

"You bribed them?" I whispered. I couldn't have Lois going around the county bribing people for information.

"Not in the traditional way, but I said I could get them a prime spot as a vendor at the next festival on Harvest's village square."

"But you don't know that you can do that. Margot said the spots were full for the rest of the year!"

"I don't know for sure." She shrugged. "But I probably can. Margot would love to score a big restaurant like the Amish Corner Bench at one of her events. I'm sure she'd make an exception and add another spot just for them. If the restaurant wants to bring their fried chicken, all the better."

I shook my head and followed Lois inside. I tried to ignore the side-eyes we got from people who had been waiting for a long time.

Inside the dining room, a long line wrapped around the buffet and salad bar.

"Bus tour," Lois said, nodding at the buffet.

It certainly looked like it.

Amish girls and women moved quickly around the room, taking orders and refilling iced tea and water glasses. Teenage boys cleared tables as fast as they possibly could as the young hostesses seated new customers before the tables were even completely dry.

The blond Amish hostess smiled at us as she stopped by a window table. Lois and I sat, and before we could even glance at the menu, another young Amish woman was at our table with paper notepad in hand, ready to take our order.

"*Willkumm* to the Amish Corner Bench; would you like something to drink? Oh, Millie, it's so *gut* to see you." The young woman's pretty face lit up.

"Phoebe, I didn't know you worked here," I said, surprised to see a young woman from my district there.

"I just started. I wanted to make a little extra money before I need to keep a home."

Lois cocked her head. "Before you *keep* a home. What kind of old—"

"Lois!" I interrupted because I didn't know what she was about to say. I guessed that it would not be well received by Phoebe Yoder, though. "This is Ruth's granddaughter, Phoebe Yoder." I gave her a look.

Lois's mouth made a little O shape. I hoped that meant she would be on her best behavior.

"I've known your grandmother since we were all knee-high," Lois said.

Phoebe smiled, not knowing, of course, that Lois and Ruth's relationship—if you could even call it that—was tumultuous. "Oh, it's so nice to meet one of *Grossmaami*'s friends. She doesn't have many *Englischer* friends." She smiled at me. "Millie, of course, I know. Without you, Millie, I never would have found my match. Did you hear that Lad and I are set to be married in the fall?"

I nodded. "I was very happy to hear that. You are well suited for each other."

She sighed. "We are, and I'm so very happy. It's been such a long time. Lad was very nervous about marrying into the bishop's family, but Millie talked him into it for me."

Lois raised her brow at me.

I shook my head. "I didn't talk him into anything. He loves you. I just reminded him that there are challenges with any family he would join through marriage. Those challenges can't stand in the way of true love."

"Whatever you said worked," Phoebe said. "And the next day he proposed. I owe you so much, Millie."

I smiled. Theirs had been an easy match. Convincing Ruth that they were a match was the real challenge.

An older Amish waitress walked by and audibly cleared her throat. "Oh! I should get your drink order."

"Two iced teas, please," Lois said.

"Unsweetened," I said quietly.

Lois waved her hand. "Unsweetened for her. Not me. I want mine sweet. Extra sweet."

Phoebe laughed. "*Ya*, no problem. Will you be having the buffet today?"

Lois eyed the line. "Looks like too much work to me. I'll have the chicken dinner. I've been dreaming about it for days."

"*Gut* choice." Phoebe looked at me. "And for you?"

I twisted my mouth. The chicken dinner did sound *gut*, but it had been a warm day at the greenhouse. I felt I would do better with something lighter. "Chicken salad for me."

Lois shook her head. "You come all the way here and choose a salad."

"There's chicken on it," I said in my defense.

"When the only thing that comes with the chicken is a pile of lettuce, it no longer can be called real chicken."

I rolled my eyes.

Lois chuckled as if she knew what I was doing.

"Is there anything else I can get you?" Phoebe asked.

"Do you know if the owner, Nathaniel Zurich, is here?" I asked.

Phoebe's eyes went wide. "Is something wrong?"

"Nee, nee." I shook my head. "I just wanted to speak to him about an old friend of mine."

Phoebe doodled on the corner of her notepad. "Mr. Zurich doesn't usually come out into the dining room. He's not Amish and says the public prefer to see Amish people in an Amish restaurant." She lowered her voice. "Not all the women working here are Amish either. He just asks them to dress Amish in order to keep up the atmosphere."

"Do you think he could just stop by the table and talk to us for one minute?" Lois asked.

Phoebe tucked her pen and notepad back into her apron pocket. "I can ask, but he's a very busy man."

"We can wait if he can find a few minutes. We'll have your delicious chicken to pass the time," Lois said with a smile.

Phoebe was about to leave the table when I stopped her. "When you ask him if he will speak to us, will you tell him it's about Galilee Zook? That's our mutual friend."

Phoebe nodded, but there was no indication on her face that she recognized the name. Even though she would be marrying into the Zook family, she might not know Samuel and Gali's story, but Nathaniel would. I hoped it would be enough to grab his attention.

After she left, Lois leaned over the table. "She seems far too sweet to be Ruth Yoder's granddaughter."

"Lois," I said.

She held up her hands. "I'm just saying she must have taken after the bishop or the other side of her family because I don't see one lick of Ruth in her. It's nice that you helped calm her future groom's jitters."

I nodded absentmindedly.

She cocked her head. "What is it? You have that look."

I glanced up at her. "What look?"

"That *something is not right here* look. You get it when we are on a case or when you think someone is making a poor match." She lowered her voice to a whisper. "Do you think Phoebe and this Lad fellow are a bad match?"

I shook my head. "They are a *gut* match."

She leaned back in her chair and folded her arms. "Then what's with the face?"

Before I could answer, Phoebe was back, setting our drinks on the table with two additional glasses of water. "Nathaniel said he'll stop by your table when he gets a minute." With a smile, she added a basket of hot yeasty rolls and went to the next table.

Lois shook her head. "Such a sweetheart. Nothing like her grandma," she muttered. "Now, tell me what has your brain spinning."

"A lot of things right now have my brain spinning," I said. "But it wasn't about the match. Well, not exactly.

Phoebe is betrothed to Lad Zook." I let the name hang in the air.

"Zook is a pretty common name in Amishland," Lois said. "But don't tell me this Lad Zook is related to Galilee Zook."

I nodded. "He was her nephew, although she would have been gone for many years before he was born. He's only twenty-five. His father is Cyril Zook, Samuel's younger brother."

"Coincidence?" Lois asked.

"We don't run into many of those," I said.

Lois nodded. "No, we do not."

CHAPTER THIRTEEN

Another Amish waitress, not Phoebe, brought our food to the table. Lois leaned over her plate of chicken and inhaled deeply. Then, she picked up one of the rolls and broke it in half. There was a burst of hot, yeast-scented steam in her face.

"Wowee, it's like a facial in a bun." She dropped the roll on her bread plate and reached for the Amish peanut butter spread in the middle of the table. "Come to Mama!" She squeezed a healthy portion onto each half of the roll.

I pressed my lips together. "Lois, I think that should be enough for you."

She closed the squeeze bottle and then shook it at me. "I'm well past the age when I listen to someone else's advice on what I should and should not eat."

"I just don't want you to get sick to your stomach. That's a lot of sugar." I wrinkled my brow in concern.

She snorted. "This is nothing. I have more sugar in my morning coffee." She took a big bite of the roll and moaned. "It's so good." She held out the half-eaten roll to me. "Taste it. It will change your life."

"*Nee*, I have a dentist appointment next week. That is sure to give me a cavity."

"It's worth it," Lois said and took another bite. "This is the very best thing the Amish ever invented."

The peanut butter topping was a mixture of peanut butter and marshmallow fluff. It was sweet, creamy, and would rot your teeth right out of your mouth. But Lois was right. It was delicious. Even I loved it, and I usually wasn't a sweets person . . . other than blueberry pie, that is.

Lois broke a second roll and began to slather that one with peanut butter spread too. I didn't say anything this time.

"Don't judge. Detecting makes me hungry. My nerves make me eat more. We can't all be like you, Millie—your nerves make you stop eating. I have a feeling you will be taking that chicken salad home in a box."

She was probably right.

"You might ruin your appetite eating all those rolls before your dinner."

"Not likely, but if I do, that's what doggie bags are for."

I pushed a carrot around my plate with the back of my fork. I just couldn't stop thinking about a possible connection between the Yoder and Zook families. Was there more to it or was it simply the upcoming wedding between Lad and Phoebe that connected them?

Across the dining room, I spotted Phoebe speaking to an *Englischer* in his fifties. He was a big man. He was well over six feet tall and heavyset. He wore an Amish Corner Bench polo shirt neatly tucked into khaki pants.

Phoebe nodded at something the man said and pointed at our table. The man began walking our way.

"Lois," I hissed. "I think that's Nathaniel coming this way."

"Huh?" Lois asked with a piece of chicken hanging from her mouth.

"He's coming over right now."

Lois quietly chewed and swallowed just before the man reached our table.

"Hello, ladies," he said with a smile. "I'm Nathaniel Zurich, the owner of the Amish Corner Bench. How are your meals?"

Lois wiped at her mouth with a cloth napkin. "Amazing. I would love the recipe for your chicken, or if you could do home delivery so I wouldn't have to cook it myself, that would be even better. Do you DoorDash?"

He laughed. "There are a lot of people who come in here asking the same thing. I'm afraid I couldn't tell you the recipe even if I wanted to. Alice won't let me near the kitchen. It's an old Amish recipe that's been passed down in her family. We're lucky that she shared it with us. I know it's what makes our restaurant stand out from the rest of the Amish eateries in Holmes County." His amusement didn't reach his eyes, I noticed.

As he loomed over Lois and me at our table, I had the sneaking suspicion that we were being sized up. It was almost as if he was gauging how great a threat we were.

"I heard that you wanted to speak to me," he said. "And I don't think it was about the fried chicken."

"It's not," Lois said. "But personally, I could talk about this fried chicken all day."

"Ya." I spoke up for the first time. "We wanted to talk to you about Galilee Zook."

"That's what Phoebe said. Galilee worked here at the restaurant when I was a teenager. To be honest, that feels like a lifetime ago."

"You knew her well?" I asked.

"As well as any fifteen-year-old boy could know an adult. She worked at the restaurant for as long as I could remember. When I was a child, she used to watch me when both my parents were working in the restaurant."

"She was your babysitter?" Lois asked.

"When I was under ten. After that my parents brought me to the restaurant every day and put me to work. I would see Gali then, but not as often. She was always so busy. She was the most popular waitress in the place, and sometimes customers would wait an extra half hour just to be seated in her section. She was the life of this place back then. We were all devastated when she disappeared. It just didn't seem like something Gali would do, run away . . ." He shook his head as if he realized that he had said too much. I would have loved to know what he had been about to say.

Lois pointed her fork at him. "Sounds to me like the two of you were pretty close."

He laughed. "She was fifteen years older than me, at least. She was kind and friendly. I remember that. From what I heard at the time, she had a hard life but still was so happy when she was at the restaurant. The only time I ever saw her happiness fade was at the end of her shift."

"Why would she seem less happy then?" I asked.

He swallowed. "It was so long ago. What does it matter now?"

Lois and I shared a look. I gave a slight head shake. We didn't know for sure that the bones found under the covered bridge were those of Galilee Zook. Deputy Little would not look kindly on our revealing the discovery of the body if Nathaniel didn't already know. To be honest, Deputy Little wouldn't like the fact that we were speaking to Nathaniel at all.

"Her brother is back in Holmes County," I said.

"Uriah, you mean?" A sour expression crossed his face. "I'm well aware. He's been back for over a year and stops in the restaurant every chance he can to pester me or one of my employees about his sister. Honestly, when Phoebe told me that someone was here asking about Gali, I thought it was him. I was pleased to find it wasn't."

"You don't like talking about her?" Lois asked.

He pressed his lips together as if he was considering his answer. "I don't like being harassed about her or what she was doing the day she disappeared. I don't like my staff being harassed about it either. It was over forty years ago. I'm sorry that Uriah lost his sister, but I don't know what he wants me to do about it."

"Who else is there to pester?" Lois asked. "From looking around here, I'd say most of your staff is far too young to have been alive when Galilee died."

"Most are. They didn't know Galilee or about the mystery surrounding her disappearance or her husband's murder. Most of them have only heard her name when Uriah came into the restaurant to ask about her. He's not doing that anymore. I told him not to come back. I'm relieved to see that he's honored that request."

I considered this for a moment. Uriah said the cook wouldn't speak to him at the Amish Corner Bench, but he hadn't told me he had made himself such a nuisance that he'd been asked to leave and never return.

"As for the staff we have today, they know nothing of Gali's story." He shook his head as he said this. "And I'm not sure they would care anyway. Young people today, even the Amish, have no respect for history. Not like I did when I was a teen."

"Is there anyone else that still works here who was a friend of hers or knew her well?"

Nathaniel frowned. "I don't know why you're asking. It's one thing for Uriah to ask, but what relationship do you have to Gali?" He gave Lois a pointed look.

Granted, Lois, with her brightly colored clothing, spiky hair, and heavy makeup, didn't look like someone who would have Amish friends. However, looks aren't everything, because I was Amish and she was my closest friend in the world.

Before Lois or I could think of an answer, he said, "You must be here about the rumors."

"Rumors?" Lois asked innocently and then took another bite of chicken. I would not be surprised if she licked the bones clean, she was enjoying her meal so much.

"One of the servers came in today and said a human skeleton was discovered at the bottom of the ravine near the covered bridge where Samuel's body was found. As soon as I heard, I thought of Gali."

Lois and I shared a look. "We don't know yet if it was Gali," I said.

He nodded. "Then why are you here? Aren't you that matchmaker who solves murders? I've heard about you."

Lois sat up straighter in her chair. "Our reputation precedes us!"

He glanced at her. "It precedes her. I have no idea who you are."

Lois scowled. "I knew I should have given myself a code name, Amish Marple," she muttered. "If I had done that, he would have known who I was."

I cleared my throat. "I have helped the police a time or two, and based on where the bones were found, the deceased is likely to belong to a member of the Amish community even if it is not Gali. Of course I would be concerned about this discovery."

Nathaniel shook his head. "I will be saddened to hear if the bones are Gali's, but I've told you everything I know. Gali worked here. I was fifteen. My grandfather and my father, who are both now dead, were in charge of the restaurant then. I have told Uriah all of this before. I suggest you ask him to kindly leave my employees and me alone." He glanced over his shoulder. "I had better get back to work. I can't expect my employees to stay on the ball if I'm not. Enjoy your meals."

Lois finished her last piece of chicken as he walked away. "I don't understand why he even agreed to speak to us if he was annoyed with Uriah for prying."

I shook my head. "Maybe he was just curious to see who was asking about Gali."

She sipped her extra-sugary iced tea. "I think there must be people here who knew Gali back then. There must be one employee who worked with Gali."

I thought of the cook that Uriah had mentioned, and I was about to say her name when a small voice said, "You mean Alice Springer, the cook." Phoebe had inched up on our table with our bill without our even knowing it. She moved silently across the room in her white sneakers.

Lois jumped and smacked her hand against her iced tea glass. I caught it before it could spill on the table.

"That was a serious ninja move, Millie," Lois said.

"Danki," I said, assuming it was a compliment. I was never sure when Lois spoke in her *Englisch* riddles. I looked up at Phoebe, who set the bill in the middle of our table while maintaining a death grip on her tray.

"Who is Alice?" Lois asked.

Just as I expected, Phoebe said, "She's the head cook. She has worked here for decades." She lowered her voice. "She knows everything about everybody working at the restaurant. She is sort of like an honorary *grossmaami* to us all." She paused. "She is very different from my own *grossmaami,* that is for sure and certain."

Lois looked as if she was about to say something, and since I guessed it was about Ruth, I jumped in. "Is she here now? Do you think she would speak to us?"

Phoebe looked over her shoulder. Nathaniel was nowhere in sight, and I wondered who she was worried might come around the corner. "She might."

"Can you take us to her?"

"I can take Millie, but you might stand out in an Amish kitchen . . ." She trailed off.

Lois sighed. "It's the lipstick, isn't it? I knew this red color was pushing the envelope."

It was more than the lipstick, but I wisely said nothing.

CHAPTER FOURTEEN

"I do wish I could be in on this interview," Lois said. "You know that I never like to miss any of the action, but I will get the getaway car ready." Lois handed Phoebe a generous tip, grabbed the bill, and went to the counter to pay.

"Getaway car?" Phoebe asked.

"She's joking," I said, hoping I was right. Then again, Lois might peel out of the Amish Corner Bench's parking lot just for the fun of it. "Now, where can we find Alice?"

"In the kitchen. She's always in the kitchen. I would think that she slept there if I didn't know better." She glanced over her shoulder. "Actually, she *might* sleep there. I've never been to her home." Phoebe looked around the restaurant one more time and said in a low voice, "Follow me, Millie." She walked to the back corner of the restaurant.

It was not where I'd expected her to go. Right behind the buffet line was a swinging kitchen door where waitresses and busboys were going in and out with carts and trays. This door was made of heavy steel with a nickel-colored knob. I followed Phoebe through it. When we were on the other side, she must have seen the expression on my face because she said, "This way we have less of a chance of running into someone. If we go through the main door to the kitchen, we could be hit by waitresses and busboys dashing in and out."

My brow wrinkled. I knew that Nathaniel didn't like Lois and me asking questions about Gali, but I couldn't help but wonder if there was something more to it. Why was Phoebe being so secretive? It could just be the Amish need to avoid being involved with anything remotely connected to *Englisch* law enforcement, but I sensed there was something else going on.

She led me down a winding hallway lined on one side with metal shelves holding restaurant supplies, everything from to-go containers to dishes. It was all sparkling clean and organized. The sight made me want to go home and give my kitchen a good scrub.

Down the hall, a voice could be heard. "When you are pricking the edges of the piecrust, be delicate with it or it will crack. This is not a lemon you are trying to squeeze. Pastry is forgiving, but not that forgiving."

"That's Alice," Phoebe whispered. "We caught her in a good mood. She always likes telling someone what to do."

I raised my brow. That sounded a lot like Phoebe's grandmother Ruth.

"Ya, Alice*,"* a shaky young voice said.

"You need to relax, *kind*," Alice replied. "If I correct

you, it's to make you do better next time. It's not to make you feel low about a simple mistake."

This time I couldn't hear how the young person answered. There was another metal door to the right side of the hallway.

Phoebe glanced at me. "Wait here and I will see if she will speak to you."

That was a *gut* mood. I wondered how Alice would have dealt with the pie maker if she had been in a bad mood. No wonder Phoebe was nervous to introduce me to her.

Phoebe slipped through the doorway, and I caught a view of the kitchen. A short, round Amish woman with hair so white that her prayer cap disappeared into it hopped from station to station, giving the young staff criticism and pointers on how to better prepare her dishes. Her voice was authoritative. The door closed with a soft click before I could see her face.

Through the door, I could hear Phoebe's soft voice, but not exactly what she said.

But Alice's voice was clear and strong. "I can't speak to anyone right now. Don't you know that it's the start of the dinner rush and everyone wants the all-you-can-eat buffet! I have to keep that fully stocked with my chicken. No one else can make it like I can. Breaks my heart to think what will become of this place after I pass on. Everyone comes in here looking for my chicken."

Lois would agree with that.

"She wants to talk to me about Gali? Why didn't you say so? Have her come in. She can talk to me while I work. The Lord looks poorly on idle hands. Don't you know that?"

A moment later, the door opened, and Phoebe stuck her head out. "Alice can see you. Hurry before she changes her mind."

I stepped into the kitchen. It was the largest one I had ever seen. There were rows and rows of prep stations, most of them taken up by young Amish women who were hard at work filling stainless steel trays with pasta salad, mashed potatoes, and roast beef. As soon as a tray was filled, another young Amish woman rushed into the kitchen and spirited it out to the waiting buffet.

Alice had not been kidding when she said this was the dinner rush for the buffet. The senior bus tours that lumbered through the county from spring to fall made one final stop at the Amish Corner Bench, and it seemed to me they'd arrived all at the same time.

"We need more coleslaw," Alice called. "Someone make the coleslaw."

Three young women began cutting cabbage heads into thin strips as if their lives depended on it. They seemed to be utterly terrified. I had never worked in a professional kitchen, but I considered myself a fine cook, a distinction most Amish women would claim for themselves. But from the nervous reaction of these young women, I knew I could never live up to the standards that Alice expected of her staff. Thank goodness I didn't have to.

"If you want to talk to me, wash your hands. Put on a hairnet and gloves and start battering chicken," Alice bellowed. "I expect as an Amish woman you can handle that task."

It took me a minute to realize that she was bellowing at me. "Me?"

"*Ya*, you. I can't be wasting time. We're a popular res-

taurant and in the middle of the busiest time of the day."
She pointed to a row of pegs along the wall. "Take one of
those aprons and a hairnet and get to work."

I thought of Lois outside idling in the "getaway car,"
as she called it. If she were with me, she would tell me to
slap on an apron and find out what Alice knew. I hoped
she would be as understanding when I did just that without her. In a way, Lois was like my goats. All of them
were afraid of missing out on each and every adventure,
no matter how small.

I removed an apron from a peg and put it on. I then
reached into a small cardboard box that was labeled "dis-
posable hairnets." I took one from the box and put it on
my head and prayer cap. I felt silly with it resting on the
top of my head like a mangled piece of fishing net.

I washed my hands in the large industrial sink and
found another box with disposal gloves. I put those on
too. If Lois were here, she would want to take a picture of
me. I'd have to tell her not to, of course, since as an
Amish person, I couldn't have my photo taken.

"Start battering the chicken. Don't put them in the
deep fryer. I'm the only person in the kitchen who is allowed to do that. I'm the only one who knows the trick to
make them come out perfect.

"Now, tell me why you are here."

"It's about Galilee Zook. I'm trying to piece together
where she was the day before she disappeared." I kept
myself from saying "before she died."

There was still a very tiny chance she was alive until
we heard from Deputy Little whether the bones found in
the ravine actually were Gali's. I hoped the coroner
would be able to tell, because that was the kind of closure
Uriah needed.

Alice picked up some of the chicken legs to be delivered to the buffet and studied them. Finding no imperfections, she put them back in the chafing dish to be carried out by one of her servers. She shook her head. "Some people can't let the past go. Gali's disappearance was terrible; we were all in shock here at the Amish Corner Bench. But so much time has gone by now. Isn't it better to let it be and let *Gott* take care of it all?"

"I think for those closest to her, the answer is no. It's not enough to let it be. Did you know Gali well?" I asked.

"Very well, I'd say. I start all of my workers on a volunteer basis. They do it for a week. If by the end of the week they still think they want to work for us, I put them through even more tests, this time of the emotional kind. I have to know they are a *gut* fit before I start paying them. It's best to know if the job will work for a person before you start giving them a paycheck. Gali was one of the rare workers who was *gut* at every task I gave her, from the simplest to the most complicated. She never complained that I gave her menial tasks at times. I have servers who do, but never Gali." She took a breath. "So, of course, I knew Galilee. I was the one who hired her when she was just a girl out of school. She started at the restaurant bussing tables and worked her way up to being the favorite waitress in the place. Everyone who came into the Amish Corner Bench wanted to be served by her. She had the most radiant smile you ever saw in your life."

She shook her head. "Gali was a breath of fresh air in the kitchen. She was always so joyful about coming to work. She was my number one in the kitchen." She lowered her voice. "She was the only one who I ever taught how to make my chicken. After she disappeared, I decided that was it. Now the chicken recipe stays locked in my head."

"You don't think she ran away to be *Englisch*?" I asked. "Did she talk about wanting an *Englisch* life?"

"Never. Gali loved her Amish life. It was her home life that she had to flee. She never once talked about leaving the faith, and it would have come up too. We spent so many hours together. It would have been difficult for her to keep such a secret from me."

I glanced around the kitchen to see if any of the young girls were listening. They all seemed to be going about their tasks with the same level of attention as before. Phoebe was no longer in the room. I'm sure she had other work to do, but I also wondered if she had decided to make herself scarce in case Nathaniel popped into the kitchen and caught me there.

"What were her problems at home?"

Alice pressed her lips together. "I don't know exactly. Only occasionally would something come out. I would ask her if she could stay late or pick something up at the store on her way to work. She always said that she had to ask her husband." She took a step toward me. "Step aside—I need the tongs in that drawer."

I hopped out of the way. "But it is not unusual for an Amish woman to check in with her husband before agreeing to such things."

"It's not," she admitted. "Which is the exact reason that I never married myself. I'm married to this kitchen and to this chicken." She laughed as if she'd made some kind of joke.

I considered this. Hadn't Uriah implied that Alice had wanted to marry him when they were younger? I wanted to ask her about that, but I thought it was better with my limited time to keep the conversation focused on Gali and her disappearance.

If Gali had never told Alice much about her trouble at home, then how would the cook know Gali's thoughts on being *Englisch*? People guard their most important secrets. Wouldn't Gali guard the fact that she wanted to leave the Amish community? I wondered if there was anyone who Gali had been completely honest with. It was disheartening to think she might not have had anyone to confide in at all. After speaking to the bishop about her husband and not receiving the support she needed, she must have felt more isolated than ever. My heart broke for Gali Zook.

But then again, perhaps Alice would know the signs. Many times we Amish can tell when a young person is about to leave the faith. There is a nervousness about the ones who leave. There is a yearning for more, more education, more money, more opportunity. The yearning for more does not sit well in the Amish world. Contentment is the goal. The proverb says, "Contentment is not getting what we want but being satisfied with what we have." But finding contentment can be difficult.

As if she could read my mind, Alice said, "She may never have told me that she had trouble at home, but things would slip out. Unconscious signs. She'd wince when someone would ask her about her husband. She would always volunteer to work the latest shift, the one no one wants because they want to be home with their families."

What she said fit with what Uriah had said about his sister's marriage. I didn't know if Alice was aware that Gali had gone to her bishop for help with Samuel. She hadn't mentioned that fact, so my guess was it was another thing Gali hadn't told her.

Using the tongs, Alice flipped over the chicken in the deep fryer. With her other hand, she stirred batter for the next batch of chicken. "I need to get back to work. If you want to speak to me again about this, come at a less busy time. Perhaps we can have a seat and a real chat."

The offer surprised me. "Uriah said that you were not receptive to speaking about Gali."

She frowned. "I don't mind speaking about Gali. I just don't want to speak to *him*."

I wanted to ask her why, but she waved me toward the door. "You can leave the apron on the hook."

I had been dismissed. I thanked her, put my apron back where I found it, tossed my gloves and hairnet into the trash, took one more look around the kitchen, and went out the heavy metal door that Phoebe had brought me through. I took a few steps down the corridor and was immediately confused. Both sides of the wide hallway were lined with shelves of dishes and boxes of kitchen supplies, but I could not remember for the life of me which of the doors I'd come through. Behind me a door opened and I heard a deep male voice that I thought might be Nathaniel's.

"I will get you the money you need. Don't worry about a thing. I'm grateful that you are willing to help me out with this little problem I'm having."

The door creaked open wider, and not wanting to get Phoebe in trouble for taking me to the back of the restaurant, I decided to hide.

I grabbed the doorknob of the closest door, and it turned. I pushed the door open and went through. I found myself in a utility room. Mops, buckets, and shelves of cleaning supplies were all in their places. Everything was neat and tidy. There was a sliver of sunlight at the back of the dark room, and I hoped it came from a door that led outside. I hurried toward it.

As I went through the outside door, there was a young Amish boy no more than thirteen who was throwing a bag of trash into the Dumpster behind the building. "Oh!" he said when he saw me.

"Your chicken is the best. Is this the way to the parking lot?" I pointed to my left.

He nodded dumbly. I thanked him and went on my way without another word. Maybe if I hadn't been old enough to be his *grossmaami* he would have been more inclined to stop me and ask what I was doing there.

I walked around the building as though I wasn't in a rush at all. Lois's car was no longer in the parking lot but idling along the side of the road. She wore dark sunglasses and a wide-brimmed hat on her head. I supposed that she'd found both of those items in her colossal purse.

I opened the passenger door.

She lowered her sunglasses and said, "What's the code word?"

"Amish Marple." It was my best guess.

She shook her head. "Now, how did you know that, Millie? I swear, sometimes you're a mind reader. If you hadn't been born Amish, I think you would have done very well as a psychic. You could have had your own venue in Vegas."

I settled into my seat. "Lois, you are my dearest friend in the world, but honestly, I don't know what you are talking about half the time."

"You know—" She pulled away from the curb. "I hear that more often than you would think."

That didn't surprise me in the least. Lois removed her hat and tossed it into the backseat. She turned the car onto the road. "What took you so long? I was about to call Deputy Little and say that you had been kidnapped."

I gave her a look. "I wasn't anywhere close to being kidnapped, but when I left the kitchen, I did get turned around in the back of the restaurant. It's a maze back there."

"Oh!" Lois said. "I love a mazy place. I wish I could have gone with you. Curse my amazing hair that always makes me stand out. Maybe if I had thought to wear my hat inside, I could have gone in with you."

It wasn't just her hair that made Lois stand out, but I wasn't going to say that to her.

"Where to now, Amish Marple?"

I had long given up on trying to talk Lois out of using her nickname for me. Truth be told, I liked the name, but I would never tell another soul that. It wasn't appropriate for the modest Amish *aenti* that I should be.

"I really need to go to the Zooks' buggy shop. It helps that my buggy is in the shop right now. It's a *gut* excuse to drop by. But it's after five. They must be closed now."

"It can't hurt to stop by," Lois said as we reached the intersection.

"I guess not," I agreed.

Lois turned the corner. "If no one is there, it might be even better because we can snoop around."

"I know that's what you're hoping for," I said.

She grinned. "Of course I am."

CHAPTER FIFTEEN

"So you just happen to be having your buggy fixed by the Zook family?" Lois asked. "And that was the family Gali married into?"

I glanced at Lois. "They are the only buggy makers in my district, and I like to support district businesses whenever I can."

Lois nodded. "And they are related to Gali."

"Ya," I said. "It's been so many years, but if I remember rightly, the buggy shop has been in the family for generations. It was owned by Samuel, Gali's husband, and then his young brother, Cyril, Lad's father, after Samuel died."

"Lad, who is engaged to Phoebe Yoder."

I nodded. "The very one."

Lois shook her head. "It seems to me that every life in the Amish community touches another life."

"It is the *gut* part of being Amish. It can be the difficult part of living in our community too."

Lois nodded. "I can see that. I'll be honest . . . sometimes I envy the closeness of your community. I know there are many people in Harvest who would jump in and help me if I ever needed it, but I don't believe that I have a whole group behind me like you do."

"Lois, everyone in Harvest would help you."

She smiled. "I suppose so. I *am* well liked."

"Bingo," I said, using one her phrases.

"Hey, I'm the one who says bingo."

"I thought you would be proud that I was using one of your *Englisch* phrases."

"Actually, I am. If I could only get you to play bingo with me, then I would be very proud."

"Lois, you know as an Amish woman, I can't gamble, not even in bingo." I leaned back in my seat and looked out the window. Along the road blue cornflowers and black-eyed Susans bloomed. They both are late summer flowers. Autumn and winter were on the way.

"I'm not going to fight with you over your belief system." She sighed. "You just don't know the fun you're missing, and you can play bingo without exchanging money."

"Then maybe I'd give it a try."

Lois turned her car into the driveway of the buggy shop. A large hand-painted sign stood to the left of the entrance to the parking lot. The sign read ZOOKS' AMISH BUGGIES. The front parking lot was small. However, there was a parking lot three times the size of the one out front behind the buggy garage. When Cyril Zook's grandfather built the buggy shop, he started with one long barn, which he used for the workshop. Over the generations and as the business grew, new wings had been added to the building.

Samuel had been a big part of the expansion. Not long before he and Gali married, he put an extension on the barn made of metal, so that they had more indoor storage and work space. Everyone in our Amish district brought their buggies to the Zooks, and they were known for such great craftsmanship that they grew popular in other districts in the county and even in some of the surrounding counties. I never thought of taking my buggy anywhere else.

"When did you bring the buggy in?"

"Three weeks ago," I said.

"That seems like a long time," Lois said. "Why has your buggy been in the shop so long?"

"I need two new rear wheels and an axle. The shop told me that my model was older and they had to order the axle from Pennsylvania. As far as I know, my buggy is sitting on blocks just waiting for the axle to arrive."

"I hope it's not coming by buggy. That will take forever."

I rolled my eyes.

"I don't know if I should be proud or disturbed that you've adopted my habit of rolling my eyes. I can see why people find it so annoying." She grinned.

I chuckled. "Let's go see about my buggy."

"And find out what Cyril or any of the other family members might know about Gali."

"Right," I said. "That too."

We were about to walk toward the shop's door when a courting buggy came racing up the road and turned into the driveway. The horse and the buggy's wheels, which were going unbelievably fast, kicked up dirt and gravel into the air. A cloud of dust enveloped Lois and me.

Lois sneezed. "What on earth? If I have dirt in my hair, I will be perturbed. I just washed it over the weekend. You can't wash your hair every day at my age. And does anyone have any idea how long it takes me to achieve this kind of style?"

The dust settled around us, and I brushed at my skirts and patted the back of my head to make sure that my prayer cap was still in place.

"I'm so sorry!" Lad Zook jumped out of the buggy. He was a tall young Amish man with glasses and strong arms. I thought that the muscles came from working in his father's buggy shop his whole life. His Amish bowl haircut was a little long for an Amish man of our district, but Bishop Yoder, much to his wife's dismay, wasn't a bishop who made church members measure their hair to make sure that it was the correct length.

"Millie!" Lad cried. "Are you all right? I would never have driven in like that if I had known someone was here."

Lois dusted off her hair. I didn't tell her it was speckled with dirt and dust. "You should be more careful, young man. We're not spring chickens. You are lucky we didn't topple over and break both of our hips."

Lad's eyes went wide, and they looked even wider behind the lenses of his glasses. "Are you hurt?"

"We're fine, Lad," I said before Lois could answer.

He let out a breath. "I didn't expect anyone to be here. The buggy shop closed over an hour ago. Are you here about your buggy, Millie? It's not ready yet."

"I would like to have a chat about the buggy, *ya.*"

He appeared concerned again. "Is there a problem with the cost? I'm sure we can work with you on that." He placed a hand on his chest. "I am very grateful to you for helping me with the bishop's wife. I think your saying that Phoebe and I were a match really made a difference in the bishop giving his blessing for us to get married."

I didn't correct him, but I wasn't sure that my opinion of her granddaughter's match hadn't made any difference to Ruth. There must have been something else that made her change her mind. I wished I knew what it was. I had been trying to figure out Ruth since we were children, and I still didn't know what to expect from her at this advanced age.

Ruth had been unsure about the match, but to be fair, Ruth would be unsure of any match for Phoebe or any of her grandchildren. She only wanted *gut* people—her words—marrying into the Yoder family. Anyone who knew Ruth knew that her estimation of *gut* people was narrow at best.

I had told both the bishop and his wife that Lad and Phoebe were a *gut* match. The bishop was pleased, and so was Phoebe. Ruth, not nearly as much. However, I had known Ruth my whole life long, and knew that nothing really pleased her other than correcting people. Because of that, of course, she would not take well to the idea that she might have been wrong about her granddaughter's choice in a husband.

Lad scratched the top of his head. His hair was so light, it was almost white. I wondered if it would look any different when he was an old man.

"Are you sure neither of you is hurt?" Lad asked again.

"Lad, we are fine, stop worrying about it so much." I dusted off my sleeve. "I need to give this dress a *gut* wash as it is."

His shoulders relaxed. "I am glad to hear it." He bit his lip for half a second. "Millie, when you meet with my father about the buggy, please don't tell him what happened. He won't like it if he thinks I pushed a buggy that way." He took a breath. "It's a new model that my *daed* made, and he told me to take it out for a long drive to see how it handles. I wanted to see what it could do."

"It's a courting buggy," Lois said. "As far as I know—and I'm not an expert—those weren't designed for racing."

"I don't think that my *daed* pushes our buggies as fast or as far as they can go. We have the best craftsmanship in the county. Everyone knows it. He needs to capitalize on that. I think he's missing out on sales."

"And you think that racing the buggy down the road is the best answer?" I folded my arms.

"I just wanted to be sure I was right about what it could do before I made my argument."

"Well, you can tell him your courting buggy there is a speed demon," Lois said.

Lad blushed. "Millie, we just received the axle for your buggy that we had been waiting for, but it came at the end of the day. Tomorrow is Sunday. The earliest that it can be finished is Monday afternoon."

"It is all right, Lad. I just wanted to come and check on it. It's been quite a challenge for me to get around without a buggy. I have my bicycle, but I can only cycle so far, and I know that Bessie misses our little rides around town too. She is such a gentle horse, but she does become a little antsy if she can't get away from the farm now and again." I wasn't going to ride her. I didn't own a saddle, and riding bareback would be too risky. Besides, not all buggy horses were trained to be ridden. I didn't know if Bessie ever had been. I wouldn't risk being thrown to find out.

He licked his lips. "Millie, I know that you are friends with Phoebe's *grossmaami*. You won't say anything to her about this?" His Adam's apple jumped up and down like a bobber on a fishing pole. "So I guess that's two people who I don't want you to tell."

"Not to worry. There is no reason Ruth has to know about this, or your father. I don't tell tales."

His shoulders relaxed. *"Danki*, Millie.*"*

"You are marrying the bishop's granddaughter. Good luck to you, my boy," Lois said.

Lad turned pale. "I know Ruth Yoder is not excited about her granddaughter marrying me."

"Ruth would not like her granddaughter to marry anyone," I said. "She was the same with her own children, and they are all happily married now. She just wants the very best for her family. We can't blame her for that."

Lois opened her mouth as if she was going to add something. Whatever she thought to say about Ruth, I knew it would not be helpful to Lad.

"You and Phoebe are a lovely match," I reassured him. "I'm the one who would know that, right?"

His face cleared just a little. "*Ya*, you would. *Danki,* Millie. We would like to be married in the fall, but . . ." He scrunched up his face. "I don't know if it's to be, and Phoebe and I have been waiting so long already. We have been sweethearts since our last year of school."

"Ruth is giving you a hard time?" Lois asked.

"Phoebe's grandmother was hesitant, but she is not the problem now."

I wanted to ask Lad what the problem was, but we were already traveling too far off track from the real reason we'd come to the buggy shop, which was to learn what Lad's *daed* remembered about the time his brother was killed.

"Just remember, Ruth will be keeping her eyes on you," Lois said. "Don't let your guard down. She's just waiting for you to slip up."

I shook my head. "Lad, Lois is teasing you."

"I'm giving the young man sound advice." Lois adjusted her large purse on her shoulder. "I have known Ruth Yoder since she was in pigtails. She's a tough cookie."

She was, but I wasn't sure Lad needed to be reminded of that. He most certainly knew, just as we all did.

CHAPTER SIXTEEN

Lad cleared his throat. "Millie, even though your buggy isn't done yet, I'm sure *Daed* won't mind your coming in and taking a look at it. He's inside the shop. He always works until seven or eight in the summer months. You have to take advantage of the sunlight while you can."

That was very true, and it made a proverb come to mind. "If you want life's best, see to it that life gets your best."

"I can understand that," I said. "I would guess buggy repairs slow in the winter."

He nodded. "Very much so. Everyone wants to have their buggy fixed or checked out before the winter hits. During the winter months our hours are much shorter, and that's when *Daed* plays with the buggy designs." He nodded at the courting buggy. "He worked on the design of this buggy all last winter and has been adjusting it ever since then. It's finally finished. I almost hate to see the project end. Creating a new design is the most exciting part of the job. I wish this could be the courting buggy that Phoebe and I ride in on Sunday afternoons."

"Since you're a buggy maker," I said, "I would think that you already have a courting buggy."

He nodded. "I do, but she doesn't handle like this one." He stared forlornly at the buggy and then shook his head. "Let's go see if *Daed* can talk to you about your buggy now."

He led us to the side door of the building that was part of the new addition. As soon as I stepped inside the buggy shop I was confronted with the familiar scents of sawdust and wood stain. Both were easy to explain since every buggy was made of wood and there was a large board lying across two sawhorses. Cyril Zook was in the process of staining the board black. He was a short man with muscular arms from hours of manual labor. His beard was mostly brown, but it was beginning to turn gray on the edges. The same could be said for his eyebrows, which were half-hidden behind glasses that looked identical to his son's glasses.

"Millie," he said and carefully placed the paintbrush on the corner of the board. "I hope you weren't expecting the buggy to be finished. It's not quite ready for you yet."

"Lad just told us that, but he said I might be able to step in to see it. My friend Lois and I just enjoyed dinner at the Amish Corner Bench, and since we were so close, I thought we'd stop by."

"Did you see Phoebe?" Lad asked.

"We did," Lois said. "She was our server. She's such a sweet girl."

Lad blushed as if the compliment was directed at him, and he ducked his head, but not before I saw the smile on his face.

Cyril glanced at his son. "*Ya*, Lad is quite looking forward to his life with Phoebe, though I don't approve of his rushing into it so quickly."

Lois raised her eyebrows. "Why delay? I thought you planned to marry this fall."

Lad frowned at his father. "We *are* getting married this fall. The bishop gave his blessing."

His father pushed his glasses up his nose in an irritated manner.

"We will see about that," Cyril said and then looked at Lois and me. "My son has to learn a little more about the business before he settles down with a wife and family. He will be the one who is taking over the family buggy shop when the time comes. It's a great legacy and a great responsibility. It is my opinion that he would do much better if he knew more about the business and buggy-making craftsmanship before he marries and is distracted by a wife and children."

Lad listened to his father without a word, but the twitch in his jaw was telling. Being young and in love and being asked to wait was never easy. As a matchmaker, I had seen it many times, and many times I had been asked to intervene. I rarely did in cases like this. In the Amish world, the parents' blessing on a union is important. Marriages could happen without it, but in my experience as a matchmaker, it was always best to avoid starting marriage in the middle of a family conflict.

Cyril wiped his hands on a cloth. "Your buggy is in the next building. We probably won't be done with it until Monday afternoon."

I smiled. "That is fine. Lad said the axle came in at the end of the day. I'm just relieved to know that it's finally here."

He nodded. "Me too. It was such an odd size. I'm glad we were able to find one. Take *gut* care of it. I would hate to have to look for a second one when the first was so hard to track down."

"I will," I promised.

I knew to *Englischers* all buggies look the same, but that wasn't the case for the Amish. As soon as we stepped into the second room, I recognized my buggy. It had no wheels, and it was balanced on giant sawhorses that lifted it high enough into the air so that a repairman could walk underneath the buggy and work on the undercarriage.

"I know it looks like a mess now, but you will be much happier with the way it handles when we are all done with it," Cyril said. "It needed quite a bit of work. You're lucky that it didn't break down while you were on the road. From what I can tell, this buggy has not been serviced in a very long time."

I nodded. "It's possible. I got it when I moved back to Ohio and I bought it used."

"*Ya*, I thought it might be something like it. Buggies last much longer than automobiles, but this one, I would guess, is almost thirty years old, which is very old for an Amish buggy."

I furrowed my brow. "It looks like you have to do a lot more work than you first thought. Will that change the price? I understand if it does." I thought about my budget, which was admittedly tight as a widow who made her living sewing quilts. I wondered if Cyril would let me pay him on shop credit. I wasn't sure how else I would be able to do it and keep a roof over my head and feed the goats too. I wasn't about to give up the goats now; they were family.

"Please don't worry about it, Millie. Kip was a *gut* friend of mine for a long time. If I can't be kind to a *gut* man's widow, what sort of man am I?"

"I can't thank you enough. My quilting covers the bills, but when extra expenses like this come up, it is a stretch to the budget."

He smiled. "I'm happy to help."

"I do appreciate it very much," I said. "And take all the time you need. Lois is a *gut* friend to me. She's been acting as my taxi driver while the buggy is repaired."

Lois grinned. "I don't mind driving Millie around, especially when we are on a case."

"On a what?" Cyril asked.

Lois's eyes went wide. "When we are on a cake," she said. "My granddaughter Darcy owns and operates the Sunbeam Café in Harvest, and there is a lot of cake there."

Cyril wrinkled his brow as if confused, understandably so. Where did Lois get the idea to say, "when we are on a cake"?

"I've been there a few times," Cyril said. "The café does look like it has excellent cakes."

"The very best," Lois agreed.

"Will you be at the church services tomorrow?" I asked.

"We always plan to go," Cyril said.

"I'm sure you heard about the skeleton that was found near the covered bridge," I said. "I suppose there will be a lot of talk about that."

A cloud passed over Cyril's face. "I have heard about it. I would not be surprised if people talk about it. Everyone in the district likes to talk and spread rumors. I much prefer to work on my buggies and stay out of everyone's way."

"Some people are saying that it's Galilee Zook." I watched his face when I said this, waiting for some kind of reaction or tell to show me what he was feeling.

His face gave away nothing. "*Ya,* I know this. The bishop was here this morning to tell me. If the body does turn out to be Gali, that will be a very sad end to a sad story." He began to pick up the tools around the shop and drop them into a red toolbox that sat on the corner of a folding table. "I tell the men to put everything back into place at the end of the day. Usually on Saturday this advice goes out the window. They are ready to go home to their families, their wives, and their children. They will not take the extra minute to care for the tools when it's the end of the work week."

"*Daed*, I can put those away," Lad said.

Cyril nodded and handed his son the tool in his hand.

Lad gathered up the rest of the tools in a matter of seconds and whisked them out of the room. It seemed he was happy to get away.

"It must have been difficult when your brother was killed," I said. "It was so long ago, I don't remember much from that time. I was a young wife then. I think at the time I was so worried about making a nice home for Kip, I missed many things that were happening in the community."

"Of course it was difficult. My brother, my only sibling, was murdered, and my sister-in-law, Gali, was missing. Gali didn't deserve what happened to her. She was a sweet woman. Many times I thought she never should have married my *bruder*. He needed a less sensitive wife who could manage his moods. Gali only crumbled when Samuel threw one of his famous fits."

"Famous fits?" Lois asked.

He pressed his lips together and touched his glasses as if he was considering how much he should say. "My *bruder* was an angry man, and he had a short temper. He had been like that since he was a child. He could be . . . difficult."

Poor Gali.

"Do you believe the theory that she ran away to be *Englisch*?" I asked.

He shook his head. "I didn't and still don't. Not many people listened to me at the time, but she was too quiet and demure to do something like that. I can't remember her ever stepping out of line. What's more out of line than joining the *Englisch*?"

Murder came to mind, but I didn't say that.

As if he saw the doubt on my face, he went on to say, "If Gali had had just a little bit more backbone, she would have left my *bruder* long before she disappeared. Samuel was a hard man, and he expected perfection at work and at home. It was impossible to live up to his standard." Cyril licked his lips. "I didn't agree with all his methods, but he was my older *bruder*. Our father was dead by the time we reached adulthood. As the eldest, Samuel had inherited the buggy shop. I worked here, but I did not own it. It became mine only after my brother's death. I am grateful I only have one son, so that as a father I don't have to deal with the push and pull of two sons running a business together. I suppose that is why I'm so hard on Lad. I want him to be able to handle this business on his own. Employees are one thing, but in my opinion, sharing the decision making of a business with another person—even if that other person is your *bruder*—leads to trouble."

"Or especially if that person is your *bruder*," I said.

He nodded. "That certainly rings true for me."

"Did you want the buggy shop?" Lois asked.

Cyril glanced at her from behind his glasses. "Every Amish son wants to make something of himself. Our mother was still alive when Samuel took over the buggy shop. It was clear that my brother had purpose. I wanted that too and to prove to her I was as capable as Samuel. I think, like everyone else, she feared to say anything, to say something to Samuel about giving me more responsibility in the shop. He could be very hotheaded. And when our father died, Cyril was the head of the family. He could ignore all of us, even our *maam*, if we said something he didn't like, so we said nothing."

"Did you know that he and Galilee had a difficult marriage?" I asked.

"I knew. Everyone in the family knew. I tried to be there for my sister-in-law, but my loyalty had to be to Samuel as my *bruder* and my boss. I was young and I wasn't brave enough to tell him to be kinder to his wife. I never spoke up with him. I regret that. If I had, maybe things would have ended differently."

"Would you do things differently now?" Lois asked.

He pressed his lips together and nodded his head. "I learned from what happened. I would never treat my own wife that way when I married. I would treat her like the jewel she was. Samuel treated his wife as a servant at best; at worst, well . . . I didn't know what it was like at home, but I could imagine that it was difficult for her. It was difficult enough for everyone in the buggy shop."

"Where were you when you heard about your *bruder*'s death?"

"I was as shocked as anyone when I heard that my brother had been killed, and even more shocked when I learned that Gali was missing. It tore my family apart. My mother died shortly after that of a broken heart. I don't know if she was brokenhearted over her eldest son's death or who he had become. I believe she felt that she'd failed him in some way."

"You inherited the buggy shop after your brother's death," Lois said.

He nodded. "There was no one else to leave it to; we have no other siblings. Samuel and Galilee had no children. I put my heart and soul into changing the shop for the better. I didn't want it or the family legacy to be remembered for what it was like when Samuel was in charge of everything. I wanted the people who worked here to feel cared for and valued. It took time because fear of Samuel was so ingrained in my buggy makers, but eventually, this became the best buggy shop to work in anywhere in Holmes County." Cyril looked at me. "It might be vain of me, but I am proud of that. I could not be more grateful for that and for what we have built here. I'm proud of the business that I will pass down to my son. I want to have full confidence that Lad will be able to carry on in this tradition." He sighed. "I saw your expression, Millie, when I said I wanted Lad to wait to marry, so that I know the shop will be in *gut* hands."

"I can understand your feelings," I said. "But you don't want to alienate your only son the way Samuel did to you." My voice was as quiet and as gentle as I could make it.

Cyril frowned as he considered my advice for a long moment. "Sometimes I think about how things would have been different if Samuel had lived. Guilt eats at my heart because I know life would have been harder if he was still with us. Not just for me, but for my family and for everyone who works here. I feel guilty because, in my heart of hearts, I know it was for the best that he died. The only thing I really lost at his death was my mother."

I stared at Cyril. Did he know he had just given himself a motive for killing his brother? The strongest one I could imagine.

CHAPTER SEVENTEEN

Lois whistled under her breath. "I like Cyril, but he's looking like a prime suspect for murder, or is that just me?"

"I'm sorry to say it, but it's not just you. I like him too." I glanced at the clock on the dashboard of Lois's car. "I need to get home before the ladies come over to quilt tonight. We'll be working on my commission quilt. I'm grateful that Cyril is doing all the repairs on my buggy for such a low price, but I still need to sell the quilt I'm making on in order to pay the bill."

Lois sighed. "I wish I could come to the Double Stitch meeting and find out what Ruth really thinks about Lad Zook courting her granddaughter, but I have been away from the café long enough and need to close up for the night. You will report back, won't you?"

I smiled. "I promise."

When Lois dropped me off at my niece's greenhouse so I could collect my bicycle and ride it home. The goats would be disappointed not to see her again that day. They always liked to see Lois, but with my other friends from the quilting circle coming over in just a little while, they would have plenty of ladies to greet.

After the short bike ride between the greenhouse and my home, I wagged my finger at the goats. "No chasing the quilting ladies when they arrive, okay? Especially Ruth."

As quickly as possible, I walked around the house and tidied up. I put out my quilting materials as if I had been hard at work on the quilt all day. I knew Ruth would not be fooled. I was glad I had spent the previous night finishing the piecing of the quilt. I had been up much later than usual, but now the ladies would stretch the quilt on the frame, and we could get to the quilting process.

"Knock, knock!" Raellen called through the screen door just as I was pulling the quilt frame out of the storage closet.

"Come in, Raellen!" I pulled the quilt frame into the middle of the room.

She stepped into the house, carrying a plate of chocolate chip cookies. "Millie!" She set the plate on the closest table. "You shouldn't be moving the quilt frame all by yourself at your age."

"Raellen Raber, it may take me a bit longer, but I'm perfectly capable of moving a quilt frame across the room."

She clicked her tongue. "I don't mean to hurt your feelings, but when you get to a certain age, you need to think about your back. You only have one. My aunt pulled her back sneezing, and she's not that much older than you. Can you imagine hurting your back by sneezing?"

Actually, I could. I thought it was the best argument she could have given to convince me to accept her help.

"Fine." I shook my head. "Let's move it together, then."

She beamed. "That's just what I wanted to do."

"Hello!" another voice called as Raellen and I put the quilt frame in place. Iris came into the house followed by Leah and Ruth.

"I'm glad everyone is here on time," Ruth said. "We have a lot of work to do. *Gut* to see the frame out as well. Let's get the quilt on it. We all have church tomorrow, and it will be at the Raber farm. I'm sure Raellen will be in a hurry to return home to get everything in order."

"Oh, Ruth," Raellen said. "Everything is in order. We've been ready for days. We are so excited to have the services at our farm."

Ruth had an expression on her face as if she didn't quite believe that.

I unfurled the quilt topper I had been working on for the last several weeks. I had to admit it was some of my best work. I was almost sorry to let it go. But that is the price of being a crafter or creator of any kind. At some point you have to let go of what you made to make room for the next project. I knew my customer was buying the quilt for her daughter as a wedding present, and she would be thrilled with it just as long as it was perfect. She was an exacting sort, and I had confidence that the Double Stitch would live up to her expectations. That was reward enough for me, and the smile on her face when I handed her the quilt would keep me going through the next time I faced such an enormous project. As the saying went, "Pride in your work puts joy in your day."

"Oh, Millie," Iris gasped. "That is the most beautiful topper I have ever seen. Your color choices are lovely. The wedding ring design is my favorite, and it is one of the most difficult patterns. Getting all the curves on the quilt to be the same circumference is not an easy feat. You did a perfect job."

I blushed. It was high praise coming from Iris, who was by far the best quilter in our circle. All of her quilts sold for top dollar.

I managed a modest *"Danki."*

The other women praised the quilt too, and my blush became even more noticeable. We always complimented one another on our work, but this was the first time I'd had a real standout that everyone loved, even Ruth.

"It is lovely," Ruth added when the quilt was spread out and all the ladies had taken their places. I could almost burst with pride, but I kept that to myself. A little part of me couldn't wait to tell Lois. It helped to have a close friend who was non-Amish. Lois would receive my bragging much better than any of my Amish friends.

On the quilt frame, the ladies and I put down the back of the quilt, the layer of batting, and then the topper over it. We laid it over the frame as if we were making a bed and then we tethered it to the frame with wooden clamps.

"That quilt isn't going anywhere," Raellen declared when we were done.

I set my needles, pincushion, small snipping scissors, and pencil in front of me on the quilt topper. Around me the ladies prepared to work in the same way.

Leah threaded her needle. "We are doing spirals?"

I nodded. "That's what the customer asked for."

Raellen clapped her hands. "*Wunderbaar*. That's my favorite. The spirals forgive mistakes, and we wouldn't want to do anything to mar this gorgeous topper, Millie."

Ruth looked at her over her reading glasses. "There will be no mistakes. Millie might be getting this commission, but everyone will know it was hand-quilted by Double Stitch. So there will be no mistakes. I will not allow it. We have to maintain our status as the best quilters in the district. You will want that reputation to stand when it comes time to quilt your own designs, Raellen."

We were all talented quilters, but if we took the time to quilt each of our pieces alone, we would never be done. To help one another finish all our projects, we took turns hand-quilting each woman's work. It was finally my turn again, and I was going to make the most of the opportunity.

"Millie." Clearly trying to change the subject, Leah asked, "What did you do today? I stopped in at the café to see if you were there and needed a ride home for the quilting meeting, but Darcy said that you and Lois had been gone all afternoon."

I ran my hand over the quilt topper in front of me. The colors were white, sky blue, turquoise, and navy. Since the quilt was for an *Englischer*, I had been able to include a floral-patterned fabric in the design, which was my favorite. "Lois and I went for a drive and had dinner at the Amish Corner Bench, and then we went to check on the status of my buggy. It's been out of commission for weeks."

My words hung in the air.

Ruth cleared her throat. "You just happened to have dinner at the Amish Corner Bench, when that was the last place Galilee Zook was seen alive?"

Before I could say anything, she went on, "And you really went to the buggy shop to check on your buggy, not because it is owned by Samuel Zook's family?"

I lifted my chin. "I never once claimed that I didn't have ulterior motives."

Raellen started to laugh, and then ducked her head when Ruth's glare fell on her. Even so, her shoulders shook as she continued to chuckle to herself.

Ruth set her needle and thread on the quilt topper. "You're meddling in another murder, aren't you? You just can't stay out of it."

I frowned. "Ruth, you're asking this after you demanded to know what we were going to do about the murder? And we don't know for sure there even was a murder."

"Samuel was murdered," Leah interjected. "No one doubts that. His death remains unsolved."

"The police said that Galilee did it and ran away," Ruth added.

Leah shook her head. "I never believed that. Anyone who ever had more than a five-minute conversation with Gali would know she didn't have the strength to commit such a crime. She never stood up to anyone about anything. Had she, she never would have married Samuel in the first place. She didn't love him."

We all stared at Leah.

"Now, how do you know that?" Ruth asked.

"She confessed it to me before they were married. She was marrying him so that her parents could save their farm. They'd had several bad seasons in a row, and Samuel promised to bring their farm back from the brink. Gali didn't have enough backbone to disagree."

"I have to think part of the problem was the time. Back in those days, maybe Galilee didn't have much of a choice," said Iris, who was the least opinionated of our group. "I am lucky that Millie was able to find the perfect match for me, but I know there is so much pressure to be married in our community. Gali probably felt that Samuel was her only option."

"Maybe," Leah mused. "But if she killed him, if Gali fought back against her husband, I'm not sure we should be blaming her for it. Samuel was a cruel man. He even chastised her in public. It's frightening to think what her home life was like."

Ruth dropped her spool of white thread on the quilt topper, and it bounced across the fabric. Iris caught it just before it could fall to the floor.

"Leah Bontrager," Ruth gasped. "As an Amish person, you are supposed to be a pacifist."

"I don't like violence or war. However, I am a mother of five and grandmother of eleven. If I had to protect myself or my family, I would. You would too, Ruth. Don't pretend otherwise. You are very protective of your family."

Ruth scowled at her.

Iris handed the spool of thread back to Ruth. "Do the police think those bones are Gali's?"

"Millie thinks so." Ruth sniffed. "Since she found the bones."

I frowned at Ruth. "I didn't find Galilee Zook. I never claimed that."

"Oh!" Iris said. "You were there when they found the bones, Millie?"

I shook my head. "*Nee*. Lois and I happened to be driving by when the police were there. She was taking me home from a concert on the square."

"But the road that runs along the ravine is not on the way home for you," Raellen argued.

"Lois wanted to avoid the construction. She thought she was taking a shortcut. It turned out to be a lot longer than either one of us expected." I glanced at Ruth. "We don't even know for sure yet if the bones are Galilee's. The police are running tests."

"It's amazing what *Englischers* can find out with their tests and machines," Raellen said.

Ruth narrowed her eyes at our youngest member. She didn't like Raellen's admiration for the *Englisch* use of technology.

I turned back to Leah. "How well did you know Gali? I would love to hear more about her. Maybe it will help me understand what happened to her. And is there anything more you can tell me about Samuel?" I glanced at Ruth. "Uriah asked me to help him find out what happened to his sister. Perhaps solving Samuel's murder will give him some answers."

Ruth made a noise that I ignored. I knew it was likely because she didn't approve of Uriah or our friendship. I had to remind myself that Ruth didn't approve of much of anything.

"I am a touch older than you, Millie," Leah said. "Old enough that Gali and I overlapped in school. I knew Samuel, of course, for the same reason. I never cared for him."

"Why?" I asked.

"He was unkind and spoke back to our teacher often. He was worse as a husband. He was controlling. He didn't want Gali leaving the home unless she was going to church or to work. I think he let her go to church to keep up appearances because he hardly ever came. Gali was always full of excuses as to why her husband couldn't make it to services." She shook her head and accepted a chocolate chip cookie and napkin from the plate that Raellen passed around the room.

"Don't get crumbs on the quilt," Ruth cautioned.

"We won't, Ruth," Leah said. "You really need to stop worrying about every little thing."

Raellen held the plate out to me, but I shook my head. "Now that you mention it, I don't remember seeing Samuel at church when I saw Gali there. Perhaps that is why Kip and I never got to know him well."

"She claimed that he used Sundays to pray and rest after working six days a week at his buggy shop, but my thought was he was sleeping off the alcohol that he drank Saturday night."

"Samuel drank?" I asked.

"Like a fish," Leah said. "My husband once had to give him a ride home when he swerved off the road because he was so drunk. He was lucky that it was my husband who happened by and not the bishop or, worse, the police."

"Could his drinking have contributed to his death?" Iris wanted to know.

"Maybe in disorienting him, but the alcohol didn't stab him in the neck with a knitting needle, and that's what killed him." I dipped my long quilting needle into the piece of fabric in front of me.

"Oh!" Iris covered her mouth.

"Did the bishop know about his drinking?" I asked.

Leah shrugged. "I'm not sure."

I looked at Ruth because she was the most likely one of the group to know what the bishop knew.

Ruth threaded her needle. "I have no idea what the

bishop knew back then. *Ya*, my husband and I were married, but he wasn't the bishop at the time. His father was."

Leah cocked her head. "Are you telling us that you didn't try to overhear what was going on in the district?"

Ruth scowled at her. Of the group, Leah was the only one who could get away with making such a comment to Ruth. It might have been because she was older than Ruth, not by much, but I thought it was mostly because Leah didn't care what Ruth thought about her.

"It's likely that your husband might remember something, though," I said.

Ruth held her needle above the quilt. "Mildred Fisher, don't you for a second think about bringing my poor husband into this mess. He already has enough pressure on him as the bishop of this community."

I knew Ruth meant business because she'd called me Mildred. However, that made no difference to me. Ruth might have warned me away from speaking to her husband about Galilee Zook, but that didn't mean I would listen to her.

CHAPTER EIGHTEEN

The ladies and I made great progress on the quilt. I had complete faith that I would be able to make the deadline the following week. However, even between quilting meetings, I would have to work on it every spare moment. It wasn't an easy task when all I wanted to do was find out what had happened to Gali Zook. The more I learned about her story, the sadder it became.

I had to hurry through the chores around my small farm and get to church. Services would be held at the Raber farm, and as her closest neighbor, I want to be on time. I knew Raellen was nervous about the service going well. It was the first time the bishop had chosen the Rabers to host Sunday church. I suspected that Ruth had been behind the delay, because she claimed the sheep smelled.

The Rabers had a large sheep farm with over one hundred head of sheep. Between the sheep and the nine children, there was always something happening at the Rabers'.

I had my own nervousness about the service. Raellen's husband, Roman, was not keen on me. He didn't like that I got involved in police investigations. He believed because Raellen was my friend and, at times, the quilting circle had helped me piece together clues related to a crime, I was putting his wife at risk. Raellen assured me that Roman was just being protective, and she didn't seem to worry about her husband's concerns.

I fed Bessie and the goats. Phillip and Peter danced around me as I used the hose to fill the water troughs.

"If the two of you keep that up, we're all going to get wet," I said. "I should have known better than to put on my Sunday dress before I finished the chores."

Peaches sat on a hay bale by the barn's open door. Suddenly, he arched his back and hissed. He jumped off the bale and streaked up the ladder to the hayloft.

A man's silhouette filled the barn door. He was backlit so that I couldn't see his face, and without thinking, I turned the hose on him.

There was a cry and he stumbled back out into the sunlight. Phillip and Peter galloped after him, and I followed. I dropped the hose and grabbed a shovel.

When I came through the door, I saw a very wet Deputy Little trying to keep the goats from jumping on him.

"Stop! Stop! That's enough!" he told the goats, but his outcry only made them more excited.

I put two fingers in my mouth and whistled high and shrill just as Kip had taught me. The goats stopped bouncing, and their hooves hit the lawn as they looked at me with guilty expressions on their faces.

Deputy Little took advantage of their distraction and stepped four giant paces back. His movement caught Phillip's attention. The goat made a move as if he was going to go after the sheriff's deputy.

I whistled again. "Phillip, *nee*, now both of you, back to the barn."

The goats didn't move.

I made a motion as if I was going to whistle again and they bolted toward the barn. Peaches stood in the doorway and had to hop aside so that they would not trample him.

"Deputy Little, what are you doing here on a Sunday morning?"

"I just got off my shift and thought I would stop by and talk to you about the Zook case. I'm sorry to drop in unannounced." He looked down at his sopping-wet uniform with the muddy hoofprints on it. "Yes, I am really sorry."

My eyes went wide. Was the deputy finally starting to see me as an actual consultant on the case?

I wrinkled my nose. "I'm sorry about the water and the goats. You scared me. I'm a little jumpy. I should have known that you were a friendly face since the goats didn't run out of the barn and try to knock you over."

"No, they did that *after* you hosed me down. It's all right," he said. "It was a long shift, and I was in desperate need of a shower anyway. You might have saved me some time." He chuckled. "And I'm happy to hear that you are on your toes, Millie, and when the time comes you're willing to protect yourself. You can never be too careful."

I wanted to ask him what he meant by that, but he said, "We got the test results back on the bones found in the ravine. BCI agreed to rush it, so that the family of the deceased could be notified quickly."

I drove my shovel into the ground next to me so it stood up on end. "It's Gali," I guessed.

He nodded.

My heart sank. Of course, it would be a tragedy for anyone to die in such a lonely place, but I think a small part of me was holding out the hope that it wasn't Galilee Zook. After learning how difficult her marriage had been, I wanted to believe that she'd run away to be *Englisch* and ended up in a better life, even if it wasn't an Amish one. I knew as well as anyone else that being Amish is not right for every person.

"The coroner believes that Gali died decades ago. His findings are consistent with the time of her disappearance. In all likelihood she died the same night as her husband." He poked his toe into a tuft of grass and kept one eye on the goats, which were only a few feet away.

"How awful," I said.

"The sheriff is considering this all a closed case, so there is not much more I can do on it. Part of the reason I'm here is to tell you the investigation is over. I have to move on to other cases. We have a terrible backlog."

"Closed?" I blinked. "Why? How? We just found out that she was the one who died."

"There was a history of abuse in the family. I've learned that from members of the community. No one said anything about it back then. I found nothing in the files. However, Sheriff Marshall believes that with what we've learned recently, it's safe to make the assumption that Gali killed her husband with the knitting needle.

When she realized what she'd done, she ran from the buggy and fell into the ravine to her ultimate death. There was a snowstorm that night. Visibility would have been terrible. It's possible."

My heart sank because I knew he was right. It was possible. It was even plausible that Gali had killed her husband. He might have pushed her too far, and she'd snapped. She'd tried to do things the right way. She'd gone to the church elders for help. She'd gone to her parents. She might have felt that she was out of choices. That didn't make murder excusable, not in the least, but it did remind me of a saying: "Even though you can hide from the earth, heaven sees you act."

I prayed both Gali and Samuel had found forgiveness and peace.

"What will you do now?" I asked.

He shrugged. "I'm afraid I have to give up the case. If the sheriff and the county prosecutor consider it closed, I don't have much choice." He sighed. "Millie, please don't look at me like that."

"Like what?" I folded my arms over my apron.

"Like you're my favorite teacher and I'm disappointing you."

"I'm not disappointed in you, Deputy Little. I'm disappointed in a system that elects a sheriff who would dismiss such a case because it happened long ago and involved an Amish woman. Where is the *Englisch* justice in that?"

"I can't tell you, but I can't spend any more of my work time on this case. Sheriff Marshall is upset that the case came back up at all. He said he would boot me from the department if I continued to work on it. Before, Aiden was a buffer between the deputies and the sheriff. Now that he's gone and working for BCI, the buffer is gone too. The sheriff has been extra cranky since Aiden left. I don't believe he really knew how much work Aiden did and how essential he was to keep the department running. The sheriff expects the rest of us to pick up the slack. That's not easy. None of us are as efficient as Aiden. Resources in the department are thin. We have too many cases and too few deputies to investigate them all."

"What do you believe happened the night Gali disappeared?" I asked.

"I don't know what I believe. It will be almost impossible to prove one way or another who the killer was. There were no fingerprints taken from the knitting needle that was the murder weapon. It was a cold, snowy night; the killer, Gali or whoever if might have been, was likely wearing gloves. In all probability, we will never know what happened that night."

An idea struck me. "Why was she not found until now? If she fell into the ravine that night, she might have been covered with snow, *ya*, that's true." I swallowed. "But when spring came, wouldn't her body have been discovered? The road and bridge were still in use back then, and hunters go through those woods all the time during hunting season."

"You're asking all the right questions, Millie. I'm sorry to say that I don't have all the right answers. There's some evidence that she was buried, but the coroner says it was inconclusive. The sheriff and the prosecutor don't think that is enough to keep the case open."

"She couldn't have buried herself." I dropped my arms to my sides.

"I know that." He wrung water out of the bottom of his shirt. I had gotten him *gut* with the hose.

"Then someone else was there that night."

Deputy Little made a face, but he didn't tell me I was wrong. He knew I was right. "There is no evidence that we can use to find that person, assuming that supposition is even true. Nothing short of a confession is going to solve this case. In my experience, confessions are hard to come by. Not to mention that if someone has kept this secret for forty years, they would be even less likely to give it up now."

I wouldn't call it hope, but determination swelled in my chest. The hope that Gali was still alive was gone, but that wasn't the end of the story. She may have been gone for decades, but I had a new determination to prove her innocence. She deserved that. After the hard life she had lived, she deserved to have her name cleared of any wrongdoing.

"Millie," Deputy Little said. "What's that expression on your face?"

I met the deputy's gaze with my own. "It's the look of someone who's not going to give up."

CHAPTER NINETEEN

After Deputy Little left, I locked up the house so I could walk the quarter mile through the pasture to the Rabers' farm for the church service. Before I was involved in murder investigations in the county, I rarely locked my house. Now, I always did. I'd learned the lesson that bad people could find me even all the way out in the country.

When I reached the property line between the Rabers' farm and my home, I realized I was being followed. I spun around just in time to see Phillip and Peter duck down into the high grass. Roman Raber had not had his sheep in this end of the pasture in the last several weeks, and the grass had grown so high it was up to my knees. The goats seemed to believe that it was *gut* cover for them to get into mischief.

I put my hands on my hips. "Where do you two think

you're going? I told you that you are not welcome at the Rabers' farm. Roman believes you mislead their sheep. Out of respect for Raellen, I have to ask you both to go home."

Slowly, the goats stood up and hung their heads. It was almost as if they understood everything I said. Ruth would not approve of my even entertaining such a thought.

I was about to chastise the goats again and tell them to go back home when, to my right, the grass moved. If I had been alone, I might have thought I'd imagined the movement, but by the way the goats' heads swiveled in that direction, I knew I had not.

"Who's there?" I called.

A young man in Amish clothes popped out of the grass fifty yards away from me and dashed across the field, jumping over the tufts of grass like a deer fleeing a hunter.

I yelped. The goats started after him, but I whistled and they stopped.

I watched the figure fly over the open field. The man could run. I shivered. Had he been watching me?

I had no idea who it was except for my impression that it was a young man in Amish clothing. I supposed I really didn't know it was an Amish person or a young man. It could have been a woman or an *Englischer* wearing an Amish shirt and trousers.

I placed a hand on my chest. My heart thundered behind my rib cage. I glanced at the goats. "You all can come with me. Roman isn't going to make a scene in front of the entire church, and I think I need your backup."

They leaped in the air, and I continued on my way to the Raber farm with Phillip and Peter close at my heels. I shook my head at my own foolishness. It was a very bad idea to take the goats with me to church. The Rabers and

Ruth Yoder would both be against it, but it couldn't be helped. After seeing that man pop up out of nowhere, I was a little too edgy to walk the rest of the way alone, and I didn't have a phone at my home to ask someone to come and get me.

The goats' eyes gleamed as soon as the hundred or so sheep came into view. The sheep were clustered together in a pasture like a huge, tightly packed cotton ball. I knew the goats were dying to race through that wall of fluffy fleece.

I shook my finger at them. "*Nee*, leave the sheep alone."

They hung their heads, but Phillip at least still had one eye on the sheep. This didn't bode well.

We walked by the sheep pasture, and I let out a breath. So far, so good. Ahead of me, I saw people milling around the Rabers' front yard, where dozens of chairs had been set up for the Sunday services. The chairs faced the Rabers' wide front porch. Bishop Yoder stood on the porch speaking with another church elder. I assumed that was the place he would give his Sunday message.

While the parents talked and gossiped, children ran around the farm, squealing and greeting their friends. Since we only have church every other week, it was likely that the previous Sunday service was the last time they'd seen their playmates. School would start up again in the fall just two short weeks away. Two weeks is like a decade to a child, and from their reactions to seeing one another, you would have thought they were meeting old friends after years apart.

My great-nephew Micah ran by with two of the Raber boys. "Micah!"

He pulled up short. "*Aenti* Millie!" His eyes went

wide. "You brought Peter and Phillip. I thought you said that the goats aren't supposed to be around the sheep."

"They aren't, but I wanted them to walk with me for . . ." I trailed off. I was thinking protection, but I didn't want to say that for fear of frightening Micah. It would be even worse if he told his mother, Edith, and my niece insisted I live at her place for a few weeks. I loved my family dearly, but I very much liked living on my own and making my own choices after all these years. I grew up in my home with my siblings and parents, married Kip and lived with him, and then moved in with my brother's family after Kip died and my sister-in-law also passed away. My brother needed help raising his twins. From my brother's home, I moved again to Michigan to care for my ailing older sister Harriet. At sixty-some years old, for the first time in my life, I was living alone. Alone, if one didn't count the goats, Bessie the horse, and Peaches the cat, of course.

Micah didn't seem to notice my hesitation as he introduced the goats to his two friends.

"Can you watch the goats for me during the service and make sure they stay away from the sheep?" I asked Micah.

He grinned. "Will do, *Aenti.*" He whistled the way I had taught him, and Phillip and Peter ran to him without a backward glance my way. At least the goats were obedient on occasion. If only their good behavior could last the rest of the church service.

As I left Phillip and Peter with Micah and the two Raber boys, I hoped for the best. I would have done better to have left the goats with Micah's older brother, Jacob. Responsible Jacob would have taken it upon himself to make sure the goats were well behaved. After his father's death when the children were small, Jacob had stepped into the role of man of the house even though he was just a young boy.

I walked toward the chairs and waved at church members as I went. All along, I looked for the young man I had seen running across the pasture. He had gone in the opposite direction from the Raber farm, but I still looked for him.

I found a seat in the back row of chairs. Typically, I sat closer to the middle, but I wanted to be able to jump up and leave if the goats began to cause trouble.

Someone tapped me on the shoulder. "Millie Fisher," Ruth Yoder hissed. "My granddaughter's heart is broken, and it's your fault."

I turned in my seat to face her. "Ruth, whatever do you mean?"

"Phoebe just left church crying her eyes out. Lad has told her he can't marry her."

I stared at Ruth. It was the very last thing that I'd expected her to say. "But I just saw Lad Zook yesterday. He had only glowing things to say about Phoebe. He thanked me for encouraging the match!"

"He must have changed his mind overnight because, as of this morning, he didn't feel that way any longer. I saw him speaking to Phoebe. When I noticed how upset my granddaughter looked and began walking in that direction, he ran away like a coward. If he was really worthy of Phoebe, he would have been brave enough to stay and explain his actions."

Her comment reminded me of the Amish man I had just seen running across the pasture. Could that have been Lad?

"He was running toward your farm," she said. "I thought it was to tell you his decision."

"I never spoke to him," I said, taking care not to say I hadn't seen him because I was certain now the young man I had seen galloping away from the Raber farm was Lad. There couldn't have been two Amish young men running away from church, could there?

I shook my head. "I'm so sorry to hear that. I know that he loves her. Perhaps this is just some misunderstanding. Poor Phoebe. I'm sure it's only cold feet. Many young men have that. He and Phoebe are a perfect match."

"Clearly, they are not a perfect match if he treats her so poorly," Ruth snapped.

I understood Ruth's anger. Had it been a child in my own family who had been treated so, I know I would feel the same. Platitudes about cold feet would do little to soothe me.

I risked asking the next question even though I suspected I would not like the answer. I had to know. "Why would you think Lad's behavior has anything to do with me?"

She put her hands on her hips. "Lad told Phoebe he had a visit from the village matchmaker yesterday, and it made him question things. He doesn't feel worthy to be part of the bishop's family. What on earth did you say to him to make him think that?"

I suppressed a wince. I hadn't said anything, but I bet Lois's teasing was the source of his comments. Sometimes my friend's *Englisch* sense of humor did not translate well into the Amish world. This would be one of those times.

Ruth folded her arms. "Honestly. He is *not* worthy to

be a member of my family, but I agreed to hold my tongue because Phoebe loved him. Also, looking at the caliber of young men in this district, she could have done much worse."

"Lad is a fine young man," I said and glanced around, noticing that we'd attracted the attention of several women standing nearby. One of them was Raellen Raber. Raellen was a talented quilter, doting wife, and wonderful mother, but she was also a gossip. In fact, she was the biggest gossip in the county. If she heard about Lad and Phoebe's breakup, it would be known throughout the county before the end of the bishop's sermon.

"Ruth, I can understand why you're upset," I said in a low voice. "I'm happy to talk to you about this more at another time, but I think this is not the right moment." I nodded in Raellen's direction.

Ruth spun around and glared at Raellen and the other two women. Raellen made a mouse-like squeak and scurried away. However, I knew it was too late. She must have heard most of our conversation. The damage was done. I hoped it would not widen the rift between Lad and Phoebe, because I knew that they were a *gut* match. I wondered if it really was Lois's comment that had caused his change of heart or if it was his father. Lad's *daed* had felt very strongly that his son was not ready to marry.

The bishop's wife turned back to me. "You don't know how embarrassing this is for our family."

"Not just for Phoebe?" I asked, knowing that Ruth was going to tell me even though I said we should talk about this at another time.

"*Ya*, this is bad for the whole family. It makes us all look bad. We have already sent the invitations for the wedding. What do we do now that he has called it all off?

The ceremony is just a month away. There'll be bishops from three states attending. They had to make arrangements with other elders in their district to preach at Sunday service while they were away. Did he even think of that? Plus, we will be the laughingstock of the entire Amish community. Our granddaughter left at the altar."

"She wasn't technically left at the altar," I said.

"Millie, you are missing my point as usual."

"*Nee,* Ruth, I am not. I hear your point loud and clear." I stopped myself from saying that she cared more about her family's reputation than her granddaughter's feelings. I knew it appeared that way on the surface, but I also knew that Ruth loved Phoebe dearly and would not want her to be unhappy.

"I'm sure that the two of them will work this out with time," I said. "Again, I believe he got cold feet, but I do not doubt for a second that he loves Phoebe. When I was at the buggy shop, he spoke so beautifully about his wife-to-be. It was clear he was wondering how he could have been so lucky to find his match in her."

"If he doesn't make this right," Ruth said, "his luck is about to run out."

CHAPTER TWENTY

During the service, I was distracted. I had so much on my mind. There was Uriah, the murder, and now Phoebe and Lad. Not to mention, I kept looking around the Rabers' farm to make sure the goats weren't getting into any kind of trouble. When it was time to stand up and sing a hymn, the congregation was well into the second verse before I realized everyone was singing and I was still in my seat.

After the bishop said the final prayer, a church luncheon was held in the side yard of the Rabers' farmhouse. It was on the opposite side of the house from the sheep pasture. I knew that was intentional. The sheep were cute and fluffy, but they also smelled.

I watched as church members stood in line for the buffet-style potluck. I didn't pick up a plate and join them. I wasn't hungry. I was heartsick over the fact that the sheriff's department considered Gali's case closed despite the evidence that her body must have been buried. And I worried that Phoebe was heartbroken. Somehow, I felt responsible for doing something about both of those sad situations.

Across the lawn, Bishop Yoder spoke with a church elder. The two men shook hands and the elder walked in the direction of the food table. Bishop Yoder hung back. Anytime there were church dinners or parties with food or drink, the bishop insisted that he should be the last to be served. He felt it was his role as bishop to serve the community and always put his flock's needs first. While most of the church members were distracted by the food, I knew it was a *gut* time to speak to the bishop.

He smiled at me. "Millie, I am happy to see you. I may have been mistaken, but I saw one of your great-nephews running behind the barn with your goats. I thought they were banished from the Raber farm."

"Don't tell," I said.

He smiled. "It is not my duty to become involved in the lives of my church members as long as they are doing the *gut* work and following *Gott*'s will for their lives."

I wasn't sure bringing the goats to the Raber farm was following *Gott*'s will, but I wasn't going to argue with him about that. He was the bishop, after all.

I expected the bishop to say something to me about Phoebe, but he did not. Was he leaving it to Ruth to deal with their granddaughter's broken heart? However, I hoped that he would speak to me about Galilee Zook. His father had been the district bishop at the time of her death. It was difficult for me to believe that our current bishop knew nothing about her troubles with her husband. Certainly, if the former bishop was grooming him to be the next leader of the district, as everyone had believed, Bishop Yoder's father must have shared some of the district's problems with his eldest son.

After a long moment of silence, I said, "I am sure you have heard about the bones that were found at the bottom of the ravine by the covered bridge."

"I have." He tugged on his white beard and looked down at the grass. I noticed his trousers were so expertly pressed that it looked as if I could get a paper cut on the creases running down the front of his legs. His shoes shone in the early afternoon sun. I saw Ruth's hand in all of it. She would not let her husband take his place in the pulpit unless his attire was perfect. Perfection was impossible to achieve, even Ruth knew that, but she would do whatever it took to bring herself and her family as close to that ideal as was humanly possible.

"Deputy Little spoke to me about the discovery," the bishop said. "He wanted to know about people who might have disappeared from the community during the last several years. We have had several members leave to join the *Englisch* with no warning. I gave him the names I knew. However, as far as I know, all of those members are still living among the *Englisch*."

"Was Galilee Zook one of the names you gave him?" I asked.

His body tensed. "She was. She was one of the oldest people who disappeared."

"The bones are those of Galilee Zook." I let the sentence hang in the air between us.

He looked up from the patch of grass he appeared to be studying. "Are you sure?"

"Deputy Little told me this morning before church."

"And what does the deputy plan to do about it?" the bishop asked.

"Nothing," I said and watched the bishop's face as I did.

His brow wrinkled in concern, and he began to pull on his white beard a little more aggressively. If he wasn't careful, he might just pluck it off his chin.

"Nothing? What do you mean?" Bishop Yoder asked.

"He can't do anything about it. Sheriff Marshall is ruling the case closed, so Deputy Little can't work on it without risking getting in trouble with the sheriff."

"Why is that?"

I glanced around us to make sure nobody was listening. No one was standing nearby, but I spotted Ruth across the field speaking with several women from the church. Even though she was having a conversation with them, she was clearly keeping me in her sight. She scowled when we made eye contact. I needed to finish this conversation with the bishop because I had a feeling his wife would be over here any minute.

"The sheriff believes the most logical explanation for what happened that winter night was that Gali killed her husband. When she realized what she had done, she ran away from the buggy. It was dark and snowy. She didn't see the ravine. She ran right into it and fell to her death," I said. "It seems that everyone knew that Gali and Samuel had a turbulent marriage. Uriah says she even went to the bishop, your father, asking for help with her husband."

"What kind of help?" the bishop asked.

"I believe she wanted the church to step in and make sure he did not mistreat her." I didn't say the word "abuse"—it was such a loaded word—but it was on the tip of my tongue.

"She may have spoken to my father. I would not know. I was not an elder at the time, so I would not be privy to information about individuals in the congregation unless they came to me personally. Galilee Zook did not."

"Your father never spoke to you about her?" I could not hide the doubt in my voice. It is always the hope that the church elders don't talk to others about district members, but I knew that wasn't always the case. Ruth always seemed to know what was happening with everyone in the district. That led me to believe the bishop either told her or she overheard because she was in the same home.

"He did not." His tone was firm. "I provided counsel to my father at times, but he never spoke to me about the Zooks. If Galilee spoke to him about her husband, I don't know what advice he gave her. However, I know that we do not tolerate abuse or mistreatment of any kind in this district. *If* it was true that Gali was in any danger from her husband, my father would have done something about it."

I wasn't so sure about that. In my opinion, abuse would not have been something the bishop of the time would have addressed.

I hated even to think it, but I knew the bishop was lying.

CHAPTER TWENTY-ONE

I didn't plan to stay for the rest of the meal. I was far too distracted thinking about Gali's death. I needed to act. As I turned to find Ruth and Raellen so that I could say my good-byes, I heard a squeal. Phillip and Peter were tearing away from the food tables with pie plates in their mouths. Micah and Raellen's sons were in hot pursuit. The goats kept running, and with the pie plates still in their teeth, leaped over the split rail fence that surrounded the sheep pasture.

The sheep squealed and baaed in terror. The two goats, who still did not want to give up their pies to the boys, ran through the sheep, heads down, knocking over a few of the ewes.

I stopped just by the fence and watched in horror.

Finally, when the two goats reached the other side of the flock, they stopped, dropped the pie plates on the ground, and began to eat the pie. Meanwhile, the sheep ran around the pasture in a circle as if they were being chased by wolves.

"Millie Fisher, if you ever bring those goats back here, you won't spend another second on my property, even if we are in the middle of a church service." Roman Raber stood just a few feet from me.

"Roman, I am so sorry. I truly don't know what got into them."

Micah and the Raber boys stood on the fence and watched the sheep run around and around. "*Aenti* Millie." Micah held on to the fence and leaned back. "I tried to stop the goats, but as soon as they saw the pie, there was no holding them back. They were going to get it no matter what we did."

I shook my head. "It's not your fault, Micah." I knew how the goats could be when they got an idea into their heads. I put my two fingers in my mouth and whistled for all I was worth.

Phillip and Peter looked up. Cherry filling dripped from Peter's mouth, and blueberry filling dripped from Phillip's. I should have known Phillip would steal the blueberry. I had been looking forward to sampling it. They didn't move. I whistled again. Finally, with heads hanging low, they walked over to us.

In the meantime, the sheep had calmed down and stopped running around the pasture. Dozens lay in the grass as if they needed a nap after all of the excitement.

The goats leaped over the fence again. And landed next to me.

"Millie Fisher, you and the goats have to leave my farm right away," Roman said.

Most of the district stood around us, and my cheeks

felt hot. At my age, it wasn't often I became embarrassed anymore, but it seemed misbehaving goats at a church service would do it. "We are leaving now, and again, Roman, I'm so very sorry. If any of the sheep were harmed, please let me know and I will pay for their care."

"That won't be necessary, Millie," Raellen said.

Her husband shot her a look. It was clear to me that Roman was not happy with Raellen giving her opinion.

"Did you even see what those goats did to my sheep? They knocked several of the ewes over, and the rest of the herd ran wildly around the pasture. They are completely disoriented. It will take them the rest of the day to calm down."

I folded my hands in front of me. I had no response to that because everything he said was true. The goats had done those things, and it was time I left and got them back home.

"We are leaving," I said.

Ruth folded her arms and shook her head as I walked by her. I sighed. I would find a way to make it up to Roman and Raellen for my goats scaring their sheep.

As I walked back across the pasture that separated our two properties, the goats followed a few paces behind me with their heads hung low. They knew they were in trouble.

I glanced over my shoulder and sighed. "I can't stay mad at you. Come up here."

They grinned and ran up on either side of me.

"Just no more going to the Raber farm. Ever."

They poked their heads around me and looked at each other.

"Ever. I mean it."

They fell back into line. I shook my head.

* * *

When we reached the farm, the goats didn't even object when I suggested they go into the barn and sleep off their pie caper.

"*Aenti* Millie," a young voice called to me when I walked out of the barn.

Micah stood next to his bike in the driveway.

"Micah, what are you doing here?"

He dropped the bike in the grass. "*Maam* asked me to check on you. She was upset over what happened with the goats. She said it was my fault that they misbehaved since I was supposed to be watching them."

I shook my head. "I would never blame anyone but Phillip and Peter for the trouble they got into."

"Well, *Maam* said that I could stay with you until the end of the church services to help you."

I cocked my head as an idea started to brew in the back of my mind. "Micah, have you had time to trade any of the baseball cards with your *Englisch* friend?"

His face lit up. "*Nee.* I haven't seen Cappy since last week. I would love to show him the baseball cards I got. There are some *gut* ones in there," he said excitedly. "I got a whole stack of All Star players. I didn't have any of those. I know Cappy will want to see them."

"Are you up for another bike ride to pay him a visit?"

Micah pumped his fist in the air.

"Do you think he will be home on a Sunday afternoon?"

"Oh *ya*. He and his family go to church, but they are only there for an hour! Can you imagine if church was just an hour long? What do they do with all the extra time?"

I had no idea.

Before we left, I checked on the goats one more time. They were fast asleep on their bed of straw in the barn. They were in a pie-and-excitement-induced coma. Peaches sat on the stall wall looking down at the goats with a confused expression on his face.

I scratched the cat's head. "I know it's not often that you see them sleeping. I would enjoy the peace and quiet while you can."

Micah and I left the farm. Since I didn't know the way to the Stoller Alpaca Farm, where Cappy lived, I let my young great-nephew take the lead.

Micah pedaled with purpose in front of me. I knew Micah was thrilled with the idea of seeing his friend Cappy, but I hadn't told him why I wanted to go to the alpaca farm, that it was the place where Uriah Schrock lived, and Uriah had not appeared at church that day.

Micah didn't slow his pace while he pedaled by the weathered covered bridge and the ravine. I slowed my bicycle just a little, so that I would not lose sight of Micah. I wanted a moment to reflect over what had happened there on a cold January night forty years ago. I whispered a prayer for Gali. Being by the bridge and knowing that Gali had died there made me feel impossibly sad. Thinking about the difficult life she'd had with Samuel made me even sadder. I prayed that Gali had finally found peace and happiness with *Gott*.

The Stoller farm was just a quarter mile away from the bridge and ravine. Micah pointed at the farm. "See the alpacas," he cried.

I spotted the large animals with their woolly coats and long necks grazing behind a wire fence. There were at least a dozen of the strange-looking animals, and the colors of their coats varied from brown, white, and black to a burnt-red shade.

As we turned our bicycles onto the driveway, a cream-colored alpaca that was closest to the fence lifted his head and a long blade of grass hung from his buckteeth.

"Come on, *Aenti*," Micah called. I had never heard him quite this excited before. Micah had always been the most outgoing and cheerful of Edith's children, but right now his voice was full of joy. He pedaled faster.

The farmhouse was two stories tall, and there was a small ranch house just to the west of it next to the barn. I slowed my bicycle. I knew this place. Memories began to stir in the back of my mind. I had been here before.

An *Englisch* boy about Micah's age dashed through the front door of the big house. "Micah!" he cried. "I never, ever expected to see you on a Sunday."

Micah hopped off his bike and adjusted his knapsack. "My *aenti* wanted to see your farm." He removed the knapsack from his shoulders. "And you have to see the cards I got with my birthday money. I have twelve All Stars." He added this last part with reverence.

"No way," said the boy, whom I assumed was Cappy. "I need to see them."

Micah held up his bag. "I have them right here."

While the boys spoke, three of the alpacas walked up to them just on the other side of the fence. I climbed off my red bike and set the kickstand in place. I walked over to the closest alpaca. "You're just like a big goat."

The creature grinned at me.

"I'd stay a few feet back, if I were you. They spit if they get annoyed," Cappy said.

I took a big step back.

"You're still too close," the *Englisch* boy said. "They can really project, if you know what I mean."

I didn't want to find out what he meant, so I took two more steps back.

"Aenti," Micah said. "I'm going to show Cappy my cards."

"All right, but we can't stay too long. We want you to be home in time to meet your mother there after church. No more than twenty minutes."

The two boys turned as if they were going to run off, and I stopped them. "Cappy, is Uriah here?"

The boy brushed his long blond bangs out of his eyes. "I thought he would be at church." Cappy shrugged as if that was no matter. "He might be in his house." He pointed to the small ranch house on the property.

I raised my brow. I'd thought that Uriah was renting a room on the Stoller farm. I didn't know he had an entire house.

The boy ran off to the barn.

"Twenty minutes, Micah!" I called after them.

My great-nephew waved his hand in the air to signal he'd heard me.

The front door of the big house opened, and a large man a few years older than I came out. He was tall and stood straight up, as if he had a board along his back to keep it rigid. He held a newspaper in his hand and removed his reading glasses, then tucked them into the breast pocket of his checked shirt. "Can I help you?"

I smiled. "I am Micah Hochstetler's *aenti*. He and I were out on a bike ride after church, and he wanted to stop by and see his friend Cappy. I hope it's okay if the boys visit for a few moments. It won't be long. We have to leave for home soon."

His face cleared. "Oh, Micah and Cappy are great friends. Yes, it's all right for them to have a little visit. I know they don't get to spend as much time together as they wish. I'm Cappy's grandfather, Max Stoller."

"Millie Fisher," I said with a smile and was relieved that he did not move to shake my hand. He must have known that Amish women generally do not shake hands with men they are not related to.

His brow wrinkled again. "Millie Fisher? Why is that name familiar to me?"

I had my guesses why.

He glanced down at the newspaper in his hand and something seemed to dawn on him. He held up the paper as if it were a baton. "I have read about you in the paper. You're that Amish woman who solves murders."

I felt myself blush. "I have been mentioned in the paper a time or two," I admitted.

He glanced around the farm. "Don't you have an English friend who helps you on your cases?"

Lois would be very happy to know that at least someone in Holmes County knew she was my partner when it came to fighting crime. She would be thrilled when I told her.

"My friend Lois isn't here today. It's just Micah and I on the bike ride."

"Well, I had no idea that it was Micah's aunt who was the Amish crime solver."

I smoothed the side of my skirt with my hand. "I would not call myself a crime solver. The sheriff's deputies do that. But there have been times when I have been able to help the sheriff's department with an investigation."

"I'm sure my wife's cousin hates that you help in any way."

My eyes widened. "Who is your wife's cousin?"

"The sheriff. He's no friend of the Amish, I can tell you that. If he knew that we had an Amish man living on our farm, he would be fit to be tied. Honestly, we don't talk to him much. He's a sour person. Life is too short to be around people like that."

I knew the general consensus in the Amish community was that Sheriff Marshall was unkind, but it was surprising to hear a similar opinion from his own family, and for the family member to be so outspoken about it.

"Uriah Schrock is living here," I said. "He's a member of my district."

Max nodded and didn't seem at all surprised that I knew Uriah was living on the alpaca farm. "He's renting a room in my little ranch house. My son and his family live in the big house, and I live in the ranch. When Uriah approached us asking for a room for rent, I thought it was a great way to supplement my retirement income. It never goes as far as you need it to." He laughed. "I suppose I'm like the Amish in one way, because I'm living in a little *daadihaus* on my son's farm."

"Uriah asked you specifically for a room."

He nodded. "He said that it would be nice to spend some time here at the farm where he grew up."

Suddenly, I knew why I recognized this place. Although the alpacas and the little ranch house were new, this was the farm where Uriah had grown up. I came with my mother when she brought a casserole to the family after Uriah's *grossmaami* died. That was the one and only time I had visited his family's farm. I supposed it was because of my relationship with Kip that I never felt comfortable visiting Uriah at his home.

"Isn't it odd he would want to come and live at the farm his family lost?" I asked.

Max shrugged. "I thought the same thing, to be honest, but Uriah said he had good memories here. He was impressed by how we took care of the land. When I bought the farm, the grounds and soil were in terrible shape, but with a little time and a lot of hard work, I was able to bring it back. We are so close to the ravine and the woods that it's not a great place for crops. The soil has a lot of clay in it, but it's ideal for grazing. I always thought so, and I knew if I ever bought this place, it would be perfect for the alpaca farm I had always dreamed of." He nodded at the alpacas behind the fence. "And that's what we have here today."

I wrinkled my brow. "So you wanted this farm back when Uriah lived here?"

"I always wanted this piece of land. I never thought that we would get it." He shook his head. "I almost bought it many years ago. The Amish family that lived here ran into some financial trouble. It looked like I would be able to buy the farm, but then they found the money they needed to pay their loans and property taxes. I was heartbroken. Then eight or nine years went by, and the Schrocks found themselves back in the same place. I learned that the Schrocks' son-in-law Samuel Zook was paying many of their bills. When he was killed, that money dried up."

"So," I said, waiting to make sure that I understood what he was saying. "When Samuel died and he stopped making payments for the Schrock farm, you were able to buy it."

The large man rocked back on his heels. "Sure did. Got it for a steal." He held up his hand. "Don't get me wrong, I felt terrible over what happened to Samuel, but you can't let another person's misfortune hold you back."

His last statement was most certainly not an Amish proverb.

CHAPTER TWENTY-TWO

"Millie, what are you doing here?"

I turned away from my conversation with Max and saw Uriah Schrock walking across the lawn from the ranch house. His face was drawn and there were dark circles under his eyes that I hadn't noticed before. He normally had perfect posture, but now he was bent slightly at the waist. For the first time since he'd come back to Ohio from Indiana, he looked his age. He was a man beaten down by grief. It was written all over his face.

"Micah wanted to come and see his friend Cappy, so I agreed to go on an afternoon bike ride with him."

Uriah folded his arms. "You're not here because of my sister?"

Max overheard Uriah's comment. "Now, Uriah, we don't know for sure that the bones found at the bottom of the ravine are those of Galilee."

"They are," Uriah said. "Deputy Little told me. It was the answer I expected."

Max shook his head. "That is a terrible shame, a complete and terrible shame. The deputies will do all they can to find out what happened to your sister. Sure, it might be a bit harder now since so much time has gone by, but they are a stellar department despite all of their challenges. And their greatest challenge is the sheriff himself."

Uriah shook his head. "They can't. The sheriff told them to drop the case. He says my sister was responsible for Samuel's death and for her own. He still believes she killed her husband, but now instead of her running away to be *Englisch*, he claims that she accidentally fell to her death as she was fleeing the scene."

Max made a clicking noise and a brown alpaca walked up to the fence and leaned his head over the top rail. The alpaca farmer scratched the animal under the chin. "My wife's cousin is set in his ways. I wish I could say I am surprised by this news, but I'm not. If he had his way, all cases dealing with the Amish would be blamed on the Amish."

"Do you know Sheriff Marshall well?" I asked.

"I suppose as well as I know any of my wife's cousins. We don't spend much time with him, to be frank. He's not that much fun to be around."

"Do you know why he dislikes the Amish so much?" I asked.

Max shook his head. "Maybe they are just an easy group to blame?" He held up his paper. "I had better get back to the important work of educating myself. I always like to know what's in the news. It helped me recognize you, Millie, didn't it? I have a perfect memory. It's something I take pride in."

Before he left, I asked, "Do you remember where you were the night Samuel Zook was killed?"

He dropped the newspaper to his side. "I do. I was at my house in town with my wife and children. I was working for a bank at the time. It's such thankless work. I was not meant to be a paper pusher, I can tell you that. It would have been a school night, so I was likely arguing with my oldest about doing his homework." He chuckled. "Why do you ask?"

I could have said I'd asked because he was a murder suspect. He certainly had a motive since he'd had his eye on the Schrock land for his dream alpaca farm.

I smiled. "You just said you had a great memory, so I wanted to test you. I can't remember what I was doing five minutes ago, let alone forty years."

He tapped the newspaper on the side of his leg. "I get that a lot. People simply can't believe what I can remember. They are always shocked. I wish I could tell you more about what happened that night. I just don't know."

I thanked him, and he walked away. Uriah watched him go before he turned back to me. "Millie, what are you really doing here?"

I frowned. "Deputy Little came to my home this morning before church and told me that the bones were Galilee's. I didn't see you at church this morning and wanted to find out how you were."

His face softened. "You have always been so kind. I knew it was Gali. I told you that before, but even so, hearing the deputy tell me that I was right came as a blow. I just did not feel up to church this morning."

"*Gott* understands."

He tugged on his beard. "I surely hope so. There is so much I need Him to understand."

"Uriah, I have spoken to the young man who found Gali's skull on Friday. They said you were there when it was found. Why? Did you know they were going to discover it?"

He shook his head. "Ever since I came back to Ohio, I went to the ravine every few days. It made me feel close to Gali. It never occurred to me that I was walking so close to her grave. I just happened to be on one of my walks there when the young men made the discovery."

"But weren't you supposed to be at the square for the concert?"

He nodded. "I thought a short walk before I left for the concert would clear my head. I have been so distracted lately. I have been here for over a year and made very little progress in finding my sister."

"It wasn't until after the bones were found that I learned you were even looking for her. Why didn't you tell anyone that was the reason you were here?" I paused. "Why didn't you tell me?"

He wrinkled his brow. "I didn't want to burden anyone, especially not you. I thought it was something I needed to do alone. I realize now that if I had asked for more help, I might have found her much sooner." He paused. "And I know you must be wondering why I would stay at this farm that my family lost."

I had been wondering that.

"I had two reasons, really. First, it was close to the covered bridge. I could go there often and think of Gali. Second, this is the place I grew up. *Ya*, it wasn't my family's any longer, but it was familiar. I thought it was the perfect place to be. I asked if I could rent a room for a few weeks, and Max agreed. Neither of us thought that I would be here so many months later."

"Max has made no secret of the fact that he wanted to buy this farm and was disappointed when Samuel took over paying your family's bills." I glanced around me. There were two alpacas at the fence now. One of them blinked at me, and I noticed how impossibly long his eyelashes were.

"Max is a *gut* man. He would not kill Samuel to get this farm."

"It's a motive," I said.

"It's the wrong one."

I frowned. I didn't know why Uriah was closing himself off to the possibility that Max had been involved in the murder.

Uriah shaded his eyes from the afternoon sun. "The deputy said the case was closed. I don't know what more I can do now. Maybe it's time to go back home to Shipshewana. I have most certainly overstayed my welcome here."

"I can't believe you would give up so easily. You've spent the last year looking for the truth—why stop now when you are so close to getting some real answers?"

He dropped his hand to his side. "I don't know that I am up to it, Millie. I'm tired. My children have written me and want me to come home. I have been away from them and my grandchildren far too long. It's time I concentrated on the living instead of the dead. As an Amish man, I don't believe in ghosts. Even so, I feel like I have been wandering around this county looking for the ghost of my sister for the past year."

I wasn't going to let it go so quickly. Uriah had asked me to find out what had happened to his sister, and I was determined to do that, whether or not it was still something he wanted.

"Deputy Little said there is evidence that she was buried. If that's the case, she must have been murdered," I said.

Uriah nodded. "But if that were true, why murder Samuel and leave him in the buggy and then bury Gali? The killer could have easily left both bodies in the buggy."

"The killer buried Gali to frame her for her husband's murder," I guessed. "She was much smaller than her husband." I winced as a gruesome image struck my mind. "She would be easier to move."

"You've been very kind, Millie," Uriah said, "helping me find out what happened, but I have to tell you, I don't have the heart for this any longer. I will bury my sister properly and then go back to Indiana as soon as I can. It's time to let the dead bury the dead."

I wanted to argue that someone very much alive had buried Gali, and that person should be held responsible. Before I could, Micah ran out of the barn. "*Aenti*, you should see these cards I traded Cappy for. I really made out."

Cappy was a few feet behind him. The arrival of the children set the talk of murder to the side . . . at least for now.

Micah and I left the alpaca farm shortly after that. I had to make sure my great-nephew was home in time to meet his mother. As we rode by the ravine and bridge on the way to the greenhouse, I thought about all I had learned since Friday evening when Gali was found.

The truth was, I was no closer to finding out what had happened to Galilee Zook that cold winter's night forty years ago than I had been on Friday night. Perhaps Deputy Little was right, and we would never know. Should I give up as both the deputy and Uriah had? He had lived in

Ohio for the last year with the hope of finding out the truth about his sister. Now that he was so close to finding the truth, I didn't understand why he was letting it all go.

Deputy Little said the only way to solve the case was with a confession, which meant I had to figure out who had been behind Gali's death and then convince them to confess. That was a tall order. The murderer had remained silent for forty years. What could I possibly do to make him crack now? What could I, an Amish matchmaker, do to make a person confess such a well-kept secret? It seemed to be an impossible task.

I reviewed the suspects in my head. There weren't many. I reminded myself that after so much time, the killer could even be dead himself. The first person on my list was Cyril Zook. As the brother of Samuel and the inheritor of the family-owned buggy shop, he had the very best motive. He was a nice man, but I had learned in my investigations that even nice men could be killers.

Second on the list was Nathaniel Zurich, the current owner of the Amish Corner Bench, who had worked with Gali all those years ago. He seemed to be infatuated with Gali. I remember Gali had been an exceptionally pretty woman, perhaps even the prettiest in the district. Could Nathaniel's boyhood crush have led to murder?

The third on my list was Max Stoller, the alpaca farmer who waited so long to buy the Schrock farm. He certainly had as *gut* a motive as Cyril Zook. In both cases, their careers had benefitted once Samuel was out of the way. Cyril would have known that Samuel was unkind to his wife, so he would have realized she was the perfect person to frame for Samuel's murder. If Max had been following the family closely because he wanted the farm as much as he'd led me to believe, he would have learned about Samuel's treatment of his wife too.

The motive for my last suspect, Bishop Yoder, remained unclear. I wasn't sure whether I would even call him a suspect or just a "person of interest," as Deputy Little would have said. In any case, Bishop Yoder knew something that he wasn't telling me. Was he protecting himself or someone else? Was the person he was protecting his father, the former bishop?

And if the bishop knew something, did that mean Ruth did too?

CHAPTER TWENTY-THREE

The next morning, I rode my bike into the village, eager to tell Lois everything that I had learned on Sunday. I cruised into the main part of the village and around the square. As I let the bike coast around the green, I felt the wind in my hair and the ties from my apron flew behind me while the fabric of my skirt pressed against my legs. For a moment, I was a teenager again, riding into the village on an assignment from my mother for a quart of milk or a dozen eggs for a cake that she planned to bake on a whim. My mother loved baking just as much as I loved quilting. She was always experimenting and creating new cake recipes. My older sister, Harriet, had been her best helper in the kitchen, but I had been the one sent into the village for supplies. It was a task I loved—a moment of quiet and respite from our busy farm. My heart ached for quiet in those days. It wasn't until now, after living with others for most of my life, that I realized I loved solitude as much as I loved times with friends and family.

There was a gas lamppost right in front of the large picture window of the café. I parked my bike beside it. I did not chain my bicycle in place as I might have somewhere else. We were in Harvest and no one would touch the bicycle while I was in the café.

I opened the café door and was surprised to see Uriah Schrock sitting at the counter drinking one of Lois's sugary concoctions from the espresso machine.

"Millie, there you are," Lois cried. "What are you doing riding your bike all the way into the village? That must have been five miles."

"Five and half," I said. "And I'm perfectly capable of doing it. The exercise keeps me young."

"You don't need to be so young that you get hit by a car on the way to prove your point. You cross some busy roads on the way to the village. You need to be careful."

"I promise you I am."

Lois rolled her eyes.

Uriah didn't show any reaction to the banter that was going back and forth between Lois and me. Typically, he would have made some comment about it, saying we fought like sisters or something to that effect. He said nothing and stared down into his half-empty coffee mug. I wondered if he was still reeling the way I was from our conversation the day before. I also realized that with him sitting there, I couldn't rehash the conversation with Lois as I had planned to.

Lois widened her eyes at me and tilted her head to

Uriah. I frowned back and slipped onto a stool two down from Uriah. I spun on my seat so I could face him. "It's *gut* to see you here, Uriah."

He looked at me with bloodshot eyes and a puffy face. My heart sank. Had he been drinking?

When he didn't say anything, I asked, "How's the coffee?"

"It's fine. Lois was kind to make it for me. I'm just waiting to talk to Margot about my plans, so she can begin to look for my replacement."

"Your replacement?" Lois asked as she filled two cups of coffee and then stepped around the counter. She set the mugs on a table for two *Englisch* women. When she returned to the counter, she asked, "What are you talking about?"

Uriah raised his brow. "I'm surprised Millie hasn't told you yet. The bones by the bridge were my sister's. I've done what I came here to do and am going back to Indiana where I belong."

Lois's mouth fell open. "You can't leave. You and Mill—"

"Uriah and I are great friends," I interrupted before she said something that would embarrass both Uriah and me. "But his family is in Indiana." I turned to Uriah. "I do think you should stay and at least try to find Gali's killer."

He shook his head. "I knew those bones were hers. I never had any doubt about it, but the confirmation has hit me harder than I expected it to."

"You are mourning," I said. "Because there was uncertainty for such a long time, you didn't have a chance to mourn before."

"That could be, but my children want me to come home." He folded his hands on his lap. My heart constricted, and I could feel Lois's eyes on me. I didn't look at her. She knew me too well, and I didn't want to give away what I was feeling, the sting of pain in my heart at the idea of Uriah leaving Ohio.

"You want to leave before you know the truth?" Lois asked. "You can't do that. Amish Marple is on the case! Millie will find out what happened."

He looked at me. "I don't want to put you out, Millie, not for my sake. Deputy Little said that the department has closed the case. There isn't much more you can do." He glanced out the window. "Oh, I see Margot stomping around the square." A small smile formed on his mouth. "Even though I plan to quit, I shouldn't keep her waiting. It's never a *gut* idea to keep her or Ruth Yoder waiting."

"Those are the truest words I've ever heard," Lois said.

He stood, thanked Lois for the coffee, and shuffled out the door. I watched him go with a pain in my chest.

Lois went to see to a few tables, and I sat at the counter deep in thought.

When she came back, she asked, "You're not dropping the case, are you?"

"Nee." I hopped off my stool. "I'm not doing this just for Uriah. It's for Gali. She doesn't deserve to be remembered as a killer when she couldn't have done it."

"How do you know that?" she asked.

"She could not have buried herself. Even Deputy Little agrees with that, though he had to give up the case."

She nodded slowly.

"If she didn't bury herself, someone else did. Someone else was there the night Samuel was killed. I intend to find out who that person was."

Lois tucked her serving tray under her left arm. "Uriah is a broken man. How are you going to comfort him?"

"How can I? He wants to leave."

She shifted her weight onto one hip. "Is that because you're not giving him a reason to stay?"

"I pray for him," I said with a wrinkled brow and pretended that I didn't understand the meaning of Lois's comment. Instead, I told her all I'd learned the day before from the bishop and from Max Stoller.

"We have another problem too," I said. "I didn't have a chance to tell you over the phone yesterday because Raellen had to make a call."

"Another problem?" Lois asked. "Isn't murder enough?"

Before I could answer, the problem came through the door. Ruth Yoder stood just inside the café with her hands on her hips, glaring at Lois and me.

"Let me guess," Lois whispered out of the side of her mouth. "She's the problem."

I nodded, but I didn't have a chance to tell her why before Ruth did. "Lois Henry, you have broken my sweet Phoebe's heart. It's not enough that you drag Millie all around the county and corrupt her with your *Englisch* ways, but now you have targeted my granddaughter."

Lois's mouth hung open. "Excuse me? What have I done to Phoebe? I have had one conversation with her in her whole life."

"It's not what you've said to Phoebe; it's what you have said to Lad that has hurt her."

Lois looked to me. "I'm confused."

Ruth waggled her finger at Lois. "I went to the buggy shop this morning to make Lad explain himself after he broke my granddaughter's heart. He owed me an explanation."

I winced as I imagined the scene.

"He claimed that Lois said something to him that got him thinking about his place in the district. He knows he's not worthy of Phoebe—he's not, of course, no one is—but he can't break her heart. I won't allow it, especially after we have gone to all this trouble to plan a wedding."

Lois put her hands on her hips. "I may have teased him about getting married, but I certainly didn't tell him to break it off. I would never do that! It was clear to me that the young man loves your granddaughter very much."

"Lois Henry, you have—"

But Ruth wasn't able to finish her thought because Juliet Brook stepped into the café. The local minister's wife wore a sleeveless blue-and-yellow polka-dotted dress, a blue silk ribbon in her hair, and held a pig under her arm. Jethro, her comfort pig, was dressed up with a bow tie that matched Juliet's dress.

"Good morning, ladies," Juliet trilled with a bright smile. Juliet was always a cheerful soul, but since she'd married Reverend Brook the previous summer, she seemed to be floating on air.

Jethro lifted his snout and inhaled deeply. He was especially fond of Darcy's blueberry pancakes. Not that I could blame him. I loved Darcy's pancakes as well, but nothing beat her blueberry pie.

Juliet pulled up short when she saw our faces. "Did I step into the middle of something?"

"No, of course not, Juliet," Lois said, even though that wasn't exactly the truth. "Are you here to pick up Reverend Brook's lunch?"

Juliet beamed. "I am. He loves Darcy's chicken salad sandwiches and homemade potato chips. I tried to make them myself, but I just can't get the recipe quite right. Darcy is a whiz in the kitchen."

"She is that," Lois agreed. "Let me grab the lunch for you. Darcy has it all packed up."

Juliet thanked Lois, who made a quick exit to the kitchen. I knew that she was thankful for Juliet's arrival. Ruth's lecture would have gone on much longer otherwise.

"I'm sorry to hear the news about Uriah's sister. I saw him on the square with Margot and shared my condolences." Juliet clicked her tongue. "It's so sad. I wasn't too surprised when I heard. Uriah has been looking for her for such a long time. My husband did what he could to help him, but I think we all knew this was how it was going to end. At least now Uriah can bury her and mourn her death properly. Closure is important."

I stared at Juliet. "You knew that Uriah was in Holmes County looking for his sister?"

She adjusted Jethro in her arms. The pig, which was used to being carried all over the place, didn't so much as bat an eye. "Yes, I did. He came to the house several times to ask my husband for guidance."

I felt as if I had been slapped in the face. Uriah went to Reverend Brook about his sister, but never to me? He said I was his friend. He'd made it clear that he wanted to be more than friends. He'd asked me on a buggy ride as if we were two schoolchildren, but he'd never told me why he was here until he couldn't avoid it.

I frowned. "Uriah spoke with Reverend Brook about his sister?"

Juliet nodded, and her forehead creased with worry as if she'd just realized that she'd revealed something she probably should not have.

Ruth folded her arms. "How dare he speak to another minister and not my husband? Bishop Yoder is the leader of the district."

"Uriah is not a member of our district any longer," I said quietly. "His membership changed when he joined the church in Indiana."

Ruth glared at me. "That may be so, but while he's here, he should show some respect to his home district. Speaking to an *Englisch* minister over my husband about a district matter is a slap in the bishop's face."

"Maybe he needed an objective opinion," I suggested.

Ruth glowered at me. "My husband is objective."

I almost said I didn't think that was true and I thought the bishop knew something about what had happened forty years ago, but thankfully, I held my tongue.

"I need to go home and comfort my granddaughter. Good day, ladies," Ruth said and stomped out of the café.

Juliet watched her go and wrinkled her nose. "What is wrong with her granddaughter?"

"Phoebe and Lad are having a little disagreement before the wedding."

"Oh." Juliet nodded. "I can understand that. Weddings are so stressful. I think every bride and groom argue a bit before the first day."

"Did you argue with Reverend Brook?" I asked.

"No, but he said I could have whatever I wanted." She shrugged and gave Jethro a tight hug. The pig snorted.

That sounded about right to me.

Lois reappeared from the kitchen. I guessed that she had been waiting just on the other side of the kitchen door for Ruth to leave. She held up the paper sack lunch.

Juliet took the sack from her hand. "Thank you. This will make my husband very happy. It has been a difficult week at the church with many meetings about fall programming. I've had meetings too and had to take Jethro to every last one." She sighed.

"Doesn't your son's girlfriend, Bailey, usually watch Jethro for you when things are busy at the church?" Lois asked.

"She does, but Bailey is away in New York filming her candy making show for Gourmet Television. Not to mention, my son is still training at the BCI headquarters for his new position in that department. I'm so proud of him for having such an important job, but I hate how far away he is now. I worry that it puts a strain on his relationship with Bailey."

"How can it not?" Lois asked.

I elbowed her in the side.

"Ouch," Lois muttered.

"When both Bailey and Aiden are away, I just don't know what to do with myself. Jethro is equally confused. He loves spending time with Bailey whenever he can. I tried to convince her to take Jethro with her on this filming trip so that he could get more screen time—the more screen time he has, the more likely he will be able to snag a big-budget film contract." She pouted. "But Bailey said that she didn't need him for the episodes they were shooting. Can you imagine? Jethro always makes every episode better. Bailey has even admitted to me that his appearances on the show are the most watched on the series. They should have him on every episode, in that case."

"Maybe if they did," I said, "it wouldn't be a special treat for the audience to see him on the television." I didn't know this for sure since I had never seen one single episode of *Bailey's Amish Sweets*. I thought it was ironic that the candy-making show was about Amish recipes, but Amish people couldn't watch it.

"I have to say that I like the episodes with the pig the most. He's always knocking stuff over. It's grade-A television," Lois said. "I agree he should be on more often."

Juliet beamed. "Thank you, Lois. I need to drop off the reverend's lunch, so I can take Jethro home for his bubble bath. He loves to be squeaky clean."

The image of Jethro in a bath surrounded by bubbles entered my mind, and I had to stifle a chuckle. Lois didn't even try to hold back her laughter and she snorted, sounding a lot like Jethro himself.

Juliet said good-bye and took her pig and her husband's lunch out the door.

Lois shook her head. "That pig really lives high on the hog."

"That he does," I said.

CHAPTER TWENTY-FOUR

"What on earth do we do about Gali Zook now?" Lois asked as she cleared a table two *Englisch* women had just left.

I walked across the room to give her a hand. "Deputy Little said the investigation is all but over, and Uriah is done with it too, but we are going to keep digging."

She eyed me as she piled half-full water glasses and coffee mugs onto her tray. "Never give up, never surrender," Lois said.

"That's definitely not an Amish proverb."

Lois cocked her head. "It's from an old sci-fi movie, so nope, not Amish."

She carried the tray back to the kitchen. I followed her through the swinging door. Darcy was at the island in the middle of the room chopping onions. Tears ran down her face. She smiled at me. "I'm making chili. Spicy chili always tastes good on a hot day, if you ask me. I know there is a way to cut onions so you don't cry, but I have never been able to master it." She picked up her cutting board and put the onions in a large pot with cooking oil, and then she grabbed another onion from the market basket in the middle of the island and began to peel it.

I frowned. I wasn't sure it was the onions. Before I could ask her what was really the matter, Lois said, "Millie and I are going out. We have to find a killer. And this is going to be a tough one to pin down since the murder happened decades ago."

"Grandma, I don't know if I want you to chase after killers all the time. You could get hurt."

"Bah, it keeps us young. Would you rather I sit in the corner of the café sipping tea and knitting a sweater for your cat?"

"I would," Darcy said and another onion tear slipped down her face.

Lois shook her head and her large plastic earrings bounced off her cheeks. "Not going to happen. You don't have the conventional grandmother."

"You don't have to remind me of that," Darcy said.

"That's good to know," Lois said. "Bryan is out front if you need help in the café."

"It should be slow. We won't have much of a lunch crowd until eleven thirty, and by then I will have everything well in hand," Darcy said. "The two of you be careful when you're out there, chasing down killers."

"We always are," Lois said. "We will take my car, Millie."

"What about my bicycle?" I asked.

Darcy wiped her hands on the dish towel hanging from her apron. "You can leave your bike here and come back for it later. I'll ask Bryan to roll it to the back of the café just so it's out of the way."

As Lois and I left the café, I saw Bryan Shell get up from his seat and knock on the kitchen door. As of yet, she had not shown more than a passing interest in him. It was for the best, in my opinion. I didn't believe they were a *gut* match. However, I would not tell Darcy that unless she asked me directly. I had learned that people rarely wanted unsolicited romantic advice. In truth, they rarely wanted solicited romantic advice if the advice did not support what they wanted to hear.

When we were on the sidewalk, Lois said, "I think we should go to the buggy shop first. I need to clear things up with Lad about Phoebe even though I'm not responsible for what he did, and we can check on your buggy again."

"I'm going there so often, the Zooks are going to begin to think I don't trust them to fix the buggy," I muttered.

On a Monday morning, the buggy shop was much busier than it had been on Saturday evening. There were several Amish men working outside the shop. I guessed that they were taking advantage of the sunshine and the lovely summer day. I could not blame them.

Lois parked her car near the building, and we both got out.

"There's Lad." I pointed at a group of young men standing under a large shade tree. The young men laughed with one another and were clearly on a work break.

Of the jovial group, Lad stood out with his hands in his pockets and his head hung low. He kicked at the ground with the toe of his work boot.

Lois shook her head. "He looks like he was the last boy picked for dodgeball. This is just not right. Anyone can see that he's upset, and I bet you all the contents of my purse it's because he realized breaking up with Phoebe was a massive mistake."

"I think you're right, and I don't want the contents of your purse. I have no idea what is in there."

Lois hiked the giant bag onto her shoulder. "I don't know either."

I didn't find that comforting. I followed Lois over to the tree.

Lad said something to his friend we couldn't hear, and the other young men put their heads down and walking back to the buggy shop. Apparently, break time was over.

Lois watched them go. "We didn't mean to scare your friends away."

Lad removed his black felt hat and ran a hand through his hair before putting the hat back in place on the top of his head. "Millie, your buggy's not done yet. It should be ready this afternoon. We will certainly let you know when it's finished."

"That's *gut*," I said. "Could the buggy be dropped off at my house? I have no way to drive my horse, Bessie, here to get it home. I'm happy to pay whatever fee the shop might charge."

"We can do that, and there's no fee. We have had the buggy for so long. We wouldn't charge you anything extra at this point. I could drop it off on my way home tonight." He paused. "You won't ever have to come back here again after that." He sounded eager for Lois and me to stop visiting the buggy shop. Was that because of his relationship with Phoebe, or because his father might be a killer?

I wrinkled my brow. "That is very kind of you. I really appreciate your doing that."

He nodded and started to walk in the direction the other men had gone.

I cleared my throat. "We heard about you and Phoebe."

My words hung in the air, and Lad froze in place. "Phoebe."

"That you're not getting married."

He turned around. "The bishop's wife told you?"

I nodded.

He bit his lower lip. "I knew she would be upset, but it can't be helped. I had to do what was right."

"Why's that?" I asked. "What makes it right? I thought you and Phoebe were a perfect match."

"We are not," he said firmly. "We're a terrible match. She's the bishop's granddaughter, and what am I? I'm a buggy builder."

"Building buggies is a very important job in the Amish community," Lois said, and then she looked at me as if to see if she was right.

"A very important job," I agreed. "And you are the first and only son in your family. This will all be yours some-day. What makes you think you are not the right person for Phoebe?"

He stared at me. "She needs a man who is stronger in his faith. Someone who can carry on the legacy of her family in the district and be a church elder, maybe even the bishop, someday. I don't want that. I just want to make buggies and have a family. I want a simple life."

"How do you know her family wants you to be in church leadership?" I asked.

"Her grandmother told me all this, and when you were here on Saturday, it just reminded me of that conversation and how the Yoder family would be watching me for the rest of my life to see if I can measure up to them. I don't want that."

"No one wants to be under a microscope like that," Lois said. "And I was only teasing you on Saturday."

"All teasing has a little bit of truth in it," Lad said. "Or it would not be humorous."

Lois couldn't argue with that.

"Lad," I said, "that may be how Ruth feels about you and Phoebe, but have you asked Phoebe?"

He wrinkled his brow. "She's a young woman. How can she know what is right for her life? She has to depend on her family to guide her."

Lois put her hands on her hips. "Now, listen here just a minute. Women have every right to guide their own lives. I don't care if they are Amish or Martian."

"Lois," I said, interrupting my friend even though I tended to agree with her.

"Millie, you can't believe that—"

"I don't." I turned to Lad. "What I was going to say to you, Lad, is Phoebe deserves to have a chance to tell you what she wants. I know she loves you, and I believe you will learn from her that she doesn't care if you don't want to be a leader in the church. In fact, it might make her love you all the more."

He stared at me. "You think so?"

"I know so."

"That doesn't change the fact that my father wants us to postpone the wedding until I take more responsibility in the buggy shop. He thinks being married will distract me."

I nodded. "It's possible that it will, but that doesn't mean you won't be able to be a *gut* husband and a *gut* worker. I think you should speak to your *daed* and tell him how you can be both."

"I was so rash." He kicked a tuft of grass at his feet. "I have been such a fool and have embarrassed myself and Phoebe in front of the entire church. Her family will be even more leery of our marrying after what I have done."

"That might very well be true. As the saying goes, 'Swallowing words before you say them is so much better than having to eat them afterward.'"

He kicked at another tuft of grass. "I've learned that. Now, I have to eat my words."

"In love and marriage, you will make many mistakes. It's *gut* to learn now how to ask for forgiveness and correct the hurts quickly. It will be practice for the future."

He nodded and then winced. "Was Ruth Yoder very mad over the breakup?"

Lois cocked her head. "Let's just say, you're not her favorite person right now."

"I never was."

"Is your father here?" I asked.

"My *daed* didn't come to work today."

"He didn't? Is he unwell?"

Lad shrugged. "I think he was. At least that was what my *maam* told me when I left for the shop this morning. She said that I had to open the shop on my own." He removed his hat and held it in his hand. "To be honest, I was surprised. I think this is the first day of work that he's ever missed in his life. I don't think he's going to be feeling much better anytime soon."

"Why's that?" I asked.

"A deputy was here a little while ago and said he wanted to talk to *Daed* about his brother, Samuel. I told him *Daed* was home sick. I think the deputy was headed that way. *Daed* does not like to talk about Samuel. There was bad blood between them."

"Bad blood?" Lois asked in the most casual tone she could muster, which for a person other than Lois was not casual at all. She sounded like she was dying to know.

"*Daed* didn't like how Samuel did things. He said he was unkind to customers and talked them into extra work they didn't need to have done on their buggies. It took my father many years to change the reputation of Zooks' Amish Buggies to what it is today. Now, we are trusted by the Amish across several districts, and we have more work than we know what to do with." He put his hat back on his head. "I suppose that's why he's so concerned about me knowing the business. He worries about the reputation of the shop. He doesn't want it to be tarnished like it was by my uncle."

"Was it Deputy Little who was asking after your father?" I asked.

"*Ya*, it seems that Deputy Little is dealing with all the Amish cases now that Aiden Brody has moved away."

What was Deputy Little still doing on the case? He said the sheriff had ordered him to drop it. If he was speaking to Cyril about his brother, he was not following that order.

"I have to get back to work. *Danki* for stopping by. I realize now that I let my fear get between Phoebe and me. I pray she'll take me back."

"She'll take you back," I said.

"But it wouldn't hurt to beg a little and take flowers and candy with you," Lois advised. "Sometimes groveling is the best thing to do when it comes to a woman's heart."

"Lois," I said with a sigh.

She held up her hands as if in surrender. "Okay, okay, I'm not giving any more relationship advice. That got me into hot water before."

That was good news for everyone. Lad said good-bye and walked back to the buggy workshop.

After he was gone, Lois said, "I don't believe for a second that Cyril is sick. His own son said that he never gets sick."

"Then why isn't he here today?" I asked.

"Isn't it obvious?" She paused. "Guilt."

CHAPTER TWENTY-FIVE

"Do you want to track down Cyril Zook?" Lois asked when we were back in her car.

I shook my head. "Not yet. Deputy Little might still be there. I do want to talk to the deputy to see why he is continuing the investigation, but if he's able to get some information from Cyril, we don't want to interrupt that."

"Let's just hope he shares that information with us," Lois muttered.

"I think he will. He can't share it with the department if he's working the case on his own time."

Lois seemed to consider this. "Then where to?"

"Back to the Amish Corner Bench. It was the last place Samuel and Gali were seen alive."

"But the only people there who were working at the time they died were Nathaniel Zurich, the owner, and Alice Springer, the cook."

"Then, those are the people we need to talk to. Nathaniel is definitely a suspect."

"I agree. He seemed a bit starry-eyed when he spoke about Gali. Mark my words, he had a thing for her." She rubbed her hands together. "And I'm always up for more of the fried chicken, so I'm game."

We arrived at the restaurant just as the early lunch crowd—which included several senior citizen tour buses—descended on the Amish Corner Bench.

"Looks like this is another bad time," Lois said.

It looked like it was a terrible time. I should have thought about lunch and dinner crowds when trying to question people at the restaurant. "Maybe we can come back later," I said.

Lois slid the sedan into a parking place. "I came all this way; I'm getting some fried chicken even if it's just carryout." She got out of the car.

I sighed. There was no point in arguing with Lois when she had her teeth set for fried chicken.

The line to get into the restaurant ran the entire length of the wraparound front porch.

And just then two more buses pulled into the parking lot. The guide stepped out of the first bus holding a red umbrella in the air to guide the group to the front door.

"Oh, no!" Lois cried. "We'll be here for hours just trying to reach the front door."

"There is another entrance," I said. "Well, technically an exit, but it's a door, so it must open both ways . . ."

She snapped her fingers. "Perfect! And if the door is locked, I always have my lock picks in my purse. I'm tired of carrying them around for no good reason."

"I wasn't suggesting that you use them," I called after

her, but it was too late—she was already around the side of the building.

I hurried after her. It was a large, single-floor building, so it took me some time to catch up with Lois. She had fried chicken on her mind, and there was no slowing her down. I was happy to see the door that I'd come out the first time I met Alice.

"I'll never get to use those lock picks," Lois lamented. "My third husband, who was a swindler by trade, taught me how to use them. I don't want to lose the skill. You never know when it will come in handy."

You never do, I thought.

"You'll have to find another door to practice on because this one is open." I grabbed her arm as she stepped toward the door. "But I don't think they would like us to go in that way."

"Probably not," she agreed. "But I'm not standing in that line for takeout. We will just weave our way through the back of the restaurant into the dining room as if we came in the normal way. I'll put in an order at the counter for fried chicken to go and you can snoop while I wait for it."

This would go horribly. I could feel it in my bones, just as my bones told me when a change in the weather was coming.

Lois went through the back door without so much as a backward glance. I had no choice but to follow her.

When we were inside, I pushed my way in front of her. "I've been here before, so at least let me show you the way to the dining room."

She held out her hand in a grand gesture. "Lead on, Amish Marple, lead on."

I sighed and wove through the shelves of dishes and

to-go containers I'd passed on Saturday. At the end of the corridor, I spotted the door Phoebe had led me through two days before. "This way."

She paused. "That's a lot of takeout boxes. They must have gotten a steal to buy that many at once. It's like Costco back here."

I didn't have a chance to reply because the door we were walking toward opened, and Nathaniel came through. He didn't see me because he was looking back at something on the other side of the door. I swallowed a yelp. He would not want to find us back here. There was a door to my right. I grabbed Lois by the arm and pulled her into the utility closet where I had hidden the last time I was in this hallway.

Lois shook me off as soon as we were inside the closet. "Yeesh, Millie, you are going to wrinkle my blouse, and I don't iron. Ever."

I turned on the light. The closet was washed with a yellow light from a single bulb hanging overhead from a chain.

"Shh," I whispered and edged to the door, pressing my ear up against it.

"Why are we hiding?" she asked. "Do you really think he will kick us out of the restaurant if he sees us?"

"I do. Shhh. And listen."

Lois pressed her ear against the door too.

"The sheriff promised me the case was closed," Nathaniel said just on the other side of the door. Hearing his voice through the door, I realized that he was the one who had been speaking the last time I hid in a closet at the restaurant. This was becoming a very odd pattern, indeed.

"He might have promised you that, but there is nothing stopping Millie Fisher and her friend from asking questions. They are troublemakers through and through," a man's voice said.

Lois bristled. "I'm more than just a friend. I'm your loyal sidekick. Every great detective needs one. Look at Holmes and Watson! And who is he calling a troublemaker?" she wanted to know.

I clapped a hand over her mouth. "Shhh!"

"Did you hear something?" Nathaniel asked.

Lois's eyes were the size of dinner plates above the hand I held over her mouth. I lowered my hand and gave her a look that clearly said *Be quiet.*

"I didn't hear a thing. It could be all the kitchen noises. I have to get going. I just came by to tell you this isn't over yet. I thought you'd want to know that."

"It is not welcome news, but I do want to know. I wish those bones had never been found. The past is in the past. Let the dead bury the dead, and let the living be."

"It's not that easy," the mystery man said.

Their voices trailed off as they moved away.

"Wow, looks to me like we have the killer in our sights." Lois batted a string hanging from the lightbulb in the ceiling out of her face. "It has to be Nathaniel. I can't say I'm surprised. I always thought there was something shady about him. Plus he definitely had a thing for Gali. I could see that from a mile away. Workplace romances always go awry . . ."

I took in the utility tub, brooms, mops, and buckets around us. "There could be many reasons why he wants the investigation to stop." I held up a hand to block the overhead light from my eyes. I wouldn't touch Lois's comment about workplace relationships. I did not think for a moment that Gali had indulged in one, especially with a teenaged boy. Adultery was not the Amish way.

"Like what?" Lois wanted to know.

"It could be hurting his business. I don't think any business owner would want the police coming around asking questions in front of customers."

"Did you see the lines when we pulled in?" Lois shook her head and adjusted the strap of her large purse on her shoulder. "The business is doing just fine. It's something more than that."

Maybe she was right. I opened the closet door and peered both ways down the corridor. I didn't see anything but shelves and supplies. "It's clear," I said, stepping out of the closet.

Lois squeezed herself and her purse out the door. "I feel like we might be real spies now. This feels like James Bond stuff."

"Lois, I really don't know what you are talking about half the time."

"It's for the best. Is that the way out?" She pointed at the door I had been trying to reach before Nathaniel had appeared.

"It is," I said.

"Then, let's go." She marched toward the door and walked into the dining room with her head held high as if she had every reason in the world to be coming through that door. I followed her through the dining room and to the counter where she could order her chicken to go. I didn't know where she planned to take the chicken. Was she going to eat it right away? It was summer, after all, and the chicken would not keep well in a hot car.

Lois asked the Amish woman at the counter, "Can I order fried chicken to go?"

The girl at the register nodded.

While she placed her order, I spotted Phoebe across the dining room. She was waiting on an elderly *Englisch* couple. She nodded at what they had said, made a note on her notepad, and gathered up their menus. She was polite but the light that Lois and I had seen in her on Saturday had been snuffed out. My heart ached for her. I prayed that Lad would be true to his word and make things right with Phoebe because the girl was clearly devastated. It was written all over her face.

As she walked back to the buffet tables, she spotted me and turned pale. She hurried toward the closest exit from the restaurant. It was as if the order she had just taken had completely left her mind.

Lois remained at the counter as she decided which sides she wanted with her chicken. She was so engrossed in her order, I knew it would take far too long to get her attention and keep up with Phoebe.

I hurried across the dining room and went out the same door Phoebe had used. I found myself on a quiet back porch of the restaurant. There was a picnic table and several outdoor wooden rockers placed around the porch. Phoebe sat at the picnic table. She had her head hidden on the tabletop in her folded arms and her body shook with sobs. She was the only person there.

"Phoebe?" I asked.

There was no answer.

I stepped close to her and touched her shoulder. "Phoebe?"

She jerked away from me. "Go away. I don't want to talk to you."

I moved to the other side of the picnic table and sat. Phoebe cried, and I waited. My mother had told me once the greatest virtue of a mother is patience. It wasn't an Amish proverb, but it should have been. I wasn't a mother, but I'd half raised Edith and her twin brother, which taught me much patience.

Within a few minutes, Phoebe's sobs became less ragged, and she lifted her head just enough to peek at me with one bloodshot eye. "What are you still doing here?"

"Waiting to speak to you," I said.

She sat up. Her nose was red and her eyes were puffy. "I need to go back to work. I haven't put my last order in. That table will be angry with me if they have to wait too long. The people who arrive here on buses have very little patience."

"This is true, but before you go, I just want to tell you how sorry I am. I know you are hurting."

"Because of you," she snapped. "It never would have entered Lad's head to break up with me if you had not spoken to him."

I wasn't so sure about that. Lois's offhand comment had only ignited fears that Lad already had about joining the Yoder family. And then there was the pressure from his father that he had to deal with. But I didn't say any of that. Those were things that he needed to tell her, not I. "I am sorry, but I know Lad cares for you. He will come around."

"Don't say that," she snapped. "I don't want to get my hopes up."

I nodded in understanding. Lad had told Lois and me he planned to make things right with Phoebe, but until he actually did, that meant little.

"I just wanted to say I'm so very sorry."

She stared at me and her shoulders sagged. "I accept your apology. I know it's part of your job as a matchmaker to challenge couples to see if they are really meant to be together. You did that for Lad and me, and we failed. It is no one's fault but our own."

I hadn't been the one to challenge their relationship. It was Lois, but Lois was my friend, and in this case I was responsible for her, so I accepted the blame.

Phoebe hung her head. "I'll never love anyone like I love Lad."

"I'm not giving up on the two of you, nor do I believe this is the end of your story, but you're right. You cannot love any two people the same way." As I said this, I thought of Kip and Uriah.

"I need to get back to work." She smoothed a stray hair that had come loose from her bun and patted the top of her prayer cap as if to make sure it was still in place. "This is the break area. No one is here right now because it's lunchtime. No one in the restaurant is allowed to take their lunch during the usual lunchtime. It is our busiest time of the day. Not many bus tours come to Amish Country in the evening." She stood up.

I stood too. "Phoebe, don't give up on Lad."

She held my gaze for a long moment. "I'll try not to." And then she disappeared through the door.

CHAPTER TWENTY-SIX

I found Lois at the front door of the restaurant holding a takeout box that smelled like fried chicken. "I see this stop was a success for you," I said.

She bent over the white box and inhaled deeply. "It was. How about you? Did you get any more snooping done? You sort of vanished on me in there."

I was about to answer her question when someone behind me cleared his throat. I turned to find Nathaniel Zurich glaring at us. "I would like to know the answer to that question as well."

"About the chicken?" Lois asked.

He scowled at her. "No, about the snooping. What are you doing, coming into my place of business and upsetting my employees? I just saw Phoebe Yoder, and the poor girl was in tears, thanks to you. What did you say that upset her so much? I hope it wasn't this nonsense about Gali Zook. Phoebe wasn't even alive when Gali disappeared."

"I didn't mean to upset Phoebe," I said. "And my conversation with her had nothing to do with Gali."

"Well, whether you meant to or not, you have, and I want you off my property."

Lois glared at him. "I have half a mind not to eat this chicken, you're being so rude to my friend, but I paid for it, so I will eat it to spite you."

I took a step toward Nathaniel. "Why are you so eager for us to stop asking questions about Gali? Is there something you know and are not sharing about her disappearance?"

He jerked back. "I don't know anything, but I do know that you are disrupting my business. We can't be associated with this murder again. It was hard enough the first time, and that was before twenty-four-hour news and social media."

"Who were you speaking to in the kitchen hallway about the murder just now?"

Nathaniel turned pale. "I—I don't know what you're talking about."

Lois stepped forward and stood shoulder to shoulder with me. "Yes, you do. You were talking about Millie and the murder investigation. And I, for one, do not appreciate being referred to as just 'her friend.' I have a way bigger role in the crime solving than that."

"Were you here the night Gali went missing?" I asked.

"No, I'm sure I wasn't. I would have had no reason to be. I was a busboy at the time and the restaurant closed early because of bad weather."

"When was the last time you saw her?" Lois asked.

"I—I don't know. Probably that day. Why does it matter?"

"Because she died that night," I said.

Nathaniel looked as if he might be ill.

"She died that night," Lois repeated. "And it sounded to us like you were planning a cover-up with another man just a few minutes ago."

He glared at Lois. "If you must know, I was speaking to my attorney. I wanted his advice on how to keep the restaurant's association with the Zooks out of the press. I don't like what you are implying. I won't stand for it." Nathaniel glared at both of us. "I have heard enough. I want you off my property right now, or I will call the sheriff and have you forcibly removed."

Lois put her hands on her hips. "Oh, yeah? I would like to see you try."

I touched Lois's arm. "Let's go."

She frowned at my hand.

"Please," I said.

"Fine." She scowled at Nathaniel. "I'm still going to eat the chicken I just bought. There's no point in having it go to waste."

We walked through the line of people waiting to get inside the restaurant and ran all the way back to the parking lot. I could feel them watching us with every step we took. We came around the back of the building where Lois had parked her car and found Alice standing outside at the kitchen door. She had a plain white mug in her hand and was gazing into the distance.

She must have heard us coming because she turned. She raised her eyebrows. "You're back again so soon?" Alice looked out over the rolling hills behind the restaurant. Sheep and cows dotted the hills, and an Amish farmer walked behind an ox and a plow in a field.

"We're here for the chicken," Lois said, holding up her prized white box. "Although Nathaniel almost made me lose my appetite for it."

Alice arched her brow. "That's my recipe. Nathaniel has no part in it, so please don't let anything he did keep you from eating it. I have been making the chicken here for near fifty years. I'm right proud of it too." She glanced at me. "I know that's not a very Amish thing to say."

"Your secret is safe with me," I said.

"You're the cook?" Lois asked. "I love your food."

"Lois, this is Alice Springer, the cook Phoebe introduced me to on Saturday."

Alice shook her head. "That poor Phoebe. She's heartsick over her lost love and has it bad. I told her to take the rest of the day off and go home to deal with it. She won't go. She says it's worse at home because her family asks her so many questions about what happened."

I winced and guessed that Ruth, Phoebe's *grossmaami*, was the main person asking all those questions.

"I told her if she can't go home, then find a place to be. She's no help to me here when she's in tears. *Englisch* customers can sense weakness, and they'll treat her poorly if she's not able to hold her chin up. I know that it will all be set to rights. Lad adores her. He'll come around. She doesn't know how rare that kind of love is," she said. "I do hope you enjoy your meal." She glanced behind her at the open door. "I should be getting back. I just needed a breath of fresh air, but if I am gone long when we are busy, the servers and kitchen staff tend to panic."

"I'm glad I got your chicken when I did," Lois said. "I don't think we will be able to come again for a while. The owner kicked us out."

"Don't worry about him," Alice said as she sipped her coffee. "Nathaniel is a bunch of hot air. He's been on pins and needles since he took this place over when his father died. He feels a lot of responsibility to keep the restaurant as successful as it has always been. I try to remind him that its success was based on my chicken recipe. Not anything his father or grandfather did."

"Did his father die recently?" I asked.

"*Nee.* It was five years ago. The man is wound tight. I think having Uriah, the deputy, and now you two here asking uncomfortable questions has him worried about what the bus tours will think if the restaurant is tangled up in this business. I told him he doesn't know *Englischers* very well, even if he's an *Englischer* himself. A little scandal and intrigue will make them want to come to the Amish Corner Bench even more."

"She's right about that," Lois said. "Maybe you all can do a murder mystery theater or an escape room. There are places in Cleveland that have done very well with that sort of thing."

"It's an idea," Alice mused.

"Neither of those ideas is very Amish," I said.

Alice glanced at me. "But Nathaniel is not Amish. He never has been. Maybe way back, five generations ago with a name like Zurich, there was some Amish or Mennonite relative, but the connection is all but gone now. His only tie to the Amish is the fact he lives in this county and owns this place." She gestured to the building behind her.

"I'm sorry to say Millie is probably right about the escape room not being the best idea, but as long as you keep making the fried chicken, the tour buses will come." Lois held up her box as if it were proof. "I wouldn't give up on the mystery theater, though."

Alice nodded as if taking the suggestion to heart. I needed to get this conversation back to the murder. "Alice, the night that Gali disappeared, what time did she leave the Amish Corner Bench?"

"It must have been after eight. We closed early that night—at seven—because of the bad weather, but Gali volunteered to stay behind with me and clean the kitchen for the next day. Everyone else went home. I saw her get into her husband's buggy, and off they went. No one could have known what was about to happen. No one could have even known she would go home by buggy that night. She usually rode her bicycle home, but as I told you, there was a bad snowstorm that night and Samuel picked her up. I could count on one hand how many times he did that in all the years that she worked here."

"Everyone went home but the two of you?" Lois asked.

Alice thought about this for a moment. "I suppose not everyone. Nathaniel, who was fifteen or sixteen at the time, was still here. His father asked him to stay the night at the restaurant to keep watch. It had been such a cold winter—the coldest I could ever remember before or since—and the pipes had frozen in the ladies' restroom the week before. Made a terrible mess. Nathaniel's father wanted him to stay at the restaurant through the cold night to keep watch."

"So Nathaniel was here at the Amish Corner Bench when Gali left with her husband that night?" I asked because I had to be sure.

Lois and I shared a look.

If that was true, why had Nathaniel said he wasn't there that night? Why had he lied?

CHAPTER TWENTY-SEVEN

After we left the Amish Corner Bench, Lois got a text message on her phone from Darcy that she was needed at the café. I asked her to drop me at my little farm. I had a lot to think about. Thankfully, I had a quilt to work on, so my hands could be busy while my mind wandered.

"What about your bicycle?" Lois asked as she turned into my driveway. The goats and Peaches ran at us full tilt. You would have thought I had been gone for a month, not just a few hours.

"I'll pick it up in the morning," I said as the car came to a stop. "I should have my buggy back by then. It's a tight squeeze, but it can fit in the backseat."

Phillip hopped outside Lois's car window. "Calm down, you crazy goat. I'm not getting out of the car."

I opened my car door and Phillip and Peter ran around

the side. They shoved their heads past me, pressing me up against the seat.

"Oh, you two knuckleheads," Lois complained and scratched them both between the ears. "Now, get out of my car. If I find goat slobber on the upholstery, I'm going to be really mad."

The goats leaped back.

Lois brushed goat hair off her hands. "How is it possible that they can be so ornery and cute all at the same time?"

"I ask myself that every day," I said as I got out of the car, shooing the goats away. "*Danki* for driving me around on this wild-goose chase again, Lois. You're a *gut* friend."

"I don't mind at all. I love a wild-goose chase. Let's just find one where I can use my lock picks, okay?"

I stood in the driveway and waved as she drove away.

With Peaches curled up at my feet, I worked on the quilt for the rest of the day and well into the evening. Only when the light was too dim for me to thread my needle did I realize how long I had been working.

I stood up and stretched, feeling a dull ache in my back. It certainly was time to stop for the day if I wanted to be able to stand up straight in the morning. I looked down at the quilt on the quilt frame. I was pleased with the work, and I hoped that the *Englisch* buyer would be too. Everyone in Double Stitch wanted to do top-quality work so the *Englischers* would continue to buy our hand-made quilts. There are many high-quality machine-made quilts and blankets that can be bought, but I knew shoppers came to us for something made with care and heart.

Peaches meowed at my feet.

"Did I forget to feed you?" I asked. "I'm sure your brother goats are outside pacing circles around the house, wanting their dinner too. If I did not have the three of you to tell me it was time to eat, I would completely lose track of time."

Peaches meowed again.

"You're persistent. Something tells me you learned that from the goats."

He pranced into the kitchen and stood by his dish.

After I fed Peaches, I went outside to feed the goats. As I expected, Phillip and Peter were circling the house impatiently as they waited for their dinner.

I went into the barn, filled their trough with their favorite feed, and threw in some carrots and lettuce as an extra treat. They buried their faces in their food as if it was going to be their very last meal.

I also fed Bessie, who was by far the most patient of my animals. When the goats weren't looking, she got two extra carrots for her good behavior.

I chuckled as I left the barn and the sun dipped behind the tree line to the west. Shadows gathered across the farm. Before I saw it, I heard the telltale clip-clop and rattle of a horse and buggy coming down the road. A large black horse pulled a wagon onto my land. My buggy was being towed by the wagon. Lad Zook sat on the wagon's bench and expertly guided the horse down my driveway.

The wagon rolled to a stop just a few yards from the barn, and Lad jumped from the seat.

I put my hands on my hips. "My, it looks brand-new! It's shining."

Lad beamed. "I threw in a fresh paint job, no charge. We had the buggy for so long at our shop that you deserved a bonus. I'm sorry about the delay with the work. Who knew it would be so hard to find the old parts that we needed?"

"I do appreciate it. It will save me the trouble. My husband, Kip, said that any *gut* Amish person puts a fresh coat of paint on his buggy every summer."

Lad nodded. "I wish more people would abide by that rule. We have had some very unkempt buggies come through our shop. With a little paint and care, they'd be as *gut* as new."

He detached my buggy from the wagon, jumped back into the driver's seat, and guided his horse and wagon away from the buggy. When they were clear, he jumped off the wagon again. "Do you want me to put the buggy in the barn?"

"*Nee.* It's not supposed to rain tonight. If you leave it out here, it will save me the trouble of pulling it out in the morning. *Danki* for delivering it."

"It's the least that I could do."

He removed his hat and held it in his large hands.

"Have you spoken to Phoebe yet?" I asked. "I saw her today, and she was still very upset."

His shoulders sagged. "*Nee*, I went to the restaurant when I had a break at the buggy shop, but the cook told me that she had sent her home. Then, she chased me out of the kitchen with her wooden spoon. Alice was angry with me for hurting Phoebe. She said if I didn't make it right, I would have to deal with her and her spoon. Phoebe has said in the past that Alice is very protective of all the people who work for her. At times, she even stood up to Nathaniel Zurich if she thought a member of her staff was being mistreated. The owner just has to take it because Alice is the only one who knows the recipe for her famous fried chicken, and that's why everyone goes to the Amish Corner Bench."

"I know my friend Lois is a big fan."

He gave me a sad smile. "I want to speak to Phoebe and ask her forgiveness, but not in front of her entire family. It's something she and I should work out. They don't need to be involved." He shook his head. I wasn't sure Ruth Yoder would agree with that.

"If you can't speak to her at work or at home, when will you?"

"I hope to do it tonight. The young people in the district are having a bonfire at the volleyball courts. Phoebe loves bonfires, and I know her friends will convince her to go. I'm not usually one for socials. There's so much to do at the buggy shop that there just doesn't seem to be the time for such things, but I'm going tonight to talk to Phoebe. She won't expect me to be there. It will be easier to speak to her there than it would be at her home with the bishop's wife nearby or at her workplace with Alice and her spoon ready to smack me."

"I pray that it goes well. It may take some time. Not all hurts heal at the same rate, even if we wish they would. If she needs time to think, you owe her that."

"That is *gut* advice, Millie. I'm going to tell her I was scared and stupid. Plain and simple. It wasn't your or Lois's fault what a mess I made of everything. It's just . . ." He swallowed hard. "Can I tell you something? Will you promise not to tell another soul or laugh?"

"Will someone be hurt if I keep this information to myself?" I peered at him over my glasses.

He shook his head. "The only thing that would be hurt is my pride. The truth is I'm fine with the bishop. He's a *gut* and fair man, but Ruth Yoder scares me half to death. She has a way of looking at you that makes you think she can see right through you to your very soul. I wasn't sure I could deal with that kind of scrutiny the rest of my life."

He took a breath. "But what I have come to realize is that the alternative, a life without Phoebe in it, is so much worse. I can put up with the bishop's wife judging me if Phoebe is at my side."

I smiled. "I'll tell you a little secret too. You're not the first person to tell me you're afraid of Ruth. I doubt you will be the last." I began to walk with him back to his wagon. "The thing is, Ruth means well. Under all those rules and that gruff exterior, she really does care about the people in our district. She's tough because she believes—however misguidedly—that that's the best way to protect them from the outside world and from themselves. You won't always agree with what she says. She and I have certainly gotten into a heated discussion a time or two, but we've always remained friends because I know that her heart is in the right place."

"I'll try to remember that," he said. "It's getting late, and I have a bonfire I need to get to. Take the buggy for a drive tomorrow. It should be *gut* to go. I drove it up and down the road in front of the buggy shop several times today to make sure everything ran smoothly. But if anything about it feels strange, bring it back in. I'll take a look at it right away."

"I will, but I don't anticipate having to do that. The only thing strange about it is it's so clean and shiny. I hate to get a single speck of dirt on it."

He chuckled and climbed back into the wagon. As he drove away, the goats, who finally reappeared after devouring their dinner in the barn, looked on with me. I prayed that he would find the right words to say to Phoebe. The honest ones were always the right ones, even if at times they were the most painful.

CHAPTER TWENTY-EIGHT

The next morning, I woke to the sound of hooves against my bedroom window. I wished I could say that this was uncommon, but anytime I left the barn door open at night so the goats could come and go, they appeared at my window at first light in search of breakfast.

The long white braid that I'd twisted my hair into the night before fell onto my shoulder as I peered out the window. The only time my hair was not pinned into a bun was at night when I slept. I remembered how Kip used to enjoy braiding it at night. He always loved my hair. He called it my crown jewel, which only he was able to see.

The goats were seeing me this morning in my braid. I threw up the blind and opened the window. Phillip and Peter danced just below the windowsill. The sun was peeking over the trees. It was almost six in the morning.

Typically, I was up at five with the goats before the sun rose. However, last night I had stayed up working on the quilt. I had gotten another burst of energy after Lad left, so I thought I should make the most of it. I felt those long hours of work in my back this morning. The ladies of Double Stitch would be coming again this week to help me, and I wanted to prove that I'd been busy. I'd accomplished so much that not even Ruth could criticize my work ethic on this project.

I shook my finger at the goats. "You two had better knock it off, or you aren't getting any breakfast. I did not sleep well last night." I pressed a fist into my lower back.

They ducked their heads, and I sighed. I couldn't stay mad at them for long, and it wasn't the goats' fault I lacked sleep. It was the quilt and my aching back. However, the quilt would soon be done, and then I could return to my normal routine.

I stopped myself. Could I return to a normal routine with Samuel's and Gali's killer still out there? I supposed most people in the community already had. The crime had been all but forgotten for the last forty years. If Uriah had not come back to Ohio, the murders would still be ignored by the members of the community. They would be ignored by *me*. I couldn't let that happen. It might take time, but I needed to know what had happened to Gali. She deserved the truth, and if Deputy Little was still looking into the case even after the sheriff had told him to stop, he thought the same. I would have to track down the deputy today. If we combined what we knew, we might come up with an answer.

"Let me dress, and I will be out," I told the goats.

They bounced away from the window and chased each other across the yard. Peaches, who was sleeping at the end of my bed, yawned and rolled over. Clearly, the cat was unimpressed by his hooved brothers' antics.

I went into the barn and fed the goats and Bessie the horse again. After she was done eating, I let Bessie out into the small pasture beside the barn, so she could enjoy the cool morning before we made our trek into the village for the day.

I watered my flower and vegetable gardens while the goats danced and bounced on their hooves. They ran at each other and butted heads. I laughed. I was worried about Uriah and the murder investigation, but Phillip and Peter's antics always raised my spirits.

The Sunbeam Café opened at six a.m. each morning; as Bessie and I left my farm a little before seven, I calculated I would arrive at the café right in the middle of the breakfast rush.

The buggy's ride was the smoothest it had been since I'd bought it. Bessie seemed to notice too. She looked back at me and gave me a horsey smile. The repair of the buggy was expensive, and I would have to sell a few more quilts to cover the cost, but it had been worth it.

Bessie seemed to agree as she lifted her legs a little bit higher and pranced down the road.

There was a straight, flat piece of road in front of us before we began to approach the hustle and bustle of the main part of the village. "Bessie, do you want to see what this buggy can do?"

Her ears flicked back and forth, and I took that as a yes.

"Let's do it!" I flicked the reins once, and Bessie took off, racing down the road at top speed. The buggy held up and the wheels spun as fast as they could. I found myself laughing in excitement just as I had as a young girl.

But then, the buggy started to veer to the right. I pulled on the reins to slow Bessie down. Her stride became erratic, and the buggy gave a mighty jerk. I pulled the reins hard to the right toward the grass along the side of the road just in time to see in the side mirror that the right side wheel had popped off the buggy and was bouncing down the road.

After that, everything occurred so quickly that it was difficult to know what was happening. As the buggy tipped, I slid across the wooden bench seat and tumbled out onto the ground. Even while I was falling, all my thoughts were on Bessie and if she was okay.

I don't know how long I lay on the side of the road. It could have been seconds or hours. I moved my hands and feet. Everything seemed to be in working order. I struggled to my knees and then onto my feet. My skirt was torn and my palm had a small cut on it, but other than that I was fine.

When I stood up, there was a sharp pain in my back that kept me bent at the waist. Fear shot through me that I might have hurt my back, but I told myself that I wouldn't have been able to stand if I was seriously injured. I prayed that was true.

Bessie was my main concern.

The back wheel of the buggy was missing. I supposed it was in the tall grass somewhere along the side of the road. The buggy was half upright, half on its side. Bessie lay in the grass at the front of it.

I struggled over to her. Thankfully, I could reach the clasps on the harness and was able to free her from the buggy. Her eyes rolled in her head. I brushed her cheek. "Bessie, you have to get up."

I knew if the horse could stand, she would probably be all right.

I rubbed her forehead and her eyes rolled back into place. She looked at me.

"Get up, old girl" I told her in Pennsylvania Dutch.

Slowly, she struggled to her feet. Her knees wobbled but held. I stood too and grabbed her bridle. I led her away from the buggy. Wrapping my arms around her neck, I hugged her tight. "I'm so sorry. This is all my fault. I shouldn't have told you to run like that." I stepped back and ran my hands over her flanks and her knees and legs. She didn't seem to be hurt, but I promised myself that I would have her checked by the equine vet as soon as I could.

Bessie nuzzled my arm.

"Now, what are we going to do?" I looked up and down the county road. If Lois had been with me, she could have called for help on the little phone she carried in her giant purse. If one of my nephews had been with me, I could have sent him to the next farm for help. I had neither of those options.

I was five miles from my farm and maybe another three from town. I had no choice but to start walking. With the pain in my back and now a growing ache in my knees, it would be a grueling trip. I couldn't leave Bessie. "Are you up for a walk, girl?"

She shook her head. I was trying to decide if that was a *yes* or a *no* when an SUV came down the road. It slowed, and I held tightly to Bessie's bridle. I didn't know if this new arrival was friend or foe.

The SUV slowed, then pulled to a stop at the side of the road. A tall man with dark blond hair stepped out of the car. Even without the sheriff's department uniform that he had worn every day until the last few months, I recognized him. My shoulders sagged with relief. "Aiden Brody, I'm glad to see you."

"Millie Fisher, are you all right?" Aiden looked from the buggy to me and Bessie and back again. "What happened? You could have been killed!" His chocolate-colored eyes were concerned.

"I'm so glad you happened by! This is all my fault. I pushed Bessie too hard and the back wheel popped clear off the buggy. Bessie could have been killed."

"Millie, *you* could have been killed," Aiden said and pointed at the cut on my hand. "You're not standing straight either. We have to get you to the hospital."

I peered at the scrape, which had not hurt until he reminded me that it was there. "It's fine. I was just so worried about Bessie. I checked her over, but I will be contacting the vet as soon as I can."

"And you need to go to the clinic yourself. That cut looks deep to me. It could get infected. The doctor will need to check whether anything else might be wrong. People have been killed from falling out of buggies before. You're very lucky."

I knew he was right. "What are you doing here? I thought you were training for the state."

"I'm home for a couple of days. We had a break in BCI training, and I thought I would come home and surprise Bailey."

"She will be so glad to see you. She does miss you very much."

"Did she tell you that?"

"She didn't have to."

He frowned as if that wasn't the answer he'd hoped to hear.

"But I thought she was in New York. That's what her mother said, at least."

"She's supposed to get home tonight." Aiden walked to the back of the buggy and squatted next to the place where the rear wheel had been. "Millie, this accident wasn't your fault." Aiden stood up and his face was gray.

I patted Bessie's cheek one more time. "What do you mean?"

"Someone cut through the axle." He knelt again, and I knelt down beside him. My back screamed as I moved, but I wanted to see what he was looking at. "You can see clearly here. It was cut halfway through. It was cut so it would break mid-ride." He looked at me. "Millie, someone tried to kill you."

"Are you sure?" I whispered.

"Absolutely sure." He stood up and removed his cell phone from the pocket in his jeans. "I have to call this in."

I stared at the saw marks that were clearly visible. They ran halfway through the axle where it had snapped. Aiden was right. This had been done on purpose. A chill ran down my back as I thought about what could have happened. What if Micah or another of Edith's children had been with me?

Behind me, I heard Aiden say, "Little, you have a case. You had better get out here. Someone tried to kill Millie Fisher."

The words hung in the air. *Someone tried to kill Millie Fisher.* Someone tried to kill *me*. Why would anyone try to kill me? I was a quiet, quilting matchmaker. I didn't mean any harm to anyone. I swallowed hard—except for the person who'd killed Samuel and Gali Zook.

Aiden ended the call. "The cavalry is on the way. I asked for an ambulance too because I very well know that you won't heed my advice and go to the clinic. You need medical attention, and I wouldn't be surprised if they told you to lie low for a few days." He gave me a stern look. "I hope you will follow the doctor's orders."

Aiden offered me his hand and helped me to my feet. Normally, I would have insisted I could stand without assistance. No one wanted to be seen as a doddering old woman, but I was too shaken by what I had seen. I ached from head to foot. "*Danki*, young man," I said and dropped his hand. "I don't know how this could have happened. I just took the buggy into the shop. It got a complete overhaul. It was all fixed. The axle is brand-new."

"Someone tampered with it." Aiden studied me. "Millie, is there any reason someone would want to harm you?"

I could think of two reasons: Samuel and Gali Zook.

CHAPTER TWENTY-NINE

"Millie!" Lois cried as she jumped out of Deputy Little's police car. "Millie!"

I stepped out from behind Bessie, who thankfully didn't seem to be hurt at all. I kept checking to be sure. I had a feeling if I touched her leg one more time, she might kick me in the shins.

Deputy Little climbed out of his cruiser at a much slower rate. He and Aiden shook hands.

"Lois," I said.

She wrapped her arms around me and gave me a huge hug.

"Oh!" I cried.

She jumped back. "You're hurt."

"A little banged up, but not too bad."

"You fell out of a buggy. You could have been killed!"

"What are you doing with the deputy?" I asked.

"Deputy Little was at the café when Aiden called him. He was there waiting for you, Millie. I told him that you would be there soon since I knew you'd be coming in on your buggy, and then he got the call. When I heard about the accident, I thought you were dead. I swear that's what I thought." Tears sprang to her eyes. "I was so afraid."

I held her hand. "I'm all right," I said in a low voice as the gravity of the accident finally sank in. Aiden and Lois were right; I could have been killed.

I patted her shoulder. "Deputy Little let you come with him to the scene?" I asked.

"Do you really think I gave him the choice to say no?"

I didn't.

Lois stared at my hand. "What happened to your hand?"

I put my hand behind me. "Oh, this? It's just a little scrape. The *gut* news is Bessie is fine."

She grabbed my wrist. "That's more than a scrape. You need a tetanus shot and maybe stitches."

I grimaced. I hated needles, which was ironic since I was a quilter.

As if on cue, an ambulance pulled up behind Deputy Little's sheriff's department cruiser.

"Good," Lois said. "They can check you out."

"I'm fine," I insisted.

"Millie, you're not fine. I overheard the conversation between Deputy Little and Aiden. Someone tried to kill you. And you and I know it's because we are too close to the Zooks' killer. The culprit is getting nervous; we have them right where we want them. It's encouraging." She paused. "Not that we want your life to be in danger, but it is always good to know you're on the right track."

"Since no one was seriously hurt in the accident, I will agree," I said.

Lois let go of my wrist and tapped her temple with her index finger. "And we know who is behind all of this, don't we?"

"We do?" I asked even though I already knew what she was going to say.

"It has to be Zooks' Amish Buggies. They are the ones who worked on the buggy. They would know how to sabotage it. Also, Cyril Zook has the strongest motive for the double murder. The buggy shop that was his brother's is now his, free and clear. It all fits together. Did you tell Aiden all this?"

"I haven't yet," I said. "And I know what you are saying makes perfect sense, but isn't it a little too obvious? Why would Cyril Zook try to kill me?"

"Maybe he wasn't trying to kill you. Maybe he was just trying to scare you, so you would back off. He doesn't know us, or you for that matter, very well if he thought that. No, this accident only reinforces our determination to bring the scoundrel to justice."

Aiden walked over to us. "Millie, the EMTs are ready to see you."

Both he and Lois glared at me pointedly. It looked as if I didn't have any choice. I would just have to grin and bear getting poked with a needle.

While the EMT looked me over and worked on my hand, I told Deputy Little and Aiden what I remembered about the accident, including as much detail as I could. I blushed when I told them how I'd pushed Bessie to run, so that I could check out what my newly refurbished buggy could do. "I was foolish," I said. "I shouldn't have done that. It was childish."

Aiden shook his head. "It might have caused the axle to break sooner rather than later, but it was going to break eventually. It was cut almost clean through. At least you were on a flat road. Had you been going down a hill, it could have been much worse." He peered at me. "Now, tell me why someone was trying to kill you."

I glanced at Deputy Little, and he sighed.

Aiden glanced at the deputy. "Little?"

"We have another murder investigation," Deputy Little said.

"A murder!" Aiden cried. "Bailey didn't tell me anything about this."

Deputy Little shook his head. "It's a cold case. The Zook case."

Understanding crossed Aiden's face. "I looked at that case from time to time when I was in the department. There was never any new information, and there were always more pressing cases that needed my attention."

Deputy Little quickly told Aiden about the young filmmakers who'd found Gali's bones. "The sheriff believes it is an open-and-shut case. He asked me to stay away from it."

"But you don't believe that," Aiden said.

Deputy Little's jaw twitched. "I'm not sure that it matters what I think. I have to follow orders."

A strange look crossed Aiden's face. I wondered if he was thinking of the time when he'd had to follow the sheriff's orders, even if he didn't agree with them.

"Lois said that you came to the Sunbeam Café to tell me something this morning," I said to Deputy Little.

He glanced at Aiden. "I took one more look at the police report from the time of the murder. There was a problem with the sheriff's theory that Galilee killed her husband."

"Because someone buried her in the ravine?" Lois asked. "A person can't bury herself."

The EMT pressed on my back and I winced.

"Does that hurt?" she asked.

"Yes, but not too much." The last place I wanted to go was the hospital. I spent so much time in the hospital both when Kip was dying and then again with my older sister, Harriet. I'd do just about anything to avoid it.

She frowned and made a note on her chart.

"That is problematic," Deputy Little said. "Yes, but in the actual autopsy report, the coroner noted that Samuel was stabbed in the neck from behind."

"From behind?" I asked and wrinkled my brow.

"Please hold still," the EMT said as she pressed on my sides.

"I suppose Gali could have been in the backseat of the buggy. That would be unusual, though," I said. "Typically, a husband and wife would sit together in the front, but I don't think Samuel and Gali were a typical Amish couple."

"Certainly not," Lois said.

"What did Sheriff Marshall say?" Aiden asked.

"I brought it to the attention of the sheriff, but he says it's not conclusive enough to reopen the case. Too much time has passed. The case is too cold." Deputy Little's shoulders drooped.

"How can the case be cold if someone is trying to kill Millie because of it?" Lois asked.

I nodded. "I don't know of anyone else who would want to kill me."

"Right now," Lois added.

I shot her a look.

Lois held her hands aloft. "We have made our enemies as a team, Amish Marple."

I sighed.

"That's why I wanted to speak to you, Millie. Maybe through the Amish grapevine you can find someone who might know who else could have been in the buggy with the Zooks that night."

"What about the coroner? Can you speak to him about his report? Is he still alive?" I asked.

Deputy Little nodded. "He is. His name is Joe Buckholzer. He lives in a senior living community outside of Millersburg."

"Joe Buckholzer!" Lois cried.

We all stared at her.

"He and I are old friends. We even dated while I was between husbands. It didn't go anywhere because I couldn't stand the way he hit his fork on his front teeth every time he ate. I just couldn't live with someone under those conditions."

"Sorry to interrupt, but we need to get back to the station," an EMT said. "And Millie needs to go to the clinic for X-rays."

"X-rays?" I asked.

"You may not feel it now, but you got pretty banged up when you fell from the buggy. Although you are miraculously okay, I would feel a lot better if we took a closer look to be sure."

I started to open my mouth, but Lois was faster. "She'll do it, and I will nurse her back to health. Don't you worry about that."

Aiden folded his arms over his chest. "That sounds like a good plan to me."

Deputy Little matched his stance. "Me too."

"It seems I'm outnumbered," I grumbled.

"Does anyone else need checking out?" the EMT asked.

I looked at my bandaged hand. "Can you look at my horse?" I asked.

She raised her brow. "I'm not a vet, but I can check her over for any obvious injuries."

"*Danki.* I plan to contact the vet, but it would be nice to be reassured that she is all right."

Aiden pulled Deputy Little to the side while the EMT examined Bessie.

"I'm glad that Bessie will be checked out," I said.

"I'll call the vet now and then get you over to the clinic," Lois said. "We will take care of those things first."

"First?" I asked. "What will be second?"

She grinned. "Paying a visit to my old friend Joe Buckholzer, of course."

CHAPTER THIRTY

The vet was kind enough to send a horse trailer to pick up Bessie, and Deputy Little had a flatbed truck haul my buggy away to the sheriff's department to be examined further. Deputy Little volunteered to stay with Bessie until the vet came for her, so that Lois could take me to the clinic. At least no one insisted that I ride in the ambulance.

At the clinic, the doctor looked at his computer. "I don't see any broken bones, but you have some deep bruising. That is why I am recommending the rest."

"For how long?" I asked.

"At least two days." He gave Lois a stern look. "Make sure that she does it. I don't want to see either of you back here for a long time."

Outside the clinic, Lois helped me into her car. I

winced as she held on to my arm. She froze. "Did I hurt you?"

"*Nee*, I'll be all right." Slowly, I swung my legs into the car.

Lois shut the door and hurried around to her side. As she clicked in her seat belt she said, "I'm taking you straight home."

"What about Joe Buckholzer?" I asked.

"Joe can wait a couple of days, and the more I think of it, the more I believe we can trick the killer into a false sense of security if we lie low."

"But—"

"No buts, and there is no way you can get to Joe's without me. Your buggy is broken, your bike is at the café, and you can't drive."

I leaned back into my seat because she was right, and I hated it.

"Oh, I texted Darcy and told her what is going on and that I would need a few days off to keep an eye on you. She's calling in the part-time waitress, and I guess there is always Bryan." She rolled her eyes.

"Lois, you don't have to put your life on hold for me."

She glanced at me and then turned back to the road. "You would for me."

I sighed. She was right again.

When we got back to the farm, Lois tucked me into bed, and to be honest, even though it was still the middle of the day, I didn't argue with her. The aches and pains were getting worse. I accepted one of the pills the doctor had sent home with us and fell into a deep sleep.

When I woke up again, I was disoriented. Light poured in through my window. I looked at the clock on my nightstand. It read a little after seven. Seven in the evening? I wondered. Peaches lay curled up at the foot of my bed. When he heard me stir, he jumped off the bed and slid through the crack in the doorway. A moment later Peaches and Lois came into the room.

"Oh, thank heavens, you're awake. You slept so hard, I was wondering if I would have to call for help."

"Is it seven at night?"

She shook her head. "It's seven in the morning on Wednesday. You slept a solid sixteen hours. I came in every hour or so to make sure that you were breathing."

I looked down at my right arm and saw a purple bruise there from my fall out of the buggy.

"It's like I lost a whole day."

"You needed the rest," Lois said. She sat on the edge of my bed and studied me. "And your coloring is much better. Whatever was in that pill the doctor gave you did you good."

"I'm hungry," I admitted.

"Well, you're in luck. I have a large pizza in the fridge. You know I don't cook."

"How did we get pizza delivered all the way out here?" My brow wrinkled.

"Darcy delivered it. She also brought some other groceries and some clothes for me."

I smiled. "Thank her for me."

"Don't you worry about that; I already have. And if you don't want pizza, I have four fresh pies—two are blueberry—and five casseroles. All the ladies from the Double Stitch have come and gone, bringing covered dishes. Ladd Zook stopped by with a cake his mother made. He was very apologetic about what happened to the buggy."

My heart swelled. "That was so kind of them."

"Your niece Edith was here too. She wanted to spend the night and keep watch over you, but I told her you'd much rather she stay with her children."

I nodded. "You are right, but it does warm my heart that so many people thought of me."

"Millie, you are well loved in this county."

I bit down on the inside of my lip to keep myself from tearing up.

She cocked her head. "Do you need help getting dressed or do you want to stay in your PJs all day? We aren't going anywhere until tomorrow. The doctor said forty-eight hours of rest."

I sat up on my pillows. "You are taking this nurse thing very seriously."

Peaches jumped onto the bed, and Lois pulled the cat into her lap. "You scared me, Millie. You are my best friend in the world. You're my family. I can't lose you."

I held out my hand to her. "I can't lose you either."

Tears came to her eyes, and then she blinked. "I can't cry. I just finished my makeup."

I cocked my head. "You didn't have to put on makeup if it's just going to be you and me hanging around my farm today."

She frowned at me. "I *always* wear makeup."

After I got dressed, which admittedly took a bit longer than usual, Lois and I had pizza for breakfast, and I have to say, it was one of the best breakfasts I'd ever had. I felt well enough to spend a little bit of time working on the quilt, and I was just rethreading my needle when there was a knock on the screen door.

"Maybe that's Darcy with more pizza," Lois said as she hurried to the door.

I leaned back into the pillow that Lois had insisted I

put behind me while I worked. I had agreed because I knew if I spent another whole day accomplishing nothing, I might just go crazy.

I turned to see Lois open the door wide. "We didn't expect to see you here."

A second later Uriah stepped through the doorway, holding his hat. He stood up straight and his white beard was neatly combed. It was the best he'd looked since before Gali's bones were discovered.

"I hope it's all right that I stopped by," Uriah said. "Everyone in the village is talking about your tumble from the buggy. I had to see for myself that you were not badly hurt."

I smiled at him. "I'm fine, but it's very kind of you to check on me. Lois has been taking excellent care of me."

Lois looked from Uriah to me and back again. "I think I'll go check on Bessie and the goats. Bessie wasn't hurt in the accident, thank goodness," she said for Uriah's benefit. "The vet brought her back to us this morning, but she could use some extra carrots after her ordeal. I'm sure Phillip and Peter would also like some since they haven't seen Millie all day except through the window." With that, she went out the door.

I leaned back in my quilting chair and pointed to the rocking chair by the cold wood-burning stove. "Please sit."

He perched on the edge of the rocker. "You've been quilting. I take that as a *gut* sign that you are feeling better."

I picked up my needle and thread again. "I am. I slept a very long time. The painkillers the clinic prescribed made me very tired. I have a few bruises and a cut on my hand." I showed him the hand. "I'm very lucky. It could have been so much worse."

He winced when he saw the scrape.

I lowered my hand onto the quilt. "It is all right. I didn't need stitches, and as you can see, I have no trouble quilting."

Uriah braced his hands on his knees. "Millie, I am so very sorry that this happened to you. It's my fault. I never should have gotten you involved in all this. This is the exact reason I never told you that I was in Holmes County to look for my sister. I knew you would jump in and want to help. I knew you would put yourself in harm's way."

I set my needle and thread down on the quilt topper. "We have to find out what happened, not just for your sake, but for Gali's."

He pressed his lips together. "I was afraid you'd say that. Please don't ask any more questions about what happened. Let the truth be buried with Gali."

I didn't say anything because I couldn't promise him I would do that.

He sighed because he knew that he couldn't talk me out of looking for answers. "Millie, I—I have always cared for you . . ."

"You have been a *gut* friend to me," I said, suddenly feeling nervous.

"You know that I wanted to be more than your friend, Millie. I loved my late wife very much, but when I saw you again, all the old feelings came rushing back. That's why I don't want you to search for Gali's killer. If something happened to you because of me, I could never forgive myself."

"Nothing will happen to me."

"Someone already tried to kill you once."

"I think they were only trying to scare me."

"And that's better? Because it certainly scared me."

I placed my hands on the quilt frame as if I needed it to steady myself. "I will be all right. Lois won't let me out of her sight from now on."

He rose from the rocker. "I am going to be leaving Ohio soon. I spoke to Margot." He walked to the door.

I felt a pain in my chest that had nothing to do with my fall. "*Ya*, you told me that you would be doing that."

He swallowed. "I don't have a reason to stay anymore."

The words hung in the air. I knew that he wanted me to say something, anything, to give him hope or a reason to remain in Ohio, but I couldn't. Kip's face came into my mind. "I'm so grateful that you stopped by. You are a *gut* man, Uriah. A very *gut* man."

He hung his head. "*Danki*, Millie." Before he went out of the door, he added, "Please be careful . . . for me."

"I will," I whispered, but by the time I spoke, he was gone.

CHAPTER THIRTY-ONE

By mid-morning on Thursday, Lois finally thought I looked well enough to resume sleuthing.

After spending time soothing the goats and reassuring Bessie that I was okay, I carefully climbed into Lois's car.

She buckled her seat belt. "It will be interesting to see how my old flame Joe Buckholzer is doing. I wondered if he aged well. Shockingly, not many of my exes do."

I leaned back on the pillow that Lois had insisted I bring with me for the ride. "Are you sure we should speak to Joe next? I'm surprised that you're not dying to get over to the buggy shop and quiz Cyril and Lad about the condition of the buggy."

"Oh, I want to, but you know as well as I do that Cyril is not going to say anything with the police there. However, I think Joe might just have the information that we've been looking for."

Ten minutes later, Lois and I were driving to Millersburg.

"Is Darcy okay with having you away from the café so much?" I asked. "I know it's one of the busiest times."

Lois glanced at me. "She will be fine. A new part-timer has really been working out."

"Not much help from Bryan?" I asked.

"Oh, no!" She shook her head. "As much as he wants to impress Darcy with his skills, he's fallen short. Iris from your quilting circle came in looking for work, and Darcy gave her the job on the spot."

"I didn't know Iris was looking for work."

Lois shrugged. "We're happy to have her on board. It means more time I can sleuth with you." She took her right hand off the steering wheel. "There's Joe's neighborhood."

The cluster of small condos seemed to pop up out of nowhere. It was as if the real estate developer had bought the land and plopped the buildings on it, expecting that they would sell quickly. Judging by the number of cars I saw in the driveways and people walking dogs outside, he had been right.

"These über-planned neighborhoods make me nervous," Lois said as she drove her car by the guardhouse. She tapped the brakes while a couple in matching shorts and polo shirts passed by. "These people look like they were cut right out of *AARP* magazine." Lois shook her head.

This was another time I wasn't quite sure what she was saying. "All the houses look the same. How do you know which one is Joe's?"

She pointed at her phone, which sat between us. "I

looked him up. His address was listed as plain as day on the Internet."

"Is there anything you can't find on that little device?"

Lois considered this. "Most things Amish." She turned at the corner. "There's his house."

I didn't know which house she meant. They were all beige-colored ranch homes with brown shutters on the windows. She turned into a driveway where the garage door was open. A classic car sat inside the garage. I didn't know much about cars, but I knew it was classic because it had one of those historical license plates. A white-haired, tanned man in jeans shorts and a white polo shirt walked out of the garage, wiping his hands on a white rag. "Lois! I never thought I would see you again. Last time you saw me you said you were never coming back, and here you are!" His voice was deep and booming. I wouldn't be the least bit surprised if they could hear it echo all the way to the county courthouse in Millersburg.

Lois touched my arm before we got out of the car. "Let me handle this."

I wrinkled my brow. "If you say so."

Lois climbed out of the car. "Joe, you look good. The seventies is your decade."

He guffawed. "You're as full of salt and vinegar as you ever were."

"I take that as a compliment."

He nodded at me. "Who is your friend?"

"This is Millie Fisher. She's my very best friend, so be nice to her."

Joe held out his hand to me. When I didn't take it, he dropped it at his side. "Sorry about that, Millie. I forgot that most Amish women don't shake hands with strange men they don't know. Force of habit."

"And you are as strange as they come," Lois said with sparkling eyes.

I cocked my head. I could be wrong, but I thought that Lois just might have a little bit of a crush on Joe Buckholzer, despite his eating habits. Joe smiled at Lois, and I thought the feeling was mutual.

He chuckled. "Well, what brings you and your friend here, Lois? I haven't seen you in a decade or more."

"We wanted to talk to you about a case you worked on as coroner."

His brow went way up. "Of all the things you could have said, that was the last I would have expected. What case is that?"

"The Zook murder about forty years ago."

He stared at Lois. "You mean the one where the killer got away."

"The killer got away? What do you mean by that?" I asked even though Lois had told me that she wanted to take the lead. I couldn't stand there like I had no idea what was happening.

Joe looked at me, and I was startled by how clear and blue his eyes were. He was a very handsome man. I could understand why Lois preened like a schoolgirl beside me.

"The sheriff's department's theory was that Galilee Zook stabbed her husband and then ran away to be English. That was never proven, of course. I've heard they found her body recently in the ravine."

"That's right. She was buried," Lois said and then gave him a detailed account of how the documentary film team had found the bones.

Joe nodded. "Then I'm not that surprised to see the two of you involved. I have read in the local paper that you have been caught up in some murder investigations of late. Both of you have."

Lois's eyes went wide. "You have? I think Millie and I were only mentioned in one article about the flea market fire last year, and that was in the very fine print."

He smiled. "That you were. I saved the article."

Lois's face turned bright red. I no longer wondered if she had a crush on Joe; I knew she did.

"In your report, you said that Samuel was stabbed in the neck from behind."

He tossed the cloth in his hand onto the back of his car. "That's right. It was the angle of the injury. Based on how he fell and the wound, it was the only explanation. Furthermore, there was a knitting basket in the backseat of the buggy. The matching knitting needle to the one that killed him was still in the basket. It was my hypothesis that someone sitting in the backseat of the buggy killed Samuel."

"But the sheriff's department ignored your theory?" Lois asked.

He nodded. "My thought was that it was unlikely Gali was the killer since the death strike came from the back of the buggy. Have you ever seen an Amish wife ride in the backseat of a buggy when she was alone with her husband?"

I shook my head.

"Neither had I. My theory was there was someone in the backseat who picked up the needle from the basket and stabbed Samuel, which scared Gali into running." He paused. "Now, at the time, I thought maybe the deputies were right and she did run away to become English. I was sorry to hear this week that she didn't make it any farther than the ravine. It was a miserable night when they died. Six inches of snow mixed with freezing rain and howling wind. I can easily see Gali taking a misstep and falling to her death."

"The sheriff still thinks Gali did it," Lois said.

"Sheriff Marshall, who was the deputy on the case back then, is a windbag through and through. He will do anything to put the Amish in a bad light. I have always thought so."

"That's been my experience," I said.

Joe shook his head. "I'm sorry to hear that. I had hoped he would have changed."

The front door of the small house opened and a woman stepped out. She was at least a decade younger than Lois and I, so I guessed fifteen or so years younger than Joe. "Honey, Pixie and I were wondering who you are talking to out here," she said.

She was a tall, thin woman wearing a summer sun-dress and carrying a small wirehaired dog in her arms. The dog's fur poked out in all directions and his eyes bugged out of his head. One eye was blue. The other was brown. His tongue stuck out of the side of his mouth.

Beside me, I saw Lois deflate just a little. I wanted to reach out and squeeze her hand, but at the same time, I didn't want to bring attention to her reaction.

"Corrine, an old flame of mine stopped by. We were just having a nice chat," Joe said with a big smile on his face.

Corrine narrowed her eyes and Pixie followed suit. It seemed when Corrine was irritated so was Pixie. Corrine came to stand next to Joe. "What are you ladies talking about with my fiancé?"

"Oh," I said as Lois's shoulders drooped an inch more.

"You're getting married? Congratulations!" I hoped that I actually sounded happy about it. "We were just talking to Joe about an old case from when he was coroner. It's a business call."

"I see." Corrine's face cleared, and Pixie's snarl trailed off. "Joe has a wonderful memory. I'm sure he can tell you every last detail."

"They were asking me about the Zook case," Joe said. "I told you about that one."

A vague expression crossed Corrine's face. "I'm sure you have, but I can't possibly remember all the old case stories you tell me. They all run together. Is that the one with Galilee Zook and her husband?"

Joe nodded.

Lois stood up a bit straighter.

"Well, if you're done talking with your friends, I was wondering if you could keep Pixie with you so that I can take a little catnap." She held the dog out to him. "Pixie here didn't get much sleep last night either. A squirrel has built a nest in the tree outside of the bedroom window. It has been endless entertainment for him, as you can imagine, and sleepless nights for me."

Joe took the dog in his arms, and the small animal immediately began to growl. The sound came from deep in his throat, and Joe held Pixie away from his chest as if he didn't know what to do with the little dog.

Corrine turned back to us. "I hope you had a nice visit. As you can see, Joe is busy now."

Lois bristled. "He's busy holding your dog?"

"Pixie is *our* dog." She looked at Joe. "Isn't he, honey?"

"Umm, yes," Joe said, looking exceedingly uncomfortable, as if he were afraid the dog was going to bite him.

"I always felt bad for Galilee Zook," Corrine said.

I froze. "Did you know Galilee?"

She shook her head. "But I feel bad for anyone who has to work for Alice Springer."

"You've worked for Alice, but you're not Amish?" Lois asked.

"It might be hard for you to believe, but I used to be, and I worked at the Amish Corner Bench for five or six years before I left the faith. Leaving was the best decision I have ever made." She smiled at Joe. "If I had not left, Joe and I could never be together, and we wouldn't have this beautiful home with our sweet Pixie."

Sweet Pixie growled again.

"I started working for Alice maybe four years after Galilee went missing, but most of the workers there still remembered her. Alice hated when anyone talked about Galilee. She also hated the English. She had no respect for them. I told her once that it was hypocritical of her to dislike the English so much when they kept the restaurant in business. She didn't like that much. She didn't like anyone in her kitchen talking back to her. When I told her I was leaving the Amish faith, she fired me."

I blinked. "But the owners of the restaurant are *Englisch*. Couldn't they stop her from doing that?"

"They could, but it might cost them her famous fried chicken. That was a risk they were not willing to take. Why do you think she's been there so many years?"

I glanced at Lois. This was new information about Alice, and I didn't know how it all fit in with the murders or if it had anything to do with them. So Alice didn't care for *Englischers*. She would not be the first Amish person to feel that way about the *Englisch* nor the last.

"I'm going to lie down now," Corrine said. She looked pointedly at us.

"I guess that's our cue to leave," Lois joked. "Joe, it was so nice to see you again."

"You too, Lois. You haven't aged a day."

Corrine glared at her fiancé.

When we were in the car, Lois whispered, "That's the ugliest dog I've ever seen."

I would not have said it aloud myself, but she was right. Pixie was not what Lois would call a "looker." He was so ugly that he was cute.

Lois backed up the car. "I hate it when the good ones get away. Remember that, Millie, when you think of Uriah. That door might close soon and never reopen."

I looked at Joe standing in the middle of his driveway, holding Pixie at arm's length. "I'm not sure that's a bad thing."

CHAPTER THIRTY-TWO

"Why don't you take me back to the café, and I can ride my bicycle home?" I suggested. "The ladies of Double Stitch are having a meeting at my house this afternoon. We have to finish that quilt I have been working on. Many hands make light work."

Lois frowned at me. "Millie, you're not going to ride your bike five miles after being laid up. We can stop at the café, but then I will take you home."

I sighed. "Lois, you're taking the doctor's orders for rest a little too seriously."

"You bet I am," she said.

I thought that she might say something more, but the phone rang inside her giant purse.

"Oh, that might be important," Lois said and reached her hand deep into the bag. Despite everything that must have been in there, she came up with the phone. It was almost like an *Englisch* magic trick.

She handed me the phone. "Hello?" I said into it.

"Lois?" Deputy Little asked.

"*Nee*, this is Millie. Lois is driving so she handed me the phone."

"Oh, very well. I just wanted to let you know that it's likely I will be able to reopen the Zook case based on your accident. You are all right?"

"I'm fine." I paused. "Lois and I are off on a—" I paused again. "An errand."

"I'm going to assume *errand* means meddling in police business. Please be careful. If the case reopens, there may be even more danger for you because the killer will be angry that the sheriff's department is involved again."

I shivered. "I will." I glanced at Lois. "We both will."

Lois took me back to the café. Iris was floating around the dining room, filling coffee mugs and taking orders. A bright smile was plastered across her face. I didn't think I had ever seen her so happy before.

"Iris." I waved. "Lois said you've started working for Darcy."

Her eyes sparkled. "I have and I love it. It's so *gut* to do something different, and Darcy and Lois are so kind to me." She smiled at me. "I'm so glad you're all right, Millie. You had us all worried."

I smiled. "I appreciate that, and I'm glad to hear you like working here. Will you be able to come to the quilting meeting tonight?"

"I plan to, but it just depends on how things are at home with the children. My husband's work has been cut back, and he's home with the children right now. It's quite a change of pace for both of us."

I could imagine it was. It wasn't uncommon for an *Englisch* wife to work outside of the home, but in the Amish world, wives and mothers still tended to work only at home. I knew Iris's husband well. He was a *gut* man, and of all the Amish men I knew, he would take this change the best. But it would still be challenging.

I was about to say all that to Iris when the café door opened and Ruth Yoder walked inside. "Iris, what are you doing holding that coffeepot?"

Iris turned pale. Next to Raellen, she was the youngest member of our quilting circle, which meant that Ruth still had the power to intimidate her.

"Ruth," I said, "Iris just got a job here at the Sunbeam Café. Isn't that wonderful news?"

Ruth narrowed her eyes. "What about your children? Don't they need their mother at home?"

Iris opened and closed her mouth.

I elbowed Iris in the side.

"They are home with my husband."

Ruth scowled.

It was time to distract Ruth. "Ruth, have you seen Lad Zook?"

Her head snapped in my direction. "Why would I see Lad Zook after what he did to Phoebe?"

"He told me that he made a mistake," I said. "I wondered if you had any *gut* news to share."

"*Ya,* he made a mistake. He made a mistake ever thinking he could be a member of my family. In some ways, I should thank Lois now for putting an end to it."

"Lois didn't put an end to it," I said.

Ruth folded her arms. "She caused the rift. Where is she, anyway?"

"She and Darcy are in the kitchen," Iris said in a low voice. "Do you want me to get them for you?"

Ruth waved her hand. "I have nothing more to say to Lois Henry." She turned to me. "I saw you and Lois come in here. I wanted to make sure you are all right, Millie." She looked me over. "I stopped by your house on Tuesday, but Lois wouldn't let me check on you. She was like a guard dog."

I smiled at the image of Lois as a guard dog. I was sure she would be a much different dog from Pixie, whom we had met just an hour ago.

"I'm grateful for your concern," I said. "Lois told me all the ladies from Double Stitch stopped by. I was touched."

"Of course we stopped by," Ruth said with a sniff. "We are *gut* Amish women. Will you be up to the Double Stitch meeting later today to work on your quilt?"

"I will. It is halfway quilted. I have every confidence that the ladies can finish it in no time. Even if they don't, I will be able to finish it myself with their help in time to give it to my customer."

"Oh," Ruth said.

Perhaps she thought I was going to say that the quilt was nowhere near complete. In the last sixty-some years I have known Ruth, I have found that sometimes agreeing with her puts her more off balance than disagreeing with her. It was just as the proverb said, "There are lots of ways to cut a cake."

Darcy came out of the kitchen. "Oh, hello, Ruth. Can I get you some breakfast or a blueberry muffin, maybe?

They are fresh from the oven. I have to say they are the fluffiest batch I have made yet."

"I'm not hungry," Ruth snapped.

Darcy's face fell. "Umm, coffee?"

Ruth shook her head. "I will see you tonight, Millie and Iris, at the quilting meeting. If you see Lad Zook, tell him to stay away from my granddaughter." With that she stomped out of the café. The door rattled when she slammed it shut.

Darcy blinked, and I noticed the blueberry muffin she held in her hand. Her café owner training kicked in. "Millie, this one is for you. It's still hot from the oven."

"Bless you," I said. Everyone knew I had an obsession when it came to all things blueberry. I thought I might be able to live on just blueberries if it ever came to it. I even loved blueberry soda. Lois thought that was a clear sign of addiction because no one in their right mind would love blueberry soda.

"What was Ruth so upset about?" Darcy asked.

"It's a miscommunication. Lad will set it to rights," I assured her. What I didn't add was that I was worried. It had been several days and it seemed that Lad had not made up with Phoebe yet. Did he go to the bonfire as planned to speak to her? I still hoped the young couple could make things right.

Iris went behind the counter and refilled the coffeepot. "I hope that he does, or Ruth is going to be impossible to live with for a very long time."

I grimaced because I knew she was right.

I called to Lois in the kitchen that I would wait for her outside. I had missed feeling the sunshine on my back the last few days.

Across from me on the square, Uriah raked up grass clippings on the wide, open lawn. It was the first time I had seen him at work since before Friday night when the bones had been found.

I sighed. He hadn't seen me. I could walk away, and I wanted to after our awkward conversation at my home the day before, but I couldn't do that. Uriah was my friend, and I had to check on him. I walked across the street and onto the square. I was moving a little slower than I normally would, but the walking helped. I got stiff if I didn't move enough.

Uriah stopped raking and watched me approach. "It's *gut* to see you, Millie."

I stood a few feet away from him. I felt shy almost. It was the closest word I could think of for how I felt. "It's *gut* to see you too. It's nice that you are back to work, but I thought you told Margot you quit."

He smiled. "Margot was pretty insistent that I make sure the square is perfect before I leave. She told me work is the best remedy for grief. If I didn't know better, I would have said that woman was Amish."

I chuckled. "She does have an Amish work ethic. Maybe it's from proximity."

His face clouded over. "*Nee*, I think it's something that some people are born with and others are not. Think of your Kip. I never met a man who worked so hard in his life."

I cleared my throat. "Deputy Little is thinking about reopening Gali's case."

He shook his head. "I hope he doesn't. I think the sheriff is right on this one. Let the dead bury the dead. Knowing what happened will not bring my sister back."

"But it's not right that everyone thinks she's a killer when she's not. I'm sure she's not. Her story deserves to be heard."

"Her story deserved to be heard forty years ago when she went to the district for help because her husband hurt her. Anything now seems pointless."

I didn't agree with that. "*Ya*, it would have made a greater difference then. If the bishop at the time had stepped in, Gali might still be alive today, but she deserves justice at least. Everyone deserves that."

"You sound like an *Englischer* when you speak like that."

I frowned. Maybe I did, but that didn't mean I wasn't right.

"I'm sorry we could not have been closer when I was here, Millie. I have—I had—hopes at one point that we might be. But the hope was so small. Even dead, Kip was always there. He was one of the *gut* ones. I knew I never had a chance with you while his memory lived. And I would never ask you to forget him."

I couldn't forget him, but I didn't say that.

"Not all marriages are like yours and Kip's," he said. "I realized that I could not live up to his memory."

"We didn't have a perfect marriage. No one does." I bit my lip. "We wanted children and could not have any. That was a strain on our relationship."

"But you went through it together. You were stronger together for it."

"His love of chewing tobacco gave him cancer and took him from me early."

"But you stayed and you loved him even when he wouldn't give up the habit. You're a *gut* woman, Millie Fisher."

"I took a vow. I made a promise that I would never leave him. I loved him." I gasped out the last words. Kip had been gone for over twenty years, and there were times, like this moment, when the pain of his death was like a fresh knife cut to the heart. The wound would scab over more quickly than it used to, and it did not keep me in bed as it had when I was newly widowed. But even in a fleeting moment like this one, all the raw emotion and agony of the loss came rushing back.

"And I loved my wife and stayed by her side too," Uriah said.

I was grateful he'd started to speak again. I needed time to recover from the blow.

Uriah went on, "But it was never like you and Kip. You and Kip were special." He picked up his rake. "I should get back to work. I was glad to see you again, Millie. Very glad. I think it closed some old doors for me, once and for all. Now, I will find new ones to open." He walked away without another word.

I stood in the middle of the green with tears in my eyes. I was not sure if my grief was greater because I'd lost Kip or lost an opportunity.

CHAPTER THIRTY-THREE

I walked back to the café and waited outside for Lois.

She stepped outside. "I saw you were talking to Uriah. How did that go?"

I shrugged. "About as well as yesterday. He wants me to give up on finding Gali's killer."

She nodded. "And he still plans to leave."

"*Ya.* I think he has to. His family needs him." I opened the passenger-side door of Lois's car, which was parked in front of the café, and slipped inside.

Lois seemed to know that I didn't want to talk. My bicycle was in Lois's trunk, and she had tied down the trunk lid with rope. Lois insisted the bike would make it back to the farm just fine that way, but with every bump we hit on the country road, I winced as I heard the bike rattle in the back.

I was just happy that she'd agreed to take my bike

back to the farm. I hated feeling trapped without trans-portation, even if I was in no shape to go on a bicycle ride.

Finally, Lois said, "Uriah might want to give up on the case, but we don't. What do you say we pay Cyril a little visit?"

I had been staring out the window, and I looked at her with a grin. "I think that is a fine idea."

Lois pulled into a driveway and turned around to head to the buggy shop.

"I'm interested in hearing what Cyril and Lad have to say about my accident," I said.

"Me too!" She opened her car door. "Millie, we might just catch a killer today."

"There's always the hope."

Once again, we arrived during work hours at the buggy shop, and the business was busy. However, what caught my eye were three people standing under a tree.

Lois parked the car. "Are you seeing what I'm see-ing?"

"I sure am."

Under the large oak tree at the edge of the parking lot, Bishop Yoder stood with Phoebe and Lad. Lad spoke earnestly, waving his hands around as he spoke.

"Should we interrupt?" Lois asked.

I shook my head. "Let's see if we can find Cyril first. Maybe they will be done when we come back out."

She gave me a thumbs-up. "Good plan. Because we want those two crazy kids to get back together."

"We do," I agreed.

As soon as we walked into the main part of the shop, someone called my name. "Millie, are you all right?" Cyril Zook walked toward us with concern on his face.

"Deputy Little and Aiden Brody were here a few days ago and told me about the buggy accident. I feel just awful."

"I'm fine and my horse, Bessie, is fine too."

He placed a hand on his chest. "That's what they told me, but it's so *gut* to see with my own eyes that you are all right."

Lois put her hands on her hips. "What do you know about the accident?"

He blinked at her. "Nothing. I know nothing. I know that it must look like we were somehow involved, but I swear to you, before Lad took the buggy to your home, I gave it the once-over myself. I always do when buggies are returned to customers. Safety is our number one priority."

"Then how did the axle get cut?" Lois leaned forward.

Cyril took a big step back. "I don't know. It must have happened when the buggy was at your home that night. I never would have given it to you in that condition. I'm telling you I checked the axle myself."

"Is that possible?" Lois asked me.

I frowned and looked at Lois. "The buggy was out all night, and it is on the other side of the barn from the house. Even if I was awake, it's not impossible that someone could have cut the axle without me knowing it."

"But what about the goats? Wouldn't they have warned you?"

I frowned. "They should have."

"We aren't responsible for what happened, but Zooks' Amish Buggies will fix your buggy free of charge."

"Are you sure?" I asked.

"Yes, he's sure." Lois stepped in front of me. "We will

accept. We will have the buggy here just as soon as it's released from police evidence."

Cyril frowned.

"Thank you again for your offer." Lois pulled me toward the door.

"What are you doing?" I asked just as soon as we were outside and she let me go.

"You can't look a gift horse in the mouth. You know how expensive that buggy was to fix the last time. You can't afford to pay twice. Let him cover it."

I sighed. "I suppose you're right. I would have to sew a lot more quilts to pay that bill twice."

"When he gives the buggy back to you, though, I would check the axle for saw marks before driving it. Just saying."

I shook my head. "Oh, look, Phoebe and Lad are hugging."

The bishop was no longer with the couple under the oak tree. They were alone and clearly back together.

"That just brings a tear to my eye," Lois said. "True love finds a way."

"It does," I agreed.

Lad spotted us and waved us over. Phoebe waved too.

"They look happy," Lois mused.

They certainly did.

"Millie," Lad said. "Are you okay?"

"I'm fine. I was just telling your father that."

"I felt terrible when I heard. Just terrible. I should have checked the buggy one more time before I left."

"It is all right, Lad. I'm sure Deputy Little will sort out what happened."

"I hope he does because you could have been killed."

Lois shifted her stance. "What's going on with the two of you? Good news?"

Phoebe blushed. "Lad proposed again. We are getting married after all, just as planned, and on the original date too."

"Oh." I clapped my hands together. "I'm so happy to hear that. You are a *gut* match."

"Danki," Phoebe said, blushing even pinker.

Lad shook his head. "I was a fool. I let my fear about joining such an important family scare me away." He held Phoebe's hand. "That won't be happening any longer. I was just worried about you downgrading yourself to be a buggy maker's wife."

"I don't care about all that. When we marry, I will be more a part of your family than my own. I want to be the buggy maker's wife. For years, I have envisioned our lives together, even when I was too young to really know what being a wife meant. I just knew that I wanted to be with you the rest of my life."

"I wasn't just worried about me," Lad explained. "I don't want our marriage to have a bad impact on your relationship with your grandmother."

"It won't. Ruth Yoder has been a powerful force in my life, but she doesn't get to choose who I marry."

"And your father and the buggy shop?" I asked. "What did he say?"

Lad straightened his shoulders. "I spoke with my *daed* and told him I am capable of taking more responsibility at the buggy shop and being married. Both are important, and I plan to treat them that way."

"Gut," I said. "It is always best to be honest about what you want."

Phoebe smiled at Lad, and Lois and I said our good-byes.

"That just warms my heart," Lois said as we walked back to her car. "What a love story. May we all be so lucky."

I hoped so too.

CHAPTER THIRTY-FOUR

Lois clapped me on the shoulder. "You made another match."

I smiled. "I did, but I suppose in this case you can say *remade* a match." I walked toward her car. "We should get back to the farm. I have so much work to do on the quilt before the quilting meeting."

She nodded. "And I promised to help Darcy with the dinner crowd until Iris is fully trained. She's doing a great job. Darcy and I are so glad to have her."

I smiled, but the smile faded from my face when I saw the bishop sitting on a bench reading his Bible. "He must be waiting for Phoebe until she is ready to leave."

"He might be in for a long wait, the way those two lovebirds are looking at each other."

I glanced over my shoulder and realized that Lois was right. Phoebe and Lad were staring into each other's eyes.

"Can you wait for me while I talk to the bishop?"

"You don't want me to come with you?" Lois frowned.

"I just don't think he will speak to me freely if you are there."

"I understand." She sighed. "Sometimes being English is a bummer."

"I never thought I would hear you say that."

"I'm nothing if not full of surprises."

That was most certainly true.

I walked over to the bishop, and when I was a few feet away, he must have sensed my presence because he looked up from his Bible. "Millie, I thought it was you and Lois speaking to Lad and Phoebe."

I smiled. "I'm happy to see they are back together. They are a *gut* match."

He nodded. "They are. Even I can see that. My wife will in time too. She just has trouble letting go. She was the same way when our children got married. Now, we have to go through it all again with the grandchildren." He smiled.

"I suppose that's the cost of having children. Letting them go."

"It is."

I shifted my feet. "Can I talk to you again about Gali Zook?"

He nodded. "I had expected you to want to speak again about her, and I have given it a lot of prayer and thought. It was such a long time ago. I suppose over the years I convinced myself it was long enough ago that it no longer matters. But it does. Every life throughout the ages matters to *Gott*, and as the bishop, it should matter to me too."

I swallowed hard. Was the bishop about to tell me that

he knew something about the murders? Even worse, was he going to tell me that he was somehow involved? This kind, mild-mannered man was a killer? Could it even be possible? It felt like a sin to let the very idea enter my head.

"You might want to sit."

I sat at the other end of the bench and waited.

"The night that Samuel Zook died, I was out on the road with my father. Even though it is *Gott*'s choice as to who the next bishop will be for any district, my father was grooming me for the job. He took me out during that terrible snowstorm because he wanted to show me that I had to be willing to put my life at risk to help the members of my flock. We were making a call on a family with a sick child." He took a breath and placed a hand on his Bible as if he needed the support. "The weather was terrible that night. Wind, snow, freezing rain. We were closed up tight in the buggy. Visibility was low. My father drove the horse. We came across the covered bridge. It was still in operation back then. We had just made it to the bridge when we saw Samuel's buggy parked on the side of the road. My father opened his window because I think he was going to call out to see if Samuel was in need of help, but then we heard the yelling."

I felt ill. "Yelling?"

"I couldn't catch all the words, but Samuel was yelling at his wife. Telling her that she wasn't doing a *gut* job keeping their home." He looked down at his hands. "I'm sorry to say that my father then rolled up his window. He said we needed to leave them be. A husband and wife had to work out their own struggles. It was between them and *Gott.* That's what he said."

He could have saved her. The thought ran across my

mind. If the old bishop had been willing to intervene, it was very likely that Samuel and Gali would still be alive.

"I know what you're thinking. How could we drive away when a husband was being so unkind to his wife? I've asked myself that so many times, and I have tried to make up for it since I have become bishop. Anytime a wife or any woman comes to me and tells me that her husband or another man is unkind or treats her poorly, I act. I remove her from the situation. I believe her. Ruth and I have hosted many of these female church members in our home. I won't walk away again. I think I will have to spend the rest of my life making up for what I did to Gali that night. I should have stood up to my father. I tried, but it was a timid attempt."

My mouth was dry. "What do you mean?"

"I—I thought that I saw a third person in the buggy. I told my father this, and he said it was not possible; Samuel and Gali were headed home, and they lived alone. There would be no one else in the buggy. It was a trick of the light on the snow."

Could that third person have been the killer? I knew that he had to have been. The bishop had seen the killer before the murder. I wanted to tell him how close he had been to saving a life, to saving lives, but I wouldn't be telling him anything he didn't already know.

"I have always wondered if I was right about the third person." He lowered his voice. "It's my greatest fear that I was."

"Assuming there was a third person, who could it have been? When Gali left the Amish Corner Bench that night, there were no customers there and very few workers. Everyone had gone home early except for Gali, Nathaniel

Zurich, who was a teenager at the time, and the Amish cook Alice Springer."

He looked up at me. "Amish cook?"

I nodded. "*Ya*, Alice Springer. She's still the cook at the Amish Corner Bench all these years later. Lois swears by her fried chicken."

"Alice Springer isn't Amish."

"What did you say?" I whispered.

He shook his head. "Let me correct that. Alice Springer is Amish *now*. She wasn't born into an Amish community."

"How do you know this?"

"Because she came to my father when she was still *Englisch* and asked if she could join the church. She said that she had read a lot about the Amish and felt that *Gott* was calling her to join the community. We always welcome anyone who is sincere into our faith."

"*Ya*, I know this," I said, but something about the story felt odd to me. "But she's not a member of our district now," I said.

He nodded. "I think she wanted to marry Uriah Schrock, and when he didn't show any interest, she joined a different district."

"It's unusual for an Amish person to change districts," I said.

"Not any stranger than an *Englischer* joining the Amish in the first place."

He had a point. A strange question struck my mind. "Her chicken recipe? Is that an Amish recipe?"

"Not that I know of. I believe she's from Kentucky, and she brought the recipe with her. As you know, it's done very well for the Amish Corner Bench."

I did know. What I didn't know was who else was aware that Alice Springer hadn't grown up Amish.

CHAPTER THIRTY-FIVE

As usual, all the women from Double Stitch were there on time for the meeting. Even Iris, who'd just finished her first dinner shift as a waitress at the Sunbeam Café. Ruth glanced at the clock when Iris entered the house. I guessed that Ruth was a little bit upset Iris wasn't late so she could reprimand her.

"You have done a lot of work on this quilt, Millie. It's beautiful. I'm sure we will finish tonight," Leah said as she took her seat at the quilt frame.

"It's possible," Ruth said. "And the work is nice."

I smiled, knowing that was high praise indeed, coming from Ruth.

As soon as we set to work, I brought up Alice Springer. "The bishop told me today she was an *Englischer* who joined the community as an adult."

Leah cocked her head. "I didn't know that. I thought

she was always Amish. I think I knew she didn't grow up here, but I certainly didn't know that she was converted Amish."

"It's rare for an *Englisch* person to join the Amish, but it does happen," Ruth said. "Why are you concerned about it?"

I frowned. "I can't really tell you why. It's just been nagging at me. I wonder why it's such a secret."

"Maybe it's not a secret," Iris suggested as she looked up from her stitches. "Maybe so much time has passed, it doesn't matter anymore. At this point, she must have been Amish much longer than she was *Englisch*."

Iris made a *gut* point, but I felt it did matter. Why, I wasn't sure.

"Well, I don't know if it means much of anything," Leah said. "But the only way you are going to get an answer about that, Millie, is to go speak to Alice yourself about it."

I knew she was right.

The next morning, I was up bright and early, even before the goats. The sun was just peeking over the horizon as I walked the quarter mile to the shed phone on the Rabers' land. I felt good on my walk. It was the strongest I had felt since my spill from the buggy. I was so grateful that the accident hadn't been worse. I dialed one of the few numbers that I'd committed to memory. It was Lois's cell number. "Lois, I know that it's very early to be calling, and you will pitch a fit if I woke you up for this call. However, I just wanted you to know that I'm going to go to the Amish Corner Bench first thing this morning. I'm feeling much better and will ride my bike. I'll be fine. I wanted to get there before it opens to speak with Alice again. Every other time we have tried to talk to her, she's been so busy. This might be my chance to get her to open up. I will come straight to the café after that and tell you all about it." I ended the call.

I shook my head. Lois was going to be so steamed with me if that call woke her up. She got up early to help her granddaughter in the café, but I knew she was hoping she would get to sleep in a bit more now that Iris was on board.

I walked back to my own farm, fed the animals, and climbed on my bicycle. Like my farm, the restaurant was on the outskirts of the village of Harvest, so it was actually closer to my home than the village square was. I pedaled as fast as I dared to the Amish Corner Bench. The restaurant opened at eight, so I knew I didn't have much time to speak to Alice before she had to get to work.

As I expected when I arrived at the restaurant, the front door was locked. I walked around to the back door and it stood wide open. Two young Amish women were peeling potatoes outside of the building, but they didn't stop me from going inside. I knew I looked harmless and was viewed as another Amish *grossmaami* checking in on her family.

I peeked into the kitchen. I saw more young women working but not Alice. "Is Alice here?" I asked in Pennsylvania Dutch.

"She's in the dining room," one of the young women answered. Again, it didn't seem to strike them as the least bit odd that I was there. Had Lois been with me, I knew it would have been a different story.

I followed the long corridor to the dining room, where I found Alice checking the breakfast buffet, which was in the process of being set up.

She blinked at me. "Millie Fisher, what are you doing here so early in the morning?"

"I wondered if you had a few minutes to talk before the restaurant became too busy."

She frowned. "As you can see, the restaurant is already busy as we get everything in order. I don't really have time to chat. Is this about Gali again?"

I shook my head. "*Nee*, unless she knew that you weren't born to an Amish family."

Alice stared at me. "What did you say?"

"The bishop mentioned that you joined the faith as an adult."

She looked around as if to make sure none of her workers could hear our conversation. "Let's go out in the fresh air and chat."

I nodded and followed her back through the kitchen area and out the door I had entered through.

"Why don't you wait over there," Alice said. "I'm just going to grab some knitting from my buggy. You know an Amish woman's hands always have to be busy."

Knitting? I shook off a thought tickling the back of my mind.

I did as asked. I stood at the edge of the hill that overlooked the pasture. It was such a beautiful scene. I inhaled the scent of hay and earth from the outside, mixed with the scents of bacon and yeast wafting through the kitchen door.

Alice joined me at the overlook. "I've always had a thing about heights," she said. "I don't fear them at all.

Sometimes I think about what it would feel like to let myself fall."

"Then you could be hurt or die."

"The hurt would be a problem. I'm not sure dying would be."

I turned to look at her and saw a gun in her hand. "I—I thought you went to your buggy to get your knitting."

She shrugged. "I decided that I don't need to be industrious all the time. None of us does. Although that's what I respect most about the Amish, their work ethic. There is no other life like it."

Cars began to pull into the parking lot behind us as people got ready to wait in line for the seven o'clock opening. The Amish Corner Bench was a very popular restaurant in the county.

"There are other people here who can help me, both inside and outside of the restaurant."

"Yes, but if you call out, then you will put all those kind people at risk too. Do you want to do that?"

I felt the blood drain from my face.

She smiled. "I didn't think so."

"Did Gali figure out you weren't Amish? Was that why you killed her?"

She glared at me. "First of all, I'm as Amish as you or anyone else in the district. I believe in the tenets of the faith and I was baptized into the church."

"One of those tenets is no killing."

She smiled. "I revised it in my own mind to say killing is permissible under the right circumstances, like when a man hits a woman."

I didn't think that was what the scripture meant, but I didn't correct her.

"So you want to know why I joined the Amish faith. Let me tell you a little story."

I swallowed as my eyes fell to the gun in her hand.

"I grew up in Kentucky. I met my husband when I was young. We got married straight out of high school. I was only seventeen when I married, so I wasn't much different from the Amish when it came to that. My husband was a cruel man. He was unkind to me before we married, but I was young and blinded by love. I was also blinded by the fact that I didn't have the best childhood. I wanted to escape from my family home. At the time, he was my way out. However, I would be lying if I said I didn't love him. I loved him dearly. I loved him more than I loved myself. Proof of that was how long I stayed with him.

"He never worked. Working and keeping house were my jobs. His was to stay home, spend money, and drink. When he drank, it was the worst. I got a job at a local diner as a short-order cook. I was good. Everyone liked my cooking. My husband would get compliments from people on the street, from both men and women, about my cooking at the diner. When the men complimented me, he took offense. He thought that meant I was messing around with them on the side. I wasn't. I was a devoted wife. Too devoted." She swallowed.

"I came home one night, and he was furious. A man in the neighborhood had said that I made the best fried chicken in the world. In my husband's crazy mind that meant something else. He came at me. I had never seen him so enraged. I knew this time he was going to kill me. I grabbed a knife from the knife block and he ran right into the blade."

I felt sick.

"I was only nineteen years old, but I knew I had to get out of my town, out of Kentucky, out of my world. So I ran. I changed my name and looked for somewhere to hide. The Amish community was my best choice. It was a good fit for me. I'm an excellent cook. I knew that I could find work. I hitchhiked my way to Holmes County. I found an Amish community that I thought might take me if I proved I was devoted to their faith and obedient to their rules. I was. I did everything that was expected of me."

"Bishop Yoder said you were a member of our district for a short while," I said.

"I was, but I changed districts when I had a disagreement with a member. I'm much happier with the district I'm in now."

Uriah was the member she'd had a disagreement with, I realized, but I knew better than to say his name. I didn't want to say anything that might make her even angrier. "Then why did you kill Samuel and Gali?"

"I *didn't* kill Gali. I was trying to protect her. On our late nights working at the restaurant, she told me about how her husband treated her. I told her that she had to leave him, but she said she couldn't because she was Amish, and the Amish didn't divorce."

I didn't argue with her on this point because I knew it was true.

"I encouraged her to go to the bishop. She finally worked up the nerve and spoke with him. The most the bishop did was slap Samuel on the wrist. Worse yet, Samuel was even more cruel to her after she went to the bishop. I knew the district had failed her. I'd made a promise to myself: No man would ever hit me again, and if I saw a man hit another woman, I would stop it at any cost."

"What happened that night?" I asked.

"There was a terrible winter storm. We closed early. Everything in the county was closed, but I still had to prepare for breakfast the next day. I knew the owners would not let me open late. Gali volunteered to stay with me. I knew it was because she didn't want to go home, but I welcomed the help. Her husband planned to come and pick her up because of the snow. When he arrived, it was clear that he was put out about having to come fetch her. I had a bad feeling that he was going to hurt her, so I asked if they would take me home too. My thought was that he wouldn't hurt her while I was in the buggy. That's where I was wrong." She closed her eyes for a moment.

My heart skipped. In a split second, I wondered if I could grab the gun, but then her eyes opened again. They narrowed at me.

"We reached the covered bridge and visibility was terrible. Samuel pulled over to the side of the road because he couldn't see through the snow at all. He told Gali it was all her fault that we were out in this terrible weather, and she was always making mistakes. He slapped her." Alice closed her eyes for a half second again. "Something in me snapped. My knitting was at my feet in the back of the buggy. I grabbed one of the needles and lashed out."

The image was all too vivid in my mind.

Where was Lois? Had she gotten my phone message by now? Would she think to come here? My heart sank. Why would she? She had no reason to come here. I'd told her that I would meet her at the café. How could I have been so stupid? I should have waited and come with her to speak with Alice. This was a time that Amish Marple could really use her backup.

"I did it. I killed Samuel Zook to protect Gali. She didn't

see it that way. She thought I'd snapped and was going to hurt her too, and she ran from the buggy. Before I could even get out, I watched Gali—" She choked on the name. "I watched Galilee fall to her death."

"How awful," I whispered.

"I climbed down the ravine in the snow. Almost falling myself a number of times. I was calling her name over and over again. She never answered because she was already dead. Her neck was broken. I had no choice but to let the blame for Samuel's murder fall on her. Can't you see that? I had already restarted my life once. I couldn't do that again." Beads of sweat gathered on her forehead.

"So you buried her?" I asked.

"There had been a January thaw the week before, so the ground was still soft enough to dig a shallow grave. I did what I thought I had to do. I didn't have any choice. I had to bury her. I found a shovel in the back of Samuel's buggy. I could have gone to prison for the rest of my life. I left my old life to stay away from trouble, not to find it."

"Did you know the bishop and his son went by in their buggy?" I asked. "This was when Samuel was yelling at Gali."

She shook her head. "I didn't know the bishop and his son were there that night. The snow was so awful. I could barely see my hand in front of my face. It was a miracle I made it up and down the ravine so many times and was then able to walk home. I was at work the next day. No one ever knew." She narrowed her eyes. "No one ever knew until you. When I went to your farm at night and cut the axle on your buggy, I thought you would be scared off. Trouble is, you don't scare easily."

"Hey, Alice? What are you doing with that gun?" a familiar voice called.

Alice and I spun around to find Lois, Deputy Little, and two other deputies standing in the parking lot. The three deputies had their guns drawn.

"Millie," Deputy Little said. "Walk toward us."

I did as I was told, although it was terrifying to turn my back on Alice and her gun. When I reached Lois, she wrapped me in a hug.

Deputy Little and the other two officers approached Alice, who had given up and dropped her gun on the ground.

"Lois, how did you know I needed help? I told you I would catch up with you in the café."

"I just had a bad feeling again, like I did when you were in the buggy accident. I wasn't going to ignore it this time, and I convinced Deputy Little to call in some friends and go with me to the restaurant. I told them if it was a false alarm, I'd buy them all breakfast." She smiled at the three deputies. "Don't worry, guys, I'll still buy you breakfast just as soon as you throw this killer into the slammer."

"Breakfast sounds good," said the deputy who was walking Alice to his cruiser.

While two of the deputies put handcuffs on Alice's wrists, Deputy Little came over to me and held out his hand. "I'm glad you're okay, Millie. That's your second close call in as many days."

"What will happen to her?" I asked. "Will she go to prison for the murder of Samuel? She was trying to protect Gali."

He shook his head. "I don't know. Even if it was self-defense, Alice is in a whole lot of trouble. There may be another murder warrant out for her in Kentucky, if what she confessed to you proves true."

"Wait, you heard her confession. How long have you been here?"

"She was telling you when we arrived," Lois said. "You're really good at getting a killer to spill all their secrets, Millie. It's a real gift."

I wrinkled my brow.

"Don't worry, Millie," Deputy Little said. "We weren't going to let her hurt you. As for Alice, only time will tell how the courts look at it all." Deputy Little walked away.

"Even though she tried to kill me—" I began.

"Twice," Lois interjected.

I nodded. "Even though she tried to kill me *twice*, I feel compassion for her. In the first incident, she was protecting herself, and then she was protecting Gali. Both times, it just got out of hand."

"True," Lois said. "But then she could also say she needed to kill you to protect herself. When would the killing for protection stop?"

I didn't have the answer for that.

Epilogue

Lois sipped coffee across from me on my front porch. She had the morning off from the café because Iris was now on the breakfast shift. The young Amish woman was in her element in the café. She was the perfect fit for the restaurant, and it was clear the café was the perfect fit for her.

"I know that it's only August," Lois said. "But I have a hankering for a pumpkin pie. I love fall. It's my favorite season."

"It's mine too, but there is something melancholy about it because it reminds me of the coming winter."

"Winter can be pretty too."

I nodded. "After the events of this summer, I'm hoping for a quiet winter." I petted Peaches, who was curled up in my lap, but the cat was not asleep. He was keeping his eye on his brother goats, who were romping in the front yard. Most days I wished that I had their energy.

"My guess is Alice Springer is going to have a very quiet winter in prison," Lois said.

I nodded. The prosecutors in both Ohio and Kentucky had decided not to charge Alice with murder in either location because she'd defended herself and then defended Gali. However, in Ohio, she would still be charged with two counts of attempted murder for the times she tried to kill me. So Lois was right—she would have a quiet winter in prison.

"Who will make the chicken now?" Lois asked.

"I don't think anyone will. Phoebe Yoder is still working at the Amish Corner Bench, and from what she said, they just had to remove it from the menu. Alice vowed to take the recipe to her grave."

Lois shook her head. "That's a disappointment. That was some good chicken."

I smiled.

"Have you heard from Uriah since he moved back to Indiana?" Lois asked.

I shook my head. *"Nee."*

"That's a shame," Lois said with a sigh. "I can't help but be a hopeless romantic."

"I appreciate your hopefulness, not your hopelessness, Lois."

"Are you upset that he's gone when there was a promise of . . ." She trailed off.

"I don't know how I feel. Maybe I was destined to have just one great love. I found mine when I was young. I was blessed in that way. Perhaps I didn't appreciate it as much as I should have because it came too early and was taken from me too soon. Some people find that great love later. Perhaps they cherish it more. It's sweeter and not taken for granted." I shook my head. "I don't know . . . I'm rambling, but I do understand why Uriah went back to Indiana. He went back to the place he should be."

Lois was quiet for a moment. "I loved my second husband dearly. I suppose that he was the closest person I have had to the one love of my life, but since I married two more times after he died, I kept looking."

"There's no harm in looking." I smiled.

"Well, it's Uriah's loss. You may not have Uriah, but you have this community, your niece and her family, a sweet cat, and me." She nodded to Phillip and Peter dancing around the yard. "And those two knuckleheads."

"And *Gott*. A long time ago I made peace with being a widow. For a moment there when I saw Uriah, I thought maybe living as a widow wouldn't be my life forever. I thought that I was getting a second chance at love."

Lois set her coffee mug on the table between us. "But it wasn't?"

I shook my head. "I don't think so. Until Uriah came along, I was happy with my life. He upset the applecart a bit. Now that he's gone back to Indiana, I feel at peace. I'm no longer uncertain of my place."

"Being unsettled by another person is not a bad thing. It's how you grow," Lois said in a low voice.

"I suppose that's true." I leaned back in my chair and watched the goats chase each other around the yard.

"As for Uriah, you never know, he might come back around."

I rocked. "Maybe. But I would have to allow myself to care for someone as much as I cared for Kip. I don't know if I can do that again. I still grieve him."

She nodded. "Grief is not terminal, but it can be chronic. Don't ever let anyone tell you otherwise. Just like with any chronic illness, there will be good days and bad days. Some days you will even feel normal—but what is normal, really? You'll never stop loving or missing or wishing things could have been different. Do you know what that all means?"

I shook my head, more because I could not speak than because I didn't know the answer.

"It means you loved fully and unselfishly. It means if you could have given your life in that person's place, you would have. At the same time, you know that's not what the person you loved would have wanted. They would want you to carry on and have a good life. You have had a good life, Millie. Think of all the people you have helped."

"But it's hard," I whispered.

"So hard. It is the hardest thing you will ever do, and that's the sign of the truest love." Lois stood up, knelt by my chair, and wrapped her arm around my shoulders. "Don't you have an Amish saying for all this?"

Tears gathered in my eyes. "I'm sure that there is one, but I am drawing a blank at the moment."

"It happens to the best of us. To me more often than not."

I smiled at her. "You are a true friend, Lois."

She went back to her seat and picked up her coffee mug again. "Through thick and thin to the end."

I smiled wider. "And after."

"After too. I plan to be next-door neighbors with you and Kip on the other side. I put in my location request early that we would be neighbors in heaven just like we were when we were girls."

"How early did you put it in?" I asked.

"When we were five and I told you that you were my favorite friend."

Tears sprang to my eyes. "You're my favorite friend too. And I don't know what the bishop would say, but I think *Gott* will grant that request for both of us."

Please read on for an excerpt from
Peanut Butter Panic
an Amish Candy Shop Mystery
by
Amanda Flower

CHAPTER ONE

"Careful! Don't drop the turkeys! We will be ruined if we don't have turkey on Thanksgiving!" Margot Rawlings cried as she buzzed around the Harvest village square like a spinning top. Her short curls bounced as she pointed at the young volunteers and barked orders. "Chairs over there. No, no, no, I don't put the kids' table facing the playground. They will want to run off and play instead of eating their dinners."

A young Amish man who was carrying a crate of turkeys looked petrified as the poultry shook in his hands. After Margot yelled at him, he didn't seem to know what to do.

I smiled at him as I approached, carrying a box of display dishes for the dessert table. "You okay, Leon?"

Leon Younger was an Amish teen who volunteered

often to work at village square events, of which there were many. Since Margot had taken over Harvest's social calendar a few years ago, it seemed scarcely a week went by when there wasn't something happening on the square in our small Amish village in Holmes County, Ohio. From concerts to weddings to Christmas pageants, the square had seen it all. Thanksgiving week was no exception.

In fact, Thanksgiving was going to be bigger and grander than any event Margot had ever thrown before. There would be a community-wide Thanksgiving meal for the village. It would include both Amish and English neighbors and would be followed with a lighting-of-the-square ceremony to usher in the holiday season.

Margot had been working on it for months, which meant that everyone else in the village had been too. She was great at drafting help. I always thought if the US military brought the draft back, Margot should direct the effort.

Leon blinked his bright blue eyes at me. "She's scarier than the bishop's wife."

I hid my smile. I knew the bishop's wife, Ruth Yoder, as well as I knew Margot. I also knew Ruth would have wanted to been seen as more formidable than Margot. I certainly wasn't going to tell her what the young man said. "Why don't you take those turkeys to the church? They will be cooked later today by the church volunteers. Just leave them on the counter—the kitchen staff will know what to do."

He nodded. "*Danki*. I should have thought of that in the first place. But when Margot shouted at me to get the turkeys from Levi Wittmer's poultry farm, I brought them here where I knew she would be. I wasn't thinking." He nodded at a horse and wagon that was parked along

Main Street. "My wagon is right there. I will take them over now."

The back of the wagon was laden with crates just like the one in Leon's hands. My brow went up. How many turkeys had Margot ordered from the Wittmer farm for this event? Then again, as many as seven hundred people had said they would come for the celebration tomorrow afternoon. It was possible she would need every last turkey.

"That's a good plan, Leon, and can I give you a tip?" I asked.

He nodded.

"Give yourself a break. You are doing a fine job. Just remember, Margot is high-strung, and for better or worse, she treats everyone the same. It's not you."

He licked his lips and nodded. "*Danki*, Bailey. The Esh family is right; you are very kind for an *Englischer.*"

I smiled, taking no offense at the "for an *Englischer*" comment. It was one I had heard often since moving from New York City to Harvest.

With the crate in his arms, he hurried to his wagon, loaded the crate into the back with the others, and drove around to the church, which was just on the opposite side of the square on Church Street.

It was a gray and cloudy day, as was typical in Ohio at the end of November, but there was a bright patch of blue sky above the church's tall white steeple. The forecast for tomorrow, Thanksgiving, was clear skies and warmer temperatures. Weather was something that was never guaranteed in Ohio, but I hoped for the sake of the festivities, the report was correct.

I could only imagine the flurry of activity that must be

going on in the church kitchen at the moment. When Margot, as the village community organizer, and Juliet Brook, the pastor's wife, had put their heads together to sponsor a village-wide Thanksgiving dinner, I don't believe they realized how much work it would take.

Then again, maybe Margot, who was one of the hardest working people I had ever met, did know. However, I bet the reality had taken Juliet by surprise.

"Bailey King!" Margot pointed at me. "Just the person I wanted to see."

I sighed. Maybe I agreed with Leon just a little. Margot could be scary, and nothing was scarier than being caught in her crosshairs because she had an assignment for you, which in my case was all the time. It seemed to me that anytime Margot spotted me, she had something she wanted me to do. At least I knew I wouldn't have to drive to Wittmer Poultry Farm to collect the turkeys. I didn't think I wanted to see a bunch of turkeys walking around flapping their wings right before Thanksgiving.

She marched over to me. As usual, she wore jeans, running shoes, and a sweatshirt. However, due to the chilly temperatures, she'd added a quilted barn coat over her sweatshirt and fingerless gloves on her hands to complete her ensemble. "I stopped by Swissmen Sweets well over an hour ago looking for you. Charlotte said that you were away on an errand in Canton." She put her hands on her hips. "What are you doing traveling all that way this close to Thanksgiving? Don't you have enough to do right here at home? I hope you don't plan to go to New York this weekend. The village needs you."

I rubbed my head because I was already getting a headache as I tried to remember the sage advice I had given Leon about Margot. The advice had flown right out of my head. All I could think was he was right and she was scary.

"I'm not going to New York this weekend," I said as calmly as possible. "I only went to Canton to run an errand."

It was none of her business, but I had gone shopping for a housewarming gift for my boyfriend, Aiden Brody. I knew with Thanksgiving, Black Friday, and Small Business Saturday coming up, I would not get another chance before I saw him.

He'd just moved into a new apartment in Columbus, and I felt I had to give him a gift to show my support for the move, when in fact I wasn't feeling the least bit supportive about it. The last time we'd discussed where he would live after he completed his months of training with BCI, Ohio's Bureau of Investigations, he'd promised he'd come back to Holmes County, so his recent decision to live nearly two hours away was not great news.

For over a decade, Aiden had been a sheriff's deputy in Holmes County. That was how I'd met him, but earlier this year, he had been given the chance of a lifetime to work with BCI. He had made a good impression on the department when he collaborated with them on a case last summer. Now he had just completed six months of training with BCI. From what I had been told before, after his training he would be returning to Holmes County to work as a remote agent specializing in Amish cases. Instead, he was being moved to one of the largest cities in Ohio. I didn't know what this would mean for our relationship. Part of me had thought when Aiden returned to Holmes County, we would begin to talk seriously about marriage and having a family. All those things I knew we both wanted but were afraid to say aloud to each other.

I didn't tell Margot any of that. Instead, I said, "I came as soon as I could."

She folded her arms as if she had doubts. Margot was typically a tightly wound woman, but I don't think I had ever seen her this worked up.

"Is something wrong, Margot?"

She threw up her hands. "Something always goes wrong when it comes to these events, but it's never been anything that I couldn't handle until today."

My eyes went wide. For Margot to admit that she couldn't handle something was unheard of. "What is it?" I braced myself to hear something about Leon and the turkeys. My brain was already scrambling for a way to defend the quiet teenager.

"My mother is coming!" she wailed.

I stared at her. That was not what I had expected her to say. "Your mother?"

"I know, doesn't it sound horrible?" she moaned.

"Why is it so horrible?" I asked.

"She's never come to one of my events. Ever. My whole life long. And the first one she comes to is the village Thanksgiving dinner. Why did she have to pick this one? Why couldn't she have tried a concert or a bake sale or the Christmas parade next month? I have a camel at the Christmas parade. Everyone loves the camel. Would it have killed her to wait one more month?"

I knew Melchior the camel, who made a regular appearance at the village Christmas parade. He was nice as far as camels went but a bit of an escape artist. I wasn't sure a camel running loose was the best way for Margot to impress her mother, but what did I know?

Margot began to gasp for air.

I placed a hand on her shoulder. "Are you okay?" I

glanced around and noticed that the volunteers who were setting up for the big meal tomorrow were watching us. If Margot saw their stares, she gave no indication of it. "Do you want to sit down?"

She brushed my hand away and took a few deep breaths. "I'm fine. I don't want to sit down. I don't have time to sit down. I have to leave for the airport in an hour to pick up my mother. Everything has to be perfect here." She grabbed my arm. "Bailey, I need you!"

"Me?" I squeaked.

"Yes, I need you to oversee the preparations for Thanksgiving. Everything has to be impeccable for tomorrow. Perfect. I know that I always want things to be just right, but I'm not kidding this time. I can't fail in front of my mother again."

Again? I wanted to ask her what she meant by that, but before I could, she said, "You have to promise me." She thrust her clipboard at me. "This is the list of everything that has to be done. Guard it with your life. There's a checkmark next to the items that have been completed."

After a cursory glance, I noted that there were very few checkmarks on the page.

I tried to hand the clipboard back to her. "Margot, I'm honored that you would trust me with such an important job, but there is so much to do at Swissmen Sweets today. We are making many of the desserts for tomorrow's meal, and we're getting extra candy ready for Black Friday and Small Business Saturday. This is our biggest weekend of the year."

She would not take the clipboard. "You don't understand. You have to help me."

"What about Juliet? She's always willing to help."

"I can't ask Juliet. She's in charge of the food preparation happening at the church. You're the only one who even has a remote chance of doing the job as well as I can."

I frowned. "Thank you?"

"You don't know who my mother is. She expects perfection. Always and in all things."

I guessed Margot was in her sixties, so her mother had to be over eighty years old, and yet Margot still feared her?

She took a breath. "Mother, the honorable Zara Bevan, was a powerhouse attorney and the first female judge in Holmes County. Everything she does, she excels at." She paused. "Until she had me."

I had known Margot for a while now, and I had never known her to speak disparagingly about herself. Even when something went terribly wrong at one of her events—like the discovery of a dead body—she handled it with efficiency and confidence. However, right now she looked anything but confident. She looked terrified. The honorable Zara Bevan must have been a force to be reckoned with indeed.

"Where does your mother live now? Where is she coming from?"

"Florida. She moved there about fifteen years ago. She can play outdoor tennis all year-round down there. She says indoor tennis is not the same. She's eighty-six years old, and still plays tennis every day. She was even in the senior Olympics!"

"It seems like your mother has achieved a lot."

"You have no idea. All she does is achieve, and she expects the same level of achievement out of her family too. Out of me!"

"Has it been a long while since she visited you in Harvest?" I asked.

"You could say that. She's never been back since she left. I try to get down to Florida for at least a few days every winter to see her. But between you and me, I'm always ready to come home at the end of the visit. Actually, I'm ready to come home before the visit even starts. I don't know how I'm going to survive this weekend." She grabbed my shoulders and shook me slightly. "Bailey, I need your help. I'm desperate."

I glanced down at the clipboard again and thought about the mile-long list that I had left on the kitchen island back at Swissmen Sweets. How was I ever going to get all of this done?

But I said, "All right, I'll help you."

Really, there was nothing else I could say.

Connect with Us

Visit us online at
KensingtonBooks.com
to read more from your favorite authors, see books
by series, view reading group guides, and more.

Join us on social media

for sneak peeks, chances to win books and prize packs,
and to share your thoughts with other readers.

facebook.com/kensingtonpublishing
twitter.com/kensingtonbooks

Tell us what you think!

To share your thoughts, submit a review,
or sign up for our eNewsletters, please visit:
KensingtonBooks.com/TellUs.